THE BONE CHESS SET

AN ELA OF SALISBURY MEDIEVAL MYSTERY

J. G. LEWIS

For my mother, Mardie Gorman, whose lifelong passions for books and history have always been an inspiration to me.

ACKNOWLEDGMENTS

Once again I am very grateful to Rebecca Hazell, Betsy van der Hoek, Anne MacFarlane and Judith Tilden for their careful readings and excellent suggestions. Many thanks also to the magnificent Lynn Messina. All remaining errors are mine.

CHAPTER 1

*S*alisbury, *June 1227*

"The camel seller's here!" Richard's voice burst through the door of the ledger room. Ela stood inside, going over lists of expenses with the new steward. "You told me to come get you."

"Indeed I did," she called back to her son as she turned to open the door.

"This merchant sells camels?" asked the steward. "Aren't they from the Holy Land? I'm surprised they'd survive the sea voyage." Her newest hire, Noel Bazin, was proving rather too familiar and friendly for his role. Which meant that her children already liked him.

Ela wasn't so sure. But the steward came highly recommended by her mother and she knew better than to argue with Alianore over anything that wasn't a matter of life and death.

"Not real camels," Richard explained. "Carved ones. They're like horses but with humps on their backs."

"They're not like horses at all," protested the steward. "I've seen drawings. They're far bigger, for one thing, and they have great flat feet."

Was her new steward really going to argue with her thirteen-year-old son over the size and shape of a creature neither of them had ever seen? "Lock up please," she ordered. "We can resume later." Ela left the ledger room and headed for the hall.

"Have you seen the merchant's wares?" she asked Richard.

"He's unpacking them right now. Gerald Deschamps had him pull his wagon right into the great hall, and he's spreading them out on a table."

"What?" Ela's step quickened along the corridor. When she turned the corner she saw a covered wagon, pulled by a small brown donkey, inside her hall.

"Sir Gerald, why is there a donkey in my hall?" The garrison commander had his hands on a length of embroidered fabric. He looked up and smiled. "I know you always enjoy the merchant's visits, my lady. Your children tell me you've bought many fine gifts from trader Ziyad in the past."

"I don't believe I've entertained his donkey in my hall before."

The merchant himself hurried over to her. "At your service, my lady." A black-bearded man about her own age in a loose green robe, he bowed low. "I did explain that I could bring my wares in from the courtyard."

"No matter. You're here now and creating a clamor of excitement as usual." All her children flocked around the table, gazing at the carved boxes and inlaid bowls, the tooled leather belts and scabbards and—their favorite—the carved animals, including camels, that he always brought. Even the servants and garrison soldiers crowded around, trying to get a look at his wares.

"I have some special items for you," he said softly.

Ela nodded. Those would be hidden away inside his

wagon. Items too valuable for the maids and children to paw at. Rare and luxurious treasures that would be a fitting gift for even the highest-ranking nobles, or the king himself. "I look forward to seeing them."

Ela was annoyed with Deschamps for creating such a spectacle in her hall. She'd already had words with him this week about the soldiers making too much noise at their meals and taking too much strong drink. Perhaps her husband would have permitted such rowdy chaos in his hall, but she preferred a sense of decorum. She'd have words with him later.

"Mama, look at this dolly!" Ellie came toward her, holding high a large doll with a face carved from ivory, with painted black eyes and a brightly colored silk costume. "She looks like a princess."

"That's from a place called Egypt, little one," exclaimed Ziyad, who'd emerged from the wagon with more of his wares. "Where the people ride about on elephants."

"Can I have her, Mama?"

"She looks expensive." Ela didn't like to encourage indulgence. And the doll's dress had an excess of gold trim that seemed extravagant and distasteful. "Perhaps you could choose a silk cushion for your pins?"

Ellie's face fell. "I already have a pincushion. Petronella made it for me. I'd play with her every day and love her very much." Her eyes glowed as she stared at the lavish doll.

"She's fifty pence, my lady," said Ziyad softly. "She is dear indeed, but her face is hand carved from an elephant's tusk and her body stuffed with fine new lamb's wool. A doll fit for a little princess."

"I'm not a princess," said Ellie sadly. She thrust the doll back at Ziyad. "So you'd better keep her."

Ela laughed. In spite of herself her heart ached at Ellie's disappointment. And didn't every little girl deserve to feel like a princess at least sometimes? "We'll take her." Ziyad would compile a list of all the items bought by members of her family, and she'd pay him once his visit was done. More than once she'd given him sums that an ordinary man might not earn in his lifetime. She sometimes suspected that he came all the way to England to sell to her here at Salisbury Castle.

Not that she minded. She peered into a wooden box he'd opened. Dark blue velvet lined the interior, which held a number of small cream-colored statues. "These carvings are so delicate." She picked up the figure of a woman, about as long as her finger, carved in a delicate filigree pattern, completely hollow on the inside. "How do they do it?"

"Magic, my lady," he said with a smile. "Or perhaps a long, curved tool. But each one takes many hours. She's the queen from a chess set."

Ela realized that she was one of a collection of figures, each carved in the same style so that the light shone right through them like a lantern—the carvings so elaborate and impossibly tiny that they might have been whittled by fairies. "Where did you buy them?"

"I bought them in Toledo, but they were carved in India."

"India." Ela turned the piece over in her hand. "So very far away. It's hard to imagine such delicate things could travel such a great distance."

His dark eyes shone with amusement. "The finest craftsmen of India are unrivaled. It's worth the effort to transport their wares across the world for the enjoyment of discerning Englishmen...and women."

She turned the queen over in her hand, then put it down and picked up the bishop. "He wears a miter like one of our bishops here in England."

"Indeed he does. And if you ask me, the castle looks not entirely unlike your castle here in Salisbury."

Ela picked up the rook, a square keep with turrets, and turned it in her hand. "It looks like half the castles in Europe. And, yes, like this one."

"Look Mama, it has tiny windows, and even a slit for an archer to set his bow," said little Nicky. "An archer the size of a fly." The walls of the miniature castle featured exquisitely carved individual stones. "And look at the horse. It reminds me of Papa's destrier."

"Oh, it does. His big black one with the wavy mane."

"Bill Talbot is training Stephen on him. He won't let us call him what Papa did, though."

"Why's that?" Ela couldn't remember the horse's name. In fact, she wasn't sure she even knew it.

Nicky looked sheepish. "I'm not supposed to say it."

Ela frowned. "Oh." She'd have to ask Bill Talbot what he was talking about. She put the carved chess pieces carefully back into their velvet-lined box.

"It's a gift fit for a king, is it not?" asked Ziyad the merchant.

"Oh, indeed it is. Quite lovely."

"The work of a master craftsman. You'll not see another like it."

"Can we buy it, Mama?" pleaded Nicky. "Bill Talbot's been teaching me chess, and I almost won once."

"We already have a chess set," Ela protested. "In fact, I wouldn't be surprised if we have ten chess sets."

"But not like this one," said Ziyad. "Does your mother play chess?"

How did Ziyad know about her mother? Had he been coming to Salisbury so long that he'd come here when Alianore was still head of the household? Impossible. He didn't look old enough.

"My mother does play chess." This would be a lavish but

5

magnificent birthday present for her. Too lavish. She might be scolded for extravagance. Still….

"Your guests could hardly fail to remark on such a fine piece. I'm sure you entertain on a grand scale."

"We used to, when my husband was alive. But now that I'm a widow I live a quiet life here with my children."

The din of the great hall belied her words. Garrison soldiers mingled with the staff and a handful of townspeople there to press their suit about some matter needing her attention. Even the birds chirping high up in the rafters seemed to argue with her.

"Can we get it, Mama? Can we?" Little Ellie tugged at her gown. "I'm almost old enough to play chess."

"A doll and a chess set? Your grandmother will say I'm spoiling you."

"No, she won't." Ellie picked up a chain of gold links interspersed with deep green stones that Ziyad had pulled from a silk pouch. "She likes pretty things. She'd like this necklace."

"She would, wouldn't she? Which do you think she'd want for her birthday?"

"You can't give Grandmother the chess set," said Nicky, "because she might take it home with her and we need it here. Get her the necklace."

Apparently Nicky had already decided the chess set was theirs. "Are you buying it for us, my love?" asked Ela.

"Yes. I'll trade Papa's sword for it. It's too big for any of us anyway."

"You'll do no such thing." It occurred to Ela that she had no idea where her husband's famous longsword even rested now. Possibly in the armory. Much like his prized horse, she'd half forgotten it in the bustle of day-to-day life. "One day you might grow tall enough to carry Papa's sword yourself."

"Will tried and he said it was too heavy. It kept crashing to the ground."

"That's neither here nor there. We're keeping Papa's sword."

"I can still buy the chess set," said Nicky, "because I have two gold coins hidden under my mattress."

"What? How?"

"A man gave them to me."

"What man?"

"One of Papa's friends. After his funeral."

"Oh." Ela had been far too preoccupied with her own grief to do more than pay lip service to the many knights who'd come to pay their respects to her husband. "Well, that is nice but I suspect this chess set costs more than two gold coins."

"That depends on the value of the coins," said Ziyad, artfully folding a beautiful piece of silk cloth—blue shot through with green—that glimmered like a peacock's tail. "A single gold coin can be worth a great deal if it weighs enough. And I want you to have the chess set. It's yours for only three pounds as I want you to have it. You're a valued customer, and I know you appreciate beautiful things I bring from far away."

Three pounds was still a lot of money in the grand scheme of things, but somehow he made it sound like a bargain. "On those terms I can hardly refuse," said Ela with a smile. She fingered the green necklace. "And I'll take this as well, with a pretty box to present it in for my mother's birthday."

"Yes, my lady." He reached into his wagon and pulled out a box of dark polished wood inlaid with mother-of-pearl in a pattern that made up the phases of the moon. "Perhaps this one?"

Ela's children and other members of the household spent

much of the afternoon fingering precious silks or testing tortoiseshell combs and trying on necklaces. Even the servants shook the pennies out of their stockings to buy his treasures.

By the time Ziyad loaded the remaining goods back into his wagon, and his sweet, black-eyed donkey pulled it back through the arch, everyone had managed to spend their coins on something.

Ela left the hall to enjoy the peace of the Mass at Compline, and when she returned, Bill Talbot and Richard were locked in a battle with the new chess set. The black pieces were distinguished by an inlaid black line around the base, but otherwise both sides looked the same. Several of Richard's pieces had already fallen, including his queen, who stood forlornly to the side with her captured pawns.

"You lost your queen so soon?" she exclaimed.

"It was a worthwhile sacrifice to save my king." Richard pondered his next move without looking up.

"I shall have to instruct Richard on the importance of protecting and preserving his queen," said Bill with a sly grin. "So his lady wife isn't sacrificed to a marauding enemy at his keep."

"Indeed," said Ela. "The queen is the most useful piece. I always found that interesting."

"I like the knight," said Richard, taking the carved horse between finger and thumb. "Because he can jump behind enemy lines and take them by surprise."

"Is that a fair fight?" asked Ela.

"Sometimes whatever keeps you alive is a fair fight," said Bill. He lifted his bishop, slid it diagonally across the board, and tapped it gently against Richard's newly placed knight.

"Oh, no. I didn't see that coming."

"As a knight you must look all around you. You might see

an open plain and an empty road but the trees are full of armed men."

"I'd cut them all down," said Richard sulkily.

"Then what would you use for firewood in winter?" asked Ela. "Once a siege is over life must go back to normal."

"The queen looks a bit like you, Mama," said Richard, possibly trying to distract her from his impending defeat. "Look, she has a fillet and barbette and veil."

"I don't always wear a veil." Ela peered at the carved figure. "It might catch on the branches of the trees I just saved from your armies."

"She does have your likeness," said Bill. He picked up the defeated queen and peered at her. "Not just her clothing, either. Even her face looks like you."

"I'm hardly the most unusual-looking woman in England."

"Perhaps Ziyad had the set made especially for you."

"He said he bought it in Toledo, so that's impossible."

"I wonder if he was telling the truth. The castle, William's destrier, the queen...even Bishop Poore's miter. It's as if he gave the sculptor sketches to follow."

"Curious indeed, but I'm sure it's just a coincidence." Ela didn't like the idea of someone deliberately carving her likeness, or even that of her castle. "The carving is so unusual, though. Each piece is hollowed out inside but there's no hole large enough to fit anything bigger than a needle."

"I've never seen anything quite like it," said Bill. "The firelight moves through them and makes it look almost as if they're alive."

The early-summer night had grown chilly and a fire now glowed in the hearth. The flames sent a shower of sparks dancing upward and light flickered across the high ceiling of the great hall. The littlest children were being readied for bed. Petronella sat reading her prayer book by candlelight at a table nearby, and a group of garrison soldiers sat at another table, throwing dice and talking in hushed voices.

The light did move through the intricate carvings in such a way that they appeared almost to shift and turn.

"Your move, Richard," said Bill.

"Whatever I do, you'll take my piece." Richard surveyed the board grimly.

"But will you admit defeat and surrender, or fight to the finish?"

"I'll fight." He slid an unmoved pawn forward two places.

No sooner had he put his piece down than Bill captured it with another pawn. "En passant."

"Oh. I forgot about that," said Richard glumly. "Chess has too many moves to remember."

"It mimics life in that way," said Ela drily.

She went to sit with Petronella, who insisted on reading her some bracing passages from the Book of Job, which made her cross herself and promise never to take her blessings for granted. She kissed Ellie and Nicky good night before their maid took them upstairs to bed.

Ela took out some of the ribbon she'd bought from the merchant earlier that day. "Should I trim a gown with this, or edge a handkerchief?" she asked Petronella. The ribbon had a delicate pattern of leaves already sewn into its yellow surface. "It would look very pretty against a blue."

"Ornamentation is frivolous, Mama," scolded her pious daughter. "We should strive to live like the lilies of the field."

"The lilies of the field are lovely."

"So are you, just as God made you." Petronella glanced up from mending a stocking that should probably be given to a servant if not actually thrown away. "You don't need to cover yourself with ribbons and other fripperies."

Ela missed her two older daughters, Ida and Isabella, both now living far away with their noble husbands. They would have taken a keen interest in her frivolous ribbon and possibly even fought over who should have more of it. Her sons didn't care one way or the other. She rolled up the length of ribbon and tucked it into her sewing box. "I shall retire." She looked over at Bill and Richard. "Do put the chess set away in its box when you're finished with your game. The pieces are so delicate I don't want them getting knocked about by the soldiers."

She petted her greyhound, Grayson, who lay stretched out by the fire with her children's little dogs, then she picked up a lantern from a wrought-iron hook near the fire and headed to her chamber. Her maid, Elsie, who'd been sitting quietly nearby, rose silently to her feet and followed her.

ELSIE HELPED ELA UNDRESS, gently pulling the pins from her veil and placing them in an engraved box. The veil was shaken out and draped over the back of a chair. Then Elsie removed the fillet and barbette from Ela's hair and brushed them clean with a small, stiff brush, before wrapping them neatly and putting them in a round basket. She helped Ela lift her wool gown over her head and change into a clean linen shift scented with lavender and rose petals.

Then she turned down the quilted coverlet on Ela's bed. "Would you like a fire, my lady?"

"No, thank you, Elsie. You can go to bed now. I shall spend some time in prayer."

Ela knelt at her prie-dieu and said a few decades of the rosary, willing her mind to abandon the cares of the day and take refuge in the familiar prayers.

Nights were when she missed her husband most. When she remembered the feel of his arms around her and the tender way he kissed the back of her neck when he wanted to wake her in the night and—

Ela jerked her thoughts away from memories of marital happiness. She rose from her prie-dieu and climbed into bed. She'd sworn never to marry again. She intended to preserve her freedom and independence—and her fortune and estates —from the grasping hands of all the nobles who'd like to take them from her.

But sometimes independence could be very lonely. Especially late at night, when the sheets were cold.

~

A PIERCING SCREAM woke Ela from a deep sleep. She sat up in bed and listened.

Silence.

Had she imagined it? Dreamed it?

She climbed out of bed, walked across the wood floor with bare feet, and unlatched the leaded glass window. The cool night air rushed in, with a hint of smoke and the smell of dew-wet earth.

No sound.

She peered out at the darkness, the moon barely a sliver. She could just make out the walls that ringed the castle mound. She instinctively searched for the familiar towers of the cathedral—until she remembered that it was gone, deconsecrated and its stones carted away to build the new cathedral down the road in new Salisbury.

Stars winked, high in the heavens.

Not a soul stirred. Even the mice and the cats chasing them seemed to hold their breath.

Ela closed the casement window and latched it. A vivid dream. Nothing more. She'd had her share of them since her husband's death. He'd suffered so horribly—poisoned, she was sure of it—and felt such terror for the fate of his immortal soul.

She crossed herself. Surely that unearthly scream wasn't his soul crying out in torment?

She tried to shake the terrible thought from her head. Men didn't scream like that. It was a woman's scream.

Or perhaps a banshee or other mythical creature stalking her fevered imagination in these dark wee hours.

Ela climbed back into her bed and tried to settle under the covers. Then she heard something else.

Banging, like someone pounding on a door.

"Help! Help me!" The voice came from some distance away.

She sprang from her bed again. This was definitely a live person calling, and a woman. She threw on a robe over her shift and ran out into the hallway. "Elsie, a lantern!" Elsie slept like a fallen log. Ela rapped on her door, then pushed it open and called into the darkness for her to wake herself. The guard stood sentry at the end of the hallway lifted his head.

"Someone's downstairs," she called. The guard followed her, looking dazed and sleepy. "You must have heard them call?"

He didn't say anything. Perhaps he hadn't and didn't want to argue with his countess.

Not waiting for Elsie, Ela hurried downstairs and along the hallway to the great hall. The hall was never empty. Soldiers and servants slept in its quiet corners and sentries stood guard at all the doorways.

"Did you hear that scream?" she asked of the first soldier she saw.

"A scream? No, my lady." He was an older man, battle scarred and gruff. "I did hear someone knocking on the door, though."

"Did anyone answer it?"

"I don't know, my lady."

"Find out!"

The man startled into action and jogged stiffly across the hall, rustling the rushes on the floor. Two dogs woke and started barking. Where was Elsie with her lantern? The fire had gone out and only thin light came through the high windows.

The movement stirred other soldiers into action, and the door to the hall creaked open. Ela heard a woman's voice cry out—breathless and desperate—"Help me!"

CHAPTER 2

"Bring her in," called Ela, as she hurried toward the door. Servants stirred and lit candles, casting at least a flickering half-light on the scene.

The hood of her dark cloak hid the woman's face. She entered the hall and hesitated, then seemed to see Ela. "Help me," she pleaded.

"What's amiss?" asked Ela. She didn't recognize her, and the woman's voice had a foreign accent.

"My husband...he's gone."

"Oh." A husband leaving his wife for another woman was not as rare as one might hope. He might be persuaded to return in the cold light of morning, but it was hardly a matter to rouse the castle from their slumbers. "I'm sorry to hear that, mistress, but there's nothing we can do right now."

"He would never leave me. Never! He promised."

Ela's heart squeezed. Her husband had made so many promises when he went away to war. And he'd kept them, too, though not before everyone except her counted him as dead. "I understand. Perhaps in the morning—"

"He's dead. I'm sure of it!"

Unlikely. He was probably in another woman's bed, breaking his marriage vows and several of the Ten Commandments in one fell swoop. "What is your name, mistress?"

"My name?" She seemed surprised by the question. "My husband is Ziyad al Wahid."

"The merchant," Ela exclaimed. "He was here just yester-day, alive and well."

"I know. I was here, too."

"What?"

"I stayed inside the wagon."

Ela couldn't see her face now. The deep shadows of her hood kept it in darkness. "What's your name?"

"Safiya," she whispered. "Ziyad swore to never leave me alone at night. Never! I know he wouldn't break his vow."

Ela felt a sigh rise in her chest. No woman believed her husband would cheat on her. Not the first time, anyway. "I'm sure he'll return. You should go back to sleep until dawn."

"Go back to sleep?" The woman's voice broke. "He's in danger. Did you not hear his cry?"

Ela frowned. "I did hear a cry." It sounded like a woman. "What makes you think that was him?"

"My heart."

Ela's own heart started to pound slightly. Why would a man cry out in the dark of night? And such a sharp scream, like one in terror. "We must search for him. Guards!"

THE GUARDS SPRANG SLOWLY into action. Gerald Deschamps, grumpy at being roused from his bed in the dark, commanded them to search the area inside the castle's outer walls.

"Is your wagon attended, mistress?" Ela asked Safiya. "Your valuable goods should not be left unguarded."

"What use are they if my husband is injured or killed?" Her voice trembled. She seemed so sure that he'd come to harm. Ela now prayed that he'd just strayed into another woman's chamber.

Ela ordered guards to attend the wagon, which stood inside the walls, not far from the marketplace. She didn't want to create the opportunity for further crimes. Word of the merchant's rich and varied goods had spread across Salisbury yesterday. There were always those who couldn't help but covet their neighbor's goods—and who might seize the opportunity to break another commandment by stealing them.

Ela tried to convince Safiya to come into the hall and sit down, but she insisted on following the soldiers. Not wanting her to come to harm, Ela resolved to go with her. She asked sleepy Elsie to fetch her a cloak to cover her night-clothes. She pulled the hood up over her hair, like Safiya, and together—with a phalanx of guards—they headed out into the crisp predawn air.

Brisk winds always blew across the high castle mound, and their candle guttered even inside a horn lantern. Smoke stung Ela's nostrils as they passed through the village, where the baker's oven had already been active for some time. The baker might have been awake to hear the scream.

Ela stepped into the shop and asked the lad there if she could speak to Peter Howard, the baker. The boy fetched his master from the back room, where the ovens blazed, and Howard frowned in surprise at Ela.

"Good day, my lady. You're early for a loaf of bread, I'm afraid."

"We're seeking this lady's husband. Have you seen anyone abroad on the streets this early?"

17

"Haven't left my own house. I just come downstairs and get to work."

"Did you hear anything?"

"Can't say I did. But the roar of the ovens and the crackling of the logs drown out most noises."

Ela and Safiya headed back out into the street. The first glow of dawn now brightened the sky beyond the east wall. "We should check your wagon. Your husband may have returned and be frantic with worry." And possibly racked with guilt from being caught stepping out in the wee hours.

Back inside the castle courtyard, Safiya's hurried steps startled the guards into action and Ela heard them draw their swords as they approached. "It's just us."

The merchant wasn't there. Ela saw Safiya's face grow taut with worry.

"We should visit the Bull and Bear. It's the public house and sometimes men stay up all night there drinking and talking, and then they rent a room to sleep in if they're too drunk to ride or walk home."

"My husband's religion forbids him drink."

Again, Ela wondered if she had too much faith in her husband. "We'll look in to be sure."

Safiya hung back when the soldier knocked on the scarred door of the Bull and Bear. It took quite some time for the door to open, and when it did, the owner's wife looked like she'd just crawled out of her bed to answer it.

"Good morning, mistress. May God be with you."

The woman looked like she wished the devil's company for Ela.

"Did Ziyad the merchant visit your premises at any time during the night?"

"Here? This is a respectable house."

"He's a respectable merchant," Ela retorted. She didn't like the suggestion that he might not be worthy of this faded and musty establishment. "And he's currently missing."

"Well, he's not missing here," she snapped back. "What's missing is my good night's sleep. My lady." She tacked the last part on, remembering her manners at the last moment. No doubt she didn't want to be slapped with fines or investigated for underpayment of taxes or uncleanliness or watering ale or any other infractions that Ela might come up with in her role as sheriff.

"I'd appreciate it if you'd let me know if you see or hear of him, or if someone else does."

"Yes, my lady," she muttered, looking ready to slam the door in their faces.

Ela turned away with a sigh. "We should return to the castle. Then at least we'll hear word quickly when he turns up." If they hadn't found him by now, it was likely that he'd left Salisbury, or at least the part of it encircled by the castle walls. The area was too small for a man to go missing for long.

The sun had risen high enough behind the hills to cast a soft, pale light across the village. The first farmers now brought their goods in through the open gates, ready to set up their stalls in the market and catch the early customers for their strawberries or butter.

Hopefully Safiya's husband would be among them, ready to sell tooled leather belts and sheaths and decorative buckles and carved camels to the townspeople who didn't dare come into the castle hall yesterday.

But there was no sign of Ziyad among the people propping up their stalls on crude wooden trestles.

Ela and Safiya walked back toward the castle and were heading for the doors when Gerald Deschamps strode up to them. "My lady," he bowed his head slightly. "There is some…news."

"What news?"

He glanced at Safiya. "I'm afraid a body has been found."

Safiya let out a tiny shriek, and her hands flew to her mouth.

"Where?" asked Ela.

"In the moat."

"He drowned," said Safiya with a trembling voice. "He couldn't swim."

"He can't have drowned," said Ela, looking at Deschamps. "It's a dry moat. Take us to him."

Safiya seemed rooted to the spot. Her veil trembled, and her hands seemed to stiffen over her mouth. Ela's heart ached, and she prayed that the body in the moat was someone else.

Unlikely as that was.

She took Safiya's hand. "Come with me. We must go see what's happened."

Safiya blinked, eyes dry, clearly in shock.

Ela hesitated. Should she force the woman to view the body of her dead husband? What if it was horribly disfigured and would give her nightmares? "Would you like me to escort you to the hall to wait?"

"No," Safiya said with certainty. "I shall come."

They hurried toward the outer castle walls and followed Gerald Deschamps as he led the way to the gate. The castle stood on a great mound, built in part of earth excavated from the deep, wide ditch that ringed the castle.

The mound and the ditch around it were hundreds of years old—maybe even thousands—and her own forbears had simply built their new castle on it when they came from France with William the Conqueror more than one hundred and sixty years ago.

They passed through the archway that led out of the castle, but instead of crossing over the bridge to the other side of the moat, they took a hard right onto a narrow path that ran along the foot of the castle wall, at the top of the steep-sided ditch that ringed the castle.

Ela didn't remember the last time she'd been this way. The moat unfortunately had become a dumping ground for refuse carted out here from the castle and the town around it. Sheep grazed the grass that cloaked the higher parts of the ditch, but the lower regions were dark and dank and malodorous. Sometimes water gathered in the depths after long rains, but calling it a moat was charitable.

"Where is he?"

"Along this way, my lady."

Ela made sure Safiya was steady enough on her feet to follow the narrow path. Though a tumble down into the ditch wouldn't kill anyone, it would be most unpleasant to land at the bottom.

As they moved around the circular castle wall, a knot of men came into view, gathered at the bottom of the ditch.

Ela heard Safiya gasp. She turned to find her stopped, staring, her hands pressed to her mouth again. "You can stay here if you want."

Safiya blinked, her dark eyes fixed on the group of men. "I will. For a moment anyway."

Ela walked forward. Deschamps helped her descend the extremely steep side of the ditch, walking across the slope at an angle as a sheep would. Lifting her skirts, she half held her breath in the fetid atmosphere down at the bottom of the pit. At least the ground wasn't too damp today, and there was no garderobe near enough to have deposited refuse in the immediate area.

The dead man lay flat on his back, sightless dark eyes staring up into the sky as the sun rose above the horizon. It was unmistakably Ziyad. Even if she hadn't known him personally, his tanned skin and charcoal-dark eyes distinguished him from the local men, and his voluminous foreign-made robes, with their decorative accents, would make him stand out even in a crowd.

"Has the coroner been sent for?" asked Ela.

"He's on his way," replied Deschamps.

Ela hated that so many people had already trodden on the scene. Soon there would be more. "Please call for jurors to attend."

She looked up at the castle wall behind her. They were some distance from the main gate, and there was no visible door in the castle wall. A sheep watched them silently from the outer rim of the ditch.

"How would he end up here?" asked Ela. "Did someone push him from the top of the wall?" She peered up at the top of the defensive wall that ringed the town. It was the height of three men or more.

"He couldn't have been on top of the wall," said Deschamps. "It's manned by armed guards."

"Are you sure they were at their posts?"

Deschamps bristled. "This castle is the king's garrison, and I pride myself on keeping it under close watch at all times."

"That's commendable." No sense in getting his back up. She needed to keep him on her side in order to keep the king happy. "But if he didn't fall from the wall, how did he get here?"

"Perhaps he fell down from the outside," said Deschamps, surveying the cliff-steep outer bank. "He might have been trying to get back in after the gates were closed and lost his footing?"

"Why would he be outside the castle walls at night? And even if he was, no man would be foolish enough to try to scale this wall. He'd have waited at the gate until dawn."

Ela glanced back at Safiya. She'd inched forward along the path and now stood at the top of the steep hill.

"Sir Gerald, please have one of your men help this lady down here. This is her husband."

Two men climbed up the steep hill toward Safiya and helped her walk down it, which was good because her eyes never left her husband's lifeless body and the footing was uneven as well as sloped. When she reached him her hands flew to her mouth.

Ela stood stiffly, waiting for her to scream or cry out. She'd heard that women from the Holy Land let out terrible ululations over a dead body. Not that she actually knew where Safiya or even Ziyad came from now that she thought about it.

Safiya suddenly crumpled to the ground, falling to her knees with her head resting on her husband's dead body. Her hands grasped at his clothing, scrunching it between her fingers as if she could grip him hard enough to pull him back to life.

Ela's chest ached. That horrible realization—that her partner in life was truly gone—was all too fresh in her memory. Her husband had been dead more than a year, but she still felt the shock and grief as keenly as if he'd passed yesterday.

Safiya didn't make a sound, though. Eyes tight shut, she pressed herself against her husband, clinging to him as if she could follow him into the next life.

GILES HAUGHTON, the coroner, arrived soon after. He scrambled ably down the bank and greeted Ela and Deschamps. The same two guards who'd helped Safiya descend now gently pried her off her husband's body and lifted her to her feet. She didn't resist, but Ela wondered if she could stand unassisted. She looked ready to collapse at any moment.

"My condolences on your terrible loss, mistress," said Haughton to Safiya. She blinked mutely in response.

Haughton now knelt over the body. He tested the pulse at the neck, then slowly began to explore it with his hands, feeling the chest through Ziyad's green robe. "No obvious wounds, no blood." He felt down the arms and legs. "No broken bones."

He stood and surveyed the scene. Deschamps ordered the men to move back out of the way. Haughton glanced up the hill toward the castle's outer walls, then at the opposite bank that led up to the surrounding countryside.

"Do you think he fell from the castle wall?" asked Ela.

Haughton looked at Deschamps. "Were there footprints near the body when you first arrived?"

"I'm not sure," said Deschamps. "It wasn't fully light yet." The sun had now risen but stayed tucked behind a blanket of white clouds, casting a bleak light over the scene.

"You know how important it is to preserve the area around a crime." Haughton's voice had a slight scolding tone. Ela had noticed that the two men had a way of strutting around each other like rival roosters. "You should keep your men well back from a body."

Deschamps muttered something about seeing if he was still alive and helping Safiya down the hill, while Haughton made a circle around the body, looking for footprints in any direction.

"He must have fallen from the castle wall," he said at last. "I don't see any footprints to the site except those coming from the gate. If he'd come through the gate he would have been seen by the sentries—and he wasn't, from what they've told me. If he'd fallen from the outer edge of the ditch, he

24

would have hit the ground on the way down and there'd be abrasions on this thin turf." He pointed to the outer wall that had indeed been heavily grazed by sheep, almost down to the soil. "And I suspect he was pushed. If he'd simply slipped and fallen from the high wall, he would have likely fallen onto the bank and left a mark, especially as his body rolled down into the ditch."

Safiya let out a whimper. Ela put a hand on her shoulder, wishing her strength.

"Pushed," said Ela. "So you think it was a murder?"

"It seems that way."

Two jurors made their way around the castle wall and down the steep hill into the ditch: Thomas Price, the old thatcher, who'd been a juror as long as Ela could remember, and Stephen Hale, the cordwainer, who stitched all their shoes and who always took his responsibilities seriously.

Ela looked at them. "I heard a scream in the night," she said. "Loud enough to wake me. Did you all hear it, too?"

Thomas Price shook his head. "I'm a sound sleeper, my lady. Like trying to wake the dead, my wife says." Then he glanced at the dead body and recoiled at his words. "I beg your pardon, I…" he trailed off.

"Did you hear the cry?" Ela asked Stephen Hale. He shook his narrow head. "I didn't hear anything in particular but I did wake up in the night for no good reason. Before Matins, it was, as I lay awake trying to get back to sleep and then I heard the bells. So something might have jolted me awake." He also peered cautiously at the dead merchant's wife. Ela reflected that Safiya, with her big dark eyes and full mouth, was beautiful enough to turn heads, which may be why her husband kept her tucked away from the prying eyes of men.

"I heard it," said Safiya. "I knew it was him."

"And he didn't tell you whom he went out to meet?" Ela asked Safiya.

"No," she said quietly. "I only found him gone when I awoke in the night."

Ela looked at the blank-faced soldiers around them. "Did any of you hear it?"

One of them shrugged. None of them said anything.

"He could have cried out as he fell," said Ela. She looked at Haughton. "Could the fall itself kill him?"

"I daresay it could, if it smashed a rib and that pierced an organ."

"But you said he had no broken bones," she replied.

"I didn't find any, but we must bring him back to the castle mortuary so I can do a fuller examination." He glanced at Safiya. "His lady wife should be spared that sight."

"Indeed." Ela silently thanked him for his discretion. A cruder man might have stripped Ziyad naked right here in front of everyone. "Sir Gerald, do allow the jurors to examine the scene in all its aspects, then have the body escorted to the mortuary as quickly as possible." She turned to Haughton. "Send for me when he arrives. I'd like to attend your study of the body."

CHAPTER 3

"*L*et me take you back to your wagon," Ela said softly to Safiya, "where you can rest while we try to understand what happened."

Ascending the hill again proved quite an undertaking for both Ela and Safiya in their long skirts and smooth-soled leather boots. Even with the soldiers' help, it took some effort for them to climb back to the narrow path along the castle's outer walls.

Once back inside the gate, Safiya let out a strange low sound somewhere between a sigh and a groan. "What will become of me?"

"That's a question for tomorrow," said Ela. What indeed? Her husband was the merchant, not she. Ela had never seen her before. She didn't even know Ziyad had a wife. "For today you must rest and guard your strength. Do you have children with you?" Was Ziyad's entire family tucked away inside his wagon?

"I have no children," she said quietly. A sob rose in her throat. "And now I never shall."

Ela took Safiya's hand in hers and squeezed it gently.

"May the Lord comfort you." She knew better than to start promising a new husband and future happiness. She'd have bitten the head off anyone who'd suggested such joys to her on the day her husband died.

The sun had not fully risen, and people went about their morning business with a fresh loaf of bread under their arm or lugging a pail of milk.

"They say Allah is merciful, but is he?" Safiya's voice rose.

Ela looked around, hoping that no one had overheard. She didn't know much about this woman's religion but from what little she'd heard and read she suspected Allah was the same God as hers, just in a different robe. "He has his plan for the course of our lives. I know too well the sharp pain you're feeling right now."

"Now I'm alone in a strange country, so far from home."

"Where are you from?"

"Tangier. It's a city on the north coast of Morocco."

"Is Ziyad from there, too?"

"No, he's from Sevilla. He came to my city to buy gold. My father had a shop in the gold souk."

"And Ziyad won your heart?"

"No!" She looked like she might laugh or cry. "He bought me like I was just another finely wrought necklace. My father sold me despite my tears."

"But you became attached to him, I can see that."

"Indeed I did. I loved him deeply."

They'd reached the caravan, which had been pulled up next to a section of the outer wall, where it was convenient for people to find but not somewhere they'd be stumbling over it, cursing the inconvenience. The little donkey was tethered to a stake in the ground nearby and brightened at their approach, letting out an enthusiastic donkey greeting.

"Yafur—our donkey—will be hungry and thirsty. I must gather him some grass and take him to water."

"I'll have those brought from the castle. We keep a stock of cut hay for our horses and there's a well behind the kitchen. Unless you'd prefer to keep busy by doing it yourself? I find my grief easier to bear when I'm occupied with other things."

"I'll take him to graze outside the walls and to drink at the stream. I need to think."

"I understand. You have a lot to think about." Something puzzled her. "You speak good English. Better than Ziyad even. How did you learn it?"

"My mother taught it to me. Her father was an English trader. He kept them well and would live with her and her mother when he was in Tangier. Her mother made sure she spoke good English, and even some French, because she always hoped he'd take them both back to England with him, but he never did and he never came back after my grandmother died. My mother was pretty enough to secure a respectable marriage to the local goldsmith despite her odd upbringing."

"And here you are, one generation later." Ela saw a ray of hope. "Is your English grandfather still alive?"

"I don't know. I never met him. I doubt it. He'd be a very old man by now."

Ela couldn't tell how old Safiya was. She had the kind of smooth, bold features that might be found in a mature girl of fifteen or a youthful woman of thirty.

"And yet you've found yourself in the country of your ancestors."

"Not by my own free will. My skill in English is the reason Ziyad paid a high price for me. He wanted to build his own knowledge of the language. He often made me speak it when we were together."

"How long have you been married?"

"Five years."

"So long! How have I never seen you before?"

"It's our custom for women to stay hidden from the eyes of strangers. He never wanted me to interact with customers."

"I see. But you know how the business runs?"

"Not really. My husband managed the business." Safiya looked at her curiously. "Why are you the sheriff when there are men all around you?"

Ela blinked, taken aback. "Because I wish to see justice served for the people of Salisbury and all of Wiltshire."

Safiya regarded her curiously. "You're a very interesting woman."

Ela wasn't sure how to respond to this. Despite her life hidden in the back of a wagon, Safiya seemed oddly self-possessed. It wasn't hard to imagine her running a business. And despite her heavy accent, her English was fluent and easy to understand. "You're welcome to come to me at the castle and I'll give you what advice I can to plan how to manage your life as a widow. I was widowed myself only last year. And I'll be sure to update you with Giles Haughton's findings."

She inhaled, not sure how to say this next part. "And arrangements must be made for the body." What did people in Safiya's part of the world do with their dead? Since he wasn't a Christian, Ziyad certainly couldn't be buried in the hallowed ground of the cathedral or of a local churchyard.

Safiya stared at the wall in front of her, but Ela could tell her thoughts were focused inward. She decided to wait until after Giles Haughton's examination to raise the issue of burial.

∾

WHEN ELA ARRIVED at the mortuary, the body already lay naked on the table in the bare, stone-floored room. She crossed herself at the sight. Somehow it always felt immodest and ungodly for her to look at a naked male, even though it was an important part of her job.

Ziyad was very hairy. Not only his face and chest but his arms and legs as well. She'd never seen so much hair on a man.

She desperately wished she could turn her attention elsewhere. "Do you have any additional findings?"

"I just got him undressed, my lady. His clothes are over there. There's an odd tear on the inside of his robe."

Ela glanced at his green robe, now half folded on a chest that lay to one side against the unpainted wall. She picked it up gingerly and turned it over in her hands—there was a great deal of fabric in it—until she saw the long, jagged tear. "Do you think his robe tore on the wall?"

"No. I think it was cut with a knife."

"You think someone searched it for valuables?"

"If someone met him on the wall to make a trade, then decided to keep the item without paying, they might have tried to find the object on his person."

Ela frowned. "I wonder if they got what they wanted."

She moved closer to the corpse and realized she was half holding her breath. The body wasn't dead long enough to smell putrid, so she wondered if she was afraid of inhaling something else—a whiff of spirit still hovering around the body.

"Does a faithful infidel go to his own heaven, or does his soul wander forever in purgatory?" she pondered aloud. She didn't know if Ziyad was devout.

"I daresay every man finds the eternity he deserves based on his deeds during life," murmured Haughton.

"I do hope so." Now was not the time for a theological

discussion, but she doubted that even the most pious infidel could gain entry to the kingdom of Heaven without either baptism or last rites. "I've never presided over the death of someone who wasn't a Christian."

"We all bleed the same red blood," said Haughton. He rolled back the dead man's eyelids and studied his eyes. Then he turned his head to each side and slid his fingers into Ziyad's thick black hair. "No contusions on his skull."

He touched his neck and lifted his chin, then he paused. He leaned in and peered closely. "There's a ligature mark on his neck."

"He was strangled?"

"It's a fine mark, barely more than a single thread and right under his chin where it's not easily seen."

Ela still couldn't see it. She moved closer. Now she could just make out a thin line, barely darker than the parchment-colored skin around it. "You think this killed him?"

"It's certainly a possibility."

"But I heard him scream. If he was killed before he fell off the wall, how could he scream?"

"Perhaps he cried out as he struggled with his assailant before he strangled him."

"His attacker must have been up on the castle wall with him. Why would he go up there in the first place?" asked Ela.

"He's a trader. He'd likely go anywhere that there's money to be made for the goods he wishes to sell."

"But there are soldiers up on this wall at all hours. There'd be a sentry even at night. Perhaps especially then."

"A soldier might have killed him," suggested Haughton. He'd moved on and was now studying the dead man's hands, turning them over and palpating the palms, then looking closely at his fingernails. "His hands don't show signs of a struggle."

"Perhaps his killer surprised him from behind." She

frowned. "But when would he have found time to scream? And if he was strangled, he'd have fallen to the ground, yet he was pushed off the wall."

Haughton's hands now probed around the man's ribs. "I suggested that he was pushed because that would thrust him far enough away from the wall that he wouldn't hit the sloped bank on the way down. But that's not the only possibility. If there were two men they could have picked him up and heaved him over."

"I daresay even one man could do that if he was tall and strong enough. Ziyad wasn't a big man."

In death he looked slight. No taller than Ela herself and with the slim, un-muscled body of someone who worked with his mind rather than his body.

Haughton slid his hands underneath the body. "No ribs are broken."

"Which further suggests he was dead before he fell into the ditch."

"It does, though there may be internal bleeding that we'd find on cutting him open." He sighed. "I'm not sure that's worth doing. It will desecrate his body and upset his wife if she needs to prepare it. We already know he was strangled, so whether he was dead when he left the top of the wall or not is rather a moot point."

"I suppose you're right." Ela looked up at him. "Do you know anything about Muslim burial rituals?"

"Can't say I do. I was never in the Holy Land."

"My husband would have known," said Ela sadly. "But I shall ask Safiya when I return. The more pressing question is who killed him. I shall ask Gerald Deschamps for a list of soldiers with access to that part of the wall early this morning."

"I'd also like to find out what thin cord was used to strangle him."

"Perhaps a thin skein of embroidery thread, or three strands twisted together so as to be strong enough to pull tight without breaking," said Ela. "But it's hard to imagine soldiers with embroidery thread. What might fighting men use a thin cord for?"

"A bow string. Though that would have left more of a mark. This would be something softer. Your idea of a skein of fine threads is compelling."

"An unusual weapon suggests premeditation," said Ela. "For the killer must have brought it with him."

"It's a shame that the merchant didn't tell his wife who he was meeting."

"She was shocked that he'd gone out leaving her alone at night. The way she said it I assume they had some prior arrangement that he'd never do that."

"I know the reason most men sneak out alone at night," said Haughton gruffly.

"A woman," said Ela. "But then how would he end up on top of the castle wall? That's hardly a place for a tryst."

"Perhaps the tryst was somewhere else, and was interrupted, and the angry husband killed him and threw him from the castle wall in revenge."

"In my experience, crimes among the common people are rarely that complicated," said Ela. "If the angry husband wanted him dead, he'd have killed him on the spot with whatever weapon he had to hand."

"In his own house? And spattered his wife's kitchen floor with blood?"

"He'd hardly worry about upsetting his wife if she'd just bedded another man."

"Unless he wanted to keep it quiet and possibly get his revenge on her later."

"I think your imagination runs away with you this morning, Giles." Ela looked at the body, which Haughton had half covered with a rough linen cloth. "And I find it hard to imagine Ziyad engaging in a tryst with one of the women of Salisbury. I've known him for years and heard nothing but good tidings of his honesty."

"He comes to Salisbury every year?"

"At least once. Sometimes more often. One year he came right before Christmas, bearing a chest filled with the most luxurious inlaid boxes. I gave one to everyone I knew that year."

"You and your household were clearly a valued part of his trade. Don't you find it odd that he kept his wife hidden the whole time?"

Ela paused to inhale. "I don't know the customs of his Moorish homeland, but his wife said the men don't like strangers to gaze on their wives."

"Ah, yes, I've heard this. They don't leave the house without a male escort."

"And now his poor wife is left in a strange country with no one."

"Do you find it odd that she speaks our language so fluently?"

"She told me that she learned it as a child."

"Then she's not such a traditional wife. Perhaps she didn't like being imprisoned in his wagon away from the bustle of life."

"Are you suggesting she killed him?" asked Ela.

"The husband or wife is usually my first suspect."

Ela had not contemplated the idea that Safiya might have murdered her husband. Perhaps because the woman's grief seemed so genuine. "She appeared terrified for him when he was missing, then truly devastated by his loss."

"Would a wife not have at least a seed of doubt about her husband's intentions if he went missing in the night? Her confidence that he had come to harm is in itself suspicious."

"She heard him scream. As did I."

"Did it sound like a male scream, or a female scream?"

Ela frowned. "It woke me from my sleep, that's all I know. It was a high-pitched cry."

Haughton cleared his throat. "You may think me heartless, but I suggest searching their wagon for a fine cord of some kind."

Ela glanced again at Ziyad's lifeless body. "I suppose you're right. If nothing else it will give us more of an idea of their life together and I can press Safiya for more details about their marriage."

She shrank from probing the woman who seemed to be suffering the same terrible grief she knew too well. But as sheriff, it was her job to investigate rather than comfort. "I'll also find out what she wants to do with the body. But first we must try to find out what happened high up on the wall and who was there."

ELA AND HAUGHTON left the body in the mortuary and made their way through the castle to the outer wall, a solid mass of stone several yards thick. A few rooms and closets were tucked into its depth, and stairs inside the guard towers led to a walk along the top of the wall, where soldiers could patrol and keep an eye out for invading armies advancing across Salisbury plain.

Deschamps somehow got word of their arrival and appeared as they approached the steep stone steps. "A very sad business," he muttered.

"The merchant was strangled," said Ela. "Before someone shoved him from the top of this wall."

Deschamps eyes widened, and he looked at Haughton for confirmation. Which lit a tiny flame of annoyance in the pit of Ela's stomach. "A fine cord across his throat," said Haughton gruffly. "His killer came prepared."

Deschamps frowned. "What was a merchant doing up on the castle wall in the first place?"

"Perhaps your sentries who were stationed there at the time can answer that question for us." Ela lifted her skirts and ascended the steps.

"I've spoken to the sentries and none of them saw anything," said Deschamps, following close behind her.

"Then one or more of them is lying," said Ela coolly. "Ziyad the merchant may have been strangled elsewhere but his position in the ditch leaves no doubt that his body was thrown from the wall. If he was dead at the time that he fell —without falling against the wall, as we've already determined—his killer shoved his body with enough force to throw it out into the middle of the ditch."

"A killer pushing a merchant's body off a wall in the night?" Deschamps shook his head. "It's quite preposterous."

"Do you have a better explanation?" Ela couldn't conceal her irritation at his dismissive reply.

"My guess would be that he came up here undetected and jumped to his death, for reasons unknown to us, my lady." He said the last two words with some emphasis.

"It might be hard for him to jump after strangling himself," said Ela drily.

"Perhaps his collar was too tight and left a mark on his neck."

"The merchant's tunic was cut below the collarbone." Ela felt her eyes narrow as she peered at him. "Sir Gerald, I wonder at your insistence on blaming this man for his own death. I realize that you feel some culpability since he was killed on the castle walls manned by the garrison that you command, but, if anything, I think that should make you more eager to find the perpetrators."

Deschamps face darkened. "Perhaps he was robbed. He shouldn't have been up on the wall."

"How many men were charged with patrolling the walls?"

"Three."

"Only three men for the entire wall around all of Salisbury?" She couldn't hide her surprise.

"We're not at war or expecting a siege. They would alert others if anything was amiss."

"Except that they didn't. Where is each man posted?"

"They move around the wall, my lady." Deschamps looked slightly alarmed. Which was intriguing. "The better to survey the area around the castle."

Ela decided that she'd come up to the wall herself, unannounced, and see for herself how the men patrolled it.

ELA DIDN'T HEAD STRAIGHT BACK to Safiya. For all her need to continue her investigation, she wanted to give the widow a chance to catch her breath. If that meant she had more time to hide the murder weapon, so be it.

Ela's children had finished breaking their fast, and now the younger ones sat at their studies. Ela ordered some stewed fruit and soft cheese and sat at the high table to eat it. She'd barely taken a bite when Noel Bazin, the new steward, came rushing over, an earnest expression on his long face.

"My lady, I hear the foreign merchant fell from the castle walls!"

"We're not sure exactly what happened," she said briskly. "And it's important not to start rumors."

"We hadn't yet paid him for all the goods he brought. I was gathering the coin in readiness, but now, perhaps you might save yourself the expense." He waited for her response, a toadying look brightening his pinched features.

"The money is now owed to his wife, who is likely his heir under the circumstances," she replied coldly. "I do not look on a murder as an excuse to avoid my debts." She liked this man less and less.

"A debt to a foreigner is not the same as a debt to a countryman, my lady." He stood over her, weaving his hands together. "I'm sure anyone would find it quite understandable if you wanted to, say, donate the money to the poor or to the church." A smile pushed up the corners of his thin mouth.

"I'm sure I can find the funds to support causes close to my heart without stealing them from a freshly bereaved widow. We should look to the safety of our immortal souls before the thickness of our purses. I'll thank you to make sure that everyone else in the castle pays every penny due to Safiya for her husband's wares."

His face fell. "Yes, my lady. She is an infidel, though, and they—"

"Silence!" Ela cut him off. She'd heard quite enough of his mean-spirited drivel. "If you argue with me again on this matter I'll be forced to dismiss you from my service."

He blinked rapidly. "Begging your pardon, my lady. I didn't mean to offend."

"Immediately gather the funds to pay our debt to the merchant in full. The money you collected for the sale of the fleeces from my three southernmost manors should suffice."

"Yes, my lady."

"I do appreciate the thorough accounting you did with regards to the fleeces and the profits from each flock. It was most edifying." She could now see that some flocks produced far better wool than others and should be bred, whereas the others might be slowly sold off as they were replaced with the better stock.

"You're most welcome, my lady. Next I thought perhaps I

might order an inventory of the types and sizes of fish present in each of the fishponds on your various manors, so as to see if any of the ponds need restocking."

"An excellent idea, and perhaps the plumpest results of your investigation can be brought here for cook to prepare."

"Yes, my lady." His smile broadened. "You should enjoy the bounty of your estates while keeping good account of them."

Ela could see why her mother had praised him. Bazin showed initiative and sharpness she hadn't seen in her recent stewards. And such qualities did tend to come with arrogance and forwardness as a matter of course. Her husband had said as much about his fighting men.

Sharp people could be unusually observant. "As you know, we're seeking the killer of Ziyad the merchant. It appears he was killed up on the castle's outer walls, within hearing distance of this hall. Have you heard any talk about it?"

She kept her voice low—which was typical when she spoke about matters of business—and hoped he responded with discretion if necessary. Soldiers and castle employees moved around them, going about their business.

"There's always talk about people from foreign parts, isn't there?"

"As I recall, you yourself are from Picardy, which—last time I checked—was in a foreign country. What kind of talk?"

"Their odd ways, praying to their strange gods at all times of the day and night, for example."

"I consider piety to be a blessing regardless of the faith professed," she said stiffly. "But who was expressing disapproval of his behavior?"

"Well, the soldiers never like someone from enemy lands, do they?"

"I do wish you'd stop asking me questions that demand a particular answer. Do not presume my agreement. Our battle for Jerusalem, the heart of Christendom, does not pit us against every man and woman in the Muslim world. Did any particular soldier say something against Ziyad?"

"Let me think." He pressed a long forefinger to his temple as if that might activate his thought process. "I do recall hearing one of them ranting that such infidels should be turned away from our shores—along with all the Jews and Genoese—and that we ought not to buy any of their goods."

"Who said this?"

"One of the soldiers, I think. I couldn't say exactly who. A gruff voice. I didn't turn to see him."

"Did anyone respond?"

"I think there was a general murmur of agreement from his crude fellows." Noel Bazin peered at her as if to see how this news was being received.

Ela didn't know what to make of it. Anti-foreigner sentiment was hardly unusual—especially among soldiers whose lives were spent fighting one foreign army or another. "Did they express a desire to"—she wasn't sure how to put it—"to make any kind of mischief for him?"

"Not that I heard, but it isn't impossible. His wagon, complete with donkey, being inside the great hall excited a lot of talk."

"Ziyad's wares are highly valued by the household. We look forward each year to his visits." Though she didn't remember the wagon entering the hall before and doubted that would have happened had her husband still been castellan. She reminded herself to have a word with both Albert the porter and Gerald Deschamps about preserving the dignity of the hall.

"Indeed, my lady," said Bazin in an obsequious tone. "And

he did a great deal of business so you're far from alone in that sentiment."

"I hardly think that someone disdaining his foreignness would be inclined to kill him. What other motivation might they have?"

She knew the men talked more frankly amongst themselves when she wasn't there. Her longtime squire, Bill Talbot, overheard some of their banter, but everyone knew that he had her ear, so he wasn't privy to their unvarnished grumblings like a more distant member of her household might be.

"He had goods of considerable value. Perhaps someone wanted to acquire them without paying."

That did seem the most likely scenario—as everyone kept pointing out. But why had he left his bed in the middle of the night—without telling his wife—to meet with them?

CHAPTER 4

*E*la knew she could have Safiya summoned to the hall to meet with her, but she hoped to get a glimpse of the inside of her wagon. She now imagined a secret world in there, behind the patterned canvas, where Safiya lived out her life away from the prying eyes of strangers.

She told her guards to wait outside, and she approached the curtained door to the covered wagon.

"Safiya, it's me, Ela...Countess of Salisbury. I must speak with you."

She heard stirring inside and soon Safiya emerged, eyes red from weeping.

"May I come in and speak with you?"

Safiya hesitated, clearly unenthusiastic about the idea.

Ela reminded herself that Safiya was still a suspect. "I'm afraid that I must insist. As Sheriff of Wiltshire, I have a crime to investigate."

Surprise flashed in Safiya's eyes for a moment, before she cleared her throat and apologized for the humble nature of her home.

Ela climbed up, pulling on a brass handle that gave her enough purchase to clear the distance to the wagon's platform off the ground. Safiya pulled the curtain aside, and she entered into the dark, fragrant space.

"Is that frankincense I smell?"

Safiya nodded. "Ziyad bought it from merchants that bring it from Salalah every year. He loved the scent. To him it smelled like wealth. Burning it reminds me of him."

As Ela's eyes adjusted to the gloom, she could see the side walls of the wagon were lined with shelves of small drawers, like an apothecary might have. Further into the space was a curtained area that must be where the occupants slept and where Safiya stayed out of sight when Ziyad dealt with customers. Cooking pots hung from hooks fastened to the curved wooden hoops that held up the wagon's fabric cover.

"You must have many items of value in here. How did Ziyad protect you from robbers?"

Safiya pointed at a long knife—almost a sword—with a curved blade and a carved sheath. "He was a trained fighter. With my own eyes I've seen him kill a man who tried to rob us."

"But he didn't have this knife with him when he went out last night," observed Ela.

"If he did, he might still be alive."

"He must have not expected trouble. But you said it's highly unusual for him to go out at night?"

"He never did. He promised me that he would never leave me alone at night." Her voice trembled.

"Is there a reason why?"

Safiya's eyes lowered. "Yes."

Ela didn't want to prod her, especially in her grief, but she needed to learn more about Safiya and her relationship with her husband. "Had he...betrayed you in the past with another woman?"

"No!" her retort came swift and loud as her dark eyes flashed with indignation. "Ziyad was a good and faithful husband."

Ela frowned. "Then why did he make such a promise?"

"Because he knew I had a bad experience once." She swallowed. "When I was a girl. My father left me alone at home one evening and three men came and—" She broke off and looked at the floor. "They sullied my virtue. My father should have found them and killed them to avenge my honor—"

"Were they powerful men?"

"They had money. When he didn't seek justice I wondered if they'd paid him a high price for the right to take me."

Ela shook her head softly. "You suspect that the man charged with protecting you had bartered your innocence?"

Safiya nodded. Ela wished she could blame such horrors on the woman's unfamiliar foreign culture. But she'd heard of cruel and greedy men in London selling their daughters' innocence for a few coins to men who would never marry the poor girl.

"Then he sold me to a stranger."

Ela inhaled slowly. Women being married off to virtual strangers was almost the norm, at least among her class. How many of her contemporaries had chosen their husbands? She certainly hadn't. Her married children hadn't either. Their marriages were arranged for land and titles, just as Safiya's was arranged for gold and camels or whatever passed for influence in her country.

"I understand. And Ziyad knew this had given you a great fear of being left alone?"

"Yes. It took him a long time to win my trust. But he did. He always kept his promise to me and never left me unattended at night."

"But last night, for some reason we have yet to determine,

he was drawn into breaking his vow to you." Ela tried to imagine a reason—beyond another woman—for a man to slip away from his wife in the night. "Could he have gone outside to relieve himself?"

"It's not impossible. He was plied with some drink or other by Mistress Thornhill, the alewife, as she tried to drive a bargain on some glass cups."

Ela knew Una Thornhill, an ebullient and independent character who'd provided her with useful local gossip earlier in the year.

"But he would never have walked away from our wagon, leaving all of our wares unattended, let alone me. He has objects of great value stored in here, in places where even I don't know how to find them. He buys and brings goods for the great men of the land. Sometimes he's even called to attend one of the king's palaces."

"I'm not surprised. Your husband is known as a source of fine and unusual gifts." She peered at the many small wooden drawers, each with a tiny carved knob. "Do you know of any items of great value that he has with him on this trip?"

Safiya hesitated. "The bone chess set that you selected is one of the finest items."

"You speak like a salesman, not a woman who seeks her husband's murderer. The chess set is an extraordinary item, but perhaps he has gems or objects of ancient pedigree stored in one of these drawers."

"I don't know what's in them."

"You never peeked into them while he was outside selling?"

Safiya shook her head mutely. "It was his business to provide for us and protect us and mine to prepare food and wash his clothes and sustain us. He had no interest in the one, and I had no interest in the other."

"But you are his heir, I imagine?"

Safiya looked confused.

"By that I mean that you'll inherit his goods? Or does he have another relative that he intended to leave them to?"

"My husband has no family but me."

Ela didn't know how to verify this, but it wasn't entirely surprising. A devoted family man wouldn't spend his life on the road hawking his wares. "So this wagon and its contents are yours now. As sheriff I would like to see inside these drawers to get an idea of what else he might have for sale."

"I'm sure he brought out his finest wares in your hall." Safiya seemed reserved. "And why would someone kill him for an item that's still inside the wagon?"

"Perhaps they killed him and waited for you to leave it. Was it disturbed in any way when we returned here after finding your husband's body?"

Safiya glanced behind her, at the curtained area that must hold her bed. "Yes." She turned back to Ela. "I had a sense that someone had been here."

"Were things moved?"

"Not moved, or out of place, but there was an odd smell. I suppose that's why I lit the frankincense to get rid of it."

"What kind of smell?"

"That stale scent that men have when they don't wash. My husband never smelled like that. I washed and oiled him and scented him with rosewater every night and morning." Her eyes filled with tears. "And now I won't ever do it again."

"So a man came inside here while we were outside the castle walls," Ela mused. "Looking for something. I wonder if he found it."

She pondered asking for permission to open a drawer, then decided that since she fully intended to open one anyway, she preferred not to give Safiya the opportunity to argue with her. She approached the rows of drawers, selected a knob at random, and pulled on it.

The drawer rattled slightly as it opened, because the inside contained strands of glass beads Ela recognized as millefiori beads from Venice. She reached her fingers in and picked up a strand of them, arranged on skeins of faded red thread. "Your husband bought these in the Venetian islands?"

Safiya looked rather appalled that Ela had plunged her fingers into her husband's private drawers. "We didn't go to Venice. He might have bought them from another merchant in Sevilla or Cordoba or Toledo. The merchants each have their own route, and they barter with each other for items from the places they don't visit."

"Did he buy and sell in other European countries?"

She nodded. "Sometimes. But his best customers are here in England so he always saved his finest goods for the English."

"I see."

Ela put the millefiori beads back in their drawer and opened the drawer next to it. Pale green jade beads strung on a faded pink skein. They had odd hatchings carved into them. "Where are these from?"

"China. We didn't go there, but he bartered for them when we were in Paris."

"Who would want such a thing?"

Safiya shrugged. "We didn't talk about his business."

Ela went through several more drawers, finding a variety of strung beads and loose gemstones, some engraved silver buckles, and a large selection of dice carved from ivory.

"Do you think his most valuable items would be in these drawers, or perhaps hidden somewhere behind them?"

"I don't know."

Safiya seemed to grow increasingly tense as Ela rifled

through the contents of her husband's drawers. Ela couldn't help thinking that she knew more than she was letting on. An odd idea occurred to her. "Did your husband trade in opium?"

Safiya's mouth hardened. "One year he did, but it attracted criminals. People grow desperate for the substance and are willing to commit crimes to get their hands on it. That was the year I saw him kill a man. He never bought it again."

Ela nodded. "I've seen as much here in England. Did he buy or sell valuable gems?"

"Yes," said Safiya quietly. "He usually saved them for the abbots and bishops to decorate their holy books."

This got Ela's attention. "Was there anyone in Salisbury whom he sold them to?"

"The bishop who used to live here in the palace bought a bag of rubies one year."

"Bishop Richard Poore?"

"I don't know his name."

Bishop Poore had a taste for the finer things in life. Ela wouldn't be at all surprised by his buying luxury items from the trader. "Did your husband bring anything special for him this year?"

Safiya frowned. "We visited him at his new house down the road from the castle yesterday. I didn't hear what passed between them, but my husband was not in a good mood afterward."

Ela's interest was piqued. Bishop Poore had built himself an impressive new palace in the grounds of his extravagant new cathedral. Had he refused to pay an exorbitant price for something and ordered the merchant killed so he could take it?"

She realized she was holding her breath. Bishop Poore

was a man of fleshly desires, but she'd never thought him enough of a blackhearted villain to stoop to murder.

"I shall speak to him and see if he knows of any valuables your husband carried that might have put him in danger." And she'd peer deep into his watery, pale eyes while doing it, to see if duplicity lurked there.

"In the meantime we need to search the wagon." The difficulty would be finding someone to trust with the task. The temptation of gems and items small enough to slip up one's sleeve could make a criminal of many ordinary men. "I shall send Sir William Talbot. He's one of my most trusted friends, and I can assure you he wouldn't steal a single bead from you. I'd advise you to make a full accounting of every item in the wagon as you should sell your stock to fund your life as a widow. Unless you intend to continue the business."

"How would I continue the business? I'd just be robbed."

"It does seem to be a profession requiring an armed escort, at least if you were to continue to trade in luxuries."

"I shall have to sell them." Safiya's voice sounded flat. "But how, and to whom?"

"I'll help you look for a buyer later, but for now don't sell anything at all. Our most urgent task is to discover why your husband went outside at night, and who he encountered. I'm going to see what I can learn from the townspeople. If you need anything, come to the castle—in the meantime I'll send Bill Talbot and he'll announce himself when he arrives so as not to alarm you."

"Would it not be better to send John Dacus?" Bill Talbot was skeptical of her plan to send him to inventory Safiya's wagon.

"While Dacus has proved a willing ally so far, I don't

know him well enough to trust him entirely." Her co-sheriff, assigned by the king, had won her affection, but he was a man of fairly extravagant material tastes and she was still getting the full measure of him. "There are items of value in that wagon—possibly very great value—and I don't want the powerful forces of temptation to interfere with the pursuit of justice."

"I understand, my lady. If there are objects of great value, do you want me to remove them?"

Ela hesitated. "Yes. For now. I don't wish for them to endanger Safiya's life. She says she's unaware of what her husband had and where he put it, so be sure to check the backs and bottoms of the drawers."

"Drawers? In the wagon?"

"It's strange, but many tiny compartments line the walls. I suppose it keeps the goods secured better than baskets and bags as the wheels roll over the roads. Check the mattress and cooking pots and everywhere else as well."

"I shall bring a female maidservant to assist as I know that a Moorish woman would be uncomfortable alone with a man. I hope Safiya won't take it too hard to see me going through her private things."

"If she does, then remind her that it's her duty to see her husband's murderer brought to justice."

AFTER EATING the midday meal with her children, Ela headed into the town to Una Thornhill's ale shop. She left her attendants outside and walked through the open door into the ale shop. Two young women sat giggling on the stools she had set up in one corner for her customers. They looked up as Ela entered, stared for a moment, then went scurrying past Ela and out the door.

Mistress Thornhill emerged from the back room, wiping her hands on her apron. She stopped suddenly when she saw Ela. "My lady." She didn't conceal her surprise. "What may I get for you?"

"Nothing, thank you." Ela could still taste the bitter brew from her last visit some months ago. "I'm here to ask you about Ziyad the merchant. It sounds as if you might be one of the last people to speak with him before his death."

"Me?" She looked astonished.

"His wife said you talked to him about buying some cups."

"I always need cups for my business. They get broken. Can't serve people ale in their cupped hands."

"I'm not accusing you of anything." She could see the alewife growing defensive. "But I'm trying to determine who killed him and I'd appreciate any information you have about his last night on earth."

"Well," she frowned. "I offered him some of my best ale, but he said he didn't take strong drink on account of his religion. Then I gave him some small ale that wouldn't make even a mouse tipsy."

"And did he bring the cups to you or did you look at them in his wagon?"

"He set up a folding table outside the wagon and placed goods on it. When he sold something he'd go back inside and fetch another item to put there for sale. That way people kept coming past to see what new things he had. Clever sales trick if you ask me."

"Did you ever see his wife?"

"Never knew he had a wife." Una Thornhill pursed her lips. "Never saw her at all."

"And did you buy the cups?"

"We couldn't agree on a price." She wiped her hands on her apron again. "He wanted more than I thought they were worth. I figured I'd come back in a day or so and see if he was willing to drive a bargain."

"Who else did you see looking at his wares?"

"Oh, everyone in town at one time or another, I reckon."

"Any soldiers from the castle?"

"I daresay. I didn't pay close attention."

"Did you hear anyone talk about him?"

"I suppose so. People always talk about something new in town, don't they?"

"And did people seem kindly disposed toward Ziyad?"

Una Thornhill shrugged. "I wouldn't know. He did hold out for his prices. That gets some people's backs up."

Including hers, Ela could see. "But did you see or hear of anyone irked enough to kill him?"

"No." She spoke quickly. "I didn't, but then I'm not privy to anyone's private thoughts. I suppose most people are suspicious of foreigners, especially when they follow a different religion and take money from the purses of hard-working Englishmen."

While Ela didn't enjoy hearing the alewife's sentiments, she knew they were common. She'd heard similar mutterings even about Jewish families that had lived in Wiltshire for generations. People were suspicious of anyone who didn't follow their customs and who had a different relationship with God. Such enmity was often amplified when the person in question was successful and affluent—as Ziyad clearly had been.

"What's going to happen to all his goods?" asked Una Thornhill, suddenly. "Will they be sold off?"

"Are you hoping to get a bargain for your cups?" asked Ela sharply.

"I'd never seek to profit from a man's death," retorted the alewife, only somewhat chastened. "But I'd not be one to turn up my nose at a good price."

"Perhaps his widow will seek to sell his stock, but for now she's more concerned with finding his killer. I'll thank you to let me know if you hear any useful information in that regard."

"Yes, my lady." The alewife's lips clamped shut.

Ela reflected that she shouldn't have scolded Mistress Thornhill for showing interest in the dead man's possessions. It was more important to keep people on her side than to take the moral high ground over them. "I thank you greatly for your time, mistress. How much for a barrel of ale sent to my kitchens, where it may accompany our evening meal tonight?"

She paid almost twice what the alewife asked and left her smiling and spitting compliments.

AFTER SHE LEFT the alewife's shop, Ela trotted her horse along the road that led down to the new town that had sprung up in the water meadows at the foot of the new cathedral. Across from the cathedral sat the lavish new residence of Bishop Richard Poore, so he could gaze on his creation and congratulate himself on tearing the old cathedral from the heart of Salisbury castle.

Not that she was bitter.

Her guard rapped on the door and a servant answered. She was told that Bishop Poore was in the cathedral, discussing a detail of carving with the mason.

"I'll find him there." Catching him by surprise should work in her favor.

She left her horse outside and went in, attended by one guard. Bishop Poore's familiar voice drew her toward the tall rood screen. She heard him discussing some painted details with a workman—more gilding required—but his voice trailed off when he saw her.

"My lady Ela," he said, in his unctuous voice. "What a pleasant surprise."

She dipped her head in greeting as she approached the rotund, silver-haired bishop. "May God be with you, Bishop Poore. I'm afraid the events that bring me here are far from pleasant."

Poore excused the workman and invited Ela to walk toward the altar. "I hear a man died up at the castle. Such a sad business."

Ela startled. "How did you hear that so quickly? His body was only found this morning."

"Word travels fast between castle and cathedral. I hear he was a merchant."

"Indeed he was. And his wife tells me he visited you yesterday."

Poore's expression faltered. "Oh, dear. I didn't realize the dead man was Ziyad al Wahid."

Ela wasn't sure she believed him. Salisbury was hardly crawling with Moorish merchants. "What did you hear of the murder?"

"Well, nothing really. I heard the man fell from the wall."

"He didn't fall. He was pushed or thrown." *And strangled.* She decided to keep that secret for now. "Why did he come to see you yesterday?"

"We discussed a large ruby that he had in his possession. He knows I value the best gemstones as crown jewels in our beloved cathedral and its holy books. I've bought some fine stones from him before."

"As have I. He will be sorely missed. Did you buy the ruby?"

"No. We couldn't agree on a price."

"Who told you he was dead?"

Poore seemed to be distracted by a sudden shaft of light through the great stained glass window. "Did you see our new candlesticks?" He pointed at the largest candlesticks she'd ever seen.

"Are those solid gold?"

"Not entirely. Some of the effects are decorative, but they are beautiful, are they not?"

"Indeed they are." Even the large candles burning inside them bore an ornate geometric pattern in gold. "But please try to remember who told you that Ziyad the merchant was dead."

"I think it was one of the lay brothers, but I couldn't say which one. They go up to the castle every day to visit the market."

"Do you have any idea who would want to kill him?" She watched him closely for any reaction.

"No idea at all. A very personable man—for a foreigner."

"His wife said that he was in a dark mood after he came to visit you."

"His wife? He doesn't have a wife." Now Poore looked perplexed.

"He does. She stayed out of sight in his wagon. She heard and saw much of his business."

Poore started to twist the big ring that glittered on his plump hands. "As I mentioned, I had intended to buy a ruby from him. I tried to bargain him down to a price I considered fair, as one does with these merchants, but he kept insisting he had another buyer who would pay what he asked if I didn't."

"Who was the other buyer?"

"He didn't say. I did ask. I don't suppose it's good business to pit your clients against one another." Poore seemed to have regained his composure.

"Do you know where the ruby is now?"

"No. He didn't bring it with him. He swore up and down that it was the finest ruby any man had ever laid eyes on."

"Is it unusual for a merchant to try to sell you something of great price without you seeing it?"

"Extraordinary, I'd say. It was another reason that I didn't buy it. He said it was too valuable to carry on his person. He said even the great emperors of India didn't possess a ruby like it."

Why didn't Ziyad bring the stone with him? It seemed bizarre to expect a client to pay a vast sum for a gem they hadn't seen. Ziyad was a cunning dealer who knew how to display his wares to their best advantage. Perhaps the mysterious stone didn't exist at all?

"I thank you for your time, Bishop Poore. Do you know if Ziyad had any enemies in Salisbury?"

"Any man with valuables has an enemy in a greedy man. I'm sure you know that as well as I do."

"And I expect our Lord and Savior would prefer for us to share our wealth generously with the less fortunate." She couldn't resist the jab at him, even though it cut her just as deeply. In her defense she was planning to build two great monasteries where her family's wealth would forge communities dedicated to the service of God, where men and women would offer up daily prayers for her husband's immortal soul.

A greedy man. They were everywhere in these times. "I thank you for your time, Bishop Poore. Do let me know if you gain any insight into Ziyad the merchant's killer."

"Indeed I shall, my lady." Relief flooded his puffy features, then a sparkle of curiosity lit his pale eyes. "Is this most precious ruby now up for sale following his death?"

"The ruby has not yet been found." She wondered if Bill and Safiya had turned it up inside the wagon, or if its weight tugged at the garments and soul of Ziyad's murderer.

∼

BACK IN THE GREAT HALL, Ela found her co-sheriff, John Dacus, locked in a chess battle with her steward, Noel Bazin. So engrossed were they in their game—and surrounded by a circle of admirers, including most of her children—that they didn't notice her enter the hall and approach.

The large, elaborate carved pieces of the bone chess set seemed to hold them all in sway like the many arms of a mystic foreign idol.

Ela cleared her throat. "Elsie, could you wrest yourself away from the entertainments for a moment?"

Elsie jumped at her voice and hurried to take her cloak. "I'm so sorry, my lady. I forgot myself. I beg your pardon."

Dacus and Bazin quickly rose to their feet and regarded her with sheepish expressions. "A very fine chess set," said Dacus.

"Never seen anything like it," remarked Bazin.

"The pieces almost look like they're moving of their own accord," chimed in little Ellie.

"It's how the light moves inside them," said Stephen. "They're carved that way."

"And our new steward turns out to be a champion chess player," exclaimed Richard. "He says he once beat the King of France at chess."

"Really?" said Ela. "Is that how you ended up exiled to England?"

"Quite possibly, my lady," he looked both embarrassed and pleased with himself at the same time. "I do pride myself on my strategic thinking."

"A worthy trait in a steward, no doubt." She glanced at the chess board. Bazin had reduced his opponent's pieces to a small army of stragglers. "It appears that my co-sheriff has suffered great losses at your hands."

Dacus held up his hands. "I must admit to being besieged by a superior force." Her co-sheriff was a good-humored man who wasn't likely to feel the loss as an injury to his pride.

At that moment the doors to the hall flew open and Bill Talbot dashed in—with Safiya in his arms.

CHAPTER 5

"What's amiss?" Ela rushed toward Bill. "Is she hurt?" Bill carried Safiya into the hall. Ela could see her eyes were open and her startled gaze darted about.

Bill took her right to the main table, where the chess set was laid out, and spread her out along its length. "Someone tried to tip the wagon over," he said. "They rocked it. And it must have been more than one person as they nearly succeeded."

Ela searched the hall for Gerald Deschamps and saw him in conversation with two of his men. "Sir Gerald, have your men hitch up the wagon and bring it into the castle court-yard where the wagon and donkey must remain under guard." She turned to Bill Talbot. "Did you see who did it?"

"I didn't. The rocking wreaked havoc with the goods inside and knocked us off our feet. I think my shouts scared the perpetrators off, because by the time I scrambled back upright and looked outside, the culprits were gone."

"Why would anyone want to upset the whole wagon?"

Safiya now sat up on the table, looking mortified at the

audience of staring eyes. "I think they wanted to frighten me," she whispered.

"And to rob you, no doubt," said Bill Talbot.

"I hope they're not robbing it right now as we stand here," Ela muttered. She didn't have the greatest faith in the garrison soldiers, who could be a motley assortment of men at the best of times. "Safiya, you must stay in the castle tonight. I don't think it's safe for you to sleep in the wagon."

Safiya started to protest, but Bill Talbot and John Dacus both agreed with Ela and drowned her out. Ela issued orders for Elsie and Becca to ready a bedchamber for her and instructed Safiya to bring in whatever she needed from the wagon to make herself at home.

Safiya looked deeply uncomfortable at the prospect of staying in the castle, but she clearly knew better than to argue. "I thank you, my lady."

"I suppose you had better resume your chess game," Ela said at last, to Bazin and Dacus. "Since it appears to be a pitched battle nearing its conclusion."

"Alas I fear I can concede defeat without regret," said Dacus, with his usual disarming charm. He was a handsome man, not far from herself in age, with dark looks that he might use to charm the ladies. So far he'd shown admirable restraint.

"I never assume a bold opponent cannot turn matters around in the final moves," said Bazin brightly. Ela was surprised at her bookish steward's apparently competitive and winning manner. And however had he come to sit across a table from King Louis? "I'd be happy for you to see events through to their conclusion."

"I suspect my time would be better spent in the service of the office of sheriff," said Dacus with a wry glance at Ela. "Perhaps I should visit the Bull and Bear and take some ale there."

Ela resisted the urge to lift a brow. "That's certainly an activity off-limits to myself. And you may well gain some intelligence from people in the tavern."

"Especially if enough ale is applied to the situation," he said without smiling. "There's bound to be talk about the murder, and perhaps about the wagon, too."

"But everyone knows you're the sheriff," cut in Ela's son Stephen. "Won't that make them hold their tongues?"

"Some men, perhaps, but others fall over each other in their efforts to curry favor. Naturally I'm hoping for the latter."

"It might be better to send someone unknown to the local people," said Ela. She could see the wisdom in putting an ear to the ground. Right now they had no idea who had killed Ziyad. "But who could go unrecognized?"

After a short silence, Noel Bazin cleared his throat. "Being newly arrived in Salisbury, I'm unknown to the people here."

Ela blinked. Scrawny, foppishly dressed, and—by his accent and quirks of his dress—very obviously from France, Bazin was not likely to pass unnoticed among the locals. "What information would you give them about yourself?"

"That I'm new to Salisbury, here on business with the castle, and that I heard a murder was committed. No need for me to sully my tongue with a lie." He looked disturbingly enthusiastic.

Ela glanced at John Dacus. "If his ability to extract information from the denizens of the Bull and Bear bears any similarity to his skill at chess, I think it's worth a try."

Bazin chuckled. "At your service, my lady."

Ela somewhat reluctantly agreed that Bazin should drink and listen for information, then return immediately to the castle and relay it to Ela or Dacus. In the meantime Ela decided to take Safiya to the mortuary, where her husband's body lay.

~

"YOUR HUSBAND WAS STRANGLED." Ela said the words quickly as she approached the mortuary door. "The coroner found a thin line around his neck that suggests a fine cord pulled tight enough to cut off his air supply." She wanted to get the bad news off her chest.

Safiya's steps faltered. "So he was killed before someone pushed him off the wall?"

"It appears that way. Perhaps you can look at the mark and suggest what might have made it?"

Ziyad's body lay on the coroner's examination table, covered from head to toe in a linen cloth. She glanced at Safiya to see if she was prepared to see her dead husband's face. Safiya nodded her assent, and Ela gently pulled back the cloth.

His sun-bronzed skin disguised the mottled pallor of death. With his eyes closed and his hair combed back he looked asleep rather than dead.

Safiya stared at him for a moment. "He was so handsome. Everyone liked him. He could make friends with merchants and customers from all corners of the world." She hesitated. "Why would someone kill him?"

"Greed is a common motive."

"For theft, yes, but for murder?" Safiya gazed sadly at her husband's face.

"Did you and Bill find anything of great value when you looked through his goods?"

She looked up. "We did find that some of the drawers had false backs. Most of them were empty, but two contained some stones that looked like sapphires. Sometimes he bought the raw stones and brought them to Flanders to be dressed into jewels fit for a king's crown or a holy book. These were very fine ones, deep blue and polished to a shine."

"Sapphires do have great value."

"But they were hidden. No one knew they were there. Not even me."

"You did say that your husband didn't trouble you with the details of his business. An important customer might well have known more about the contents of his drawers than you did."

"I suppose that's true. Where's the mark of strangulation?"

Ela pointed to the thin red mark, barely visible, that ran between the hairs of his beard, where his chin joined his neck.

She heard Safiya sigh. "Why is it so hard to live sometimes, and yet so easy to kill a man?" She looked up at Ela, her dark eyes hollow. "Why would they push him off the castle wall if he was already dead?"

"Perhaps to create a spectacle to distract from the actual place and manner of death. We don't yet know where he was killed. It might be somewhere else entirely. Tonight I intend to go up on the wall and meet the men charged with guarding it. He was thrown off the wall on their watch, and I want to know why."

"Do be careful," said Safiya.

"I don't think they'll kill their countess, not while their garrison commander looks on." Though perhaps she should bring Bill Talbot with her as a second pair of eyes.

"Since we've learned all we can about your husband's body you can prepare it for burial according to your customs. I don't imagine you intend to take it back to Tangier or Sevilla."

"It's too far." Tears came to Safiya's eyes. "He'll have to be buried here among strangers."

"There's a burial ground outside the castle walls." She didn't say that it was for paupers or criminals—and infidels. "He can be laid there with whatever ceremony you wish."

"There's no imam to guide his soul to Allah. What if he gets lost on the way?"

"I don't know the teachings of your religion, but if your husband was a good man and a kind husband I'm sure he'll find his way to paradise." She wished she could offer to pray with Safiya, but that might only cause offense. "If there's anything I can do to help, please ask. I can arrange for the men to dig his grave and bury him in it. Let me know what you need in order to dress and prepare the body."

"I must do it right away. Already too much time has passed. But what if we bury him and he's forgotten and his killer walks free?"

"I will not allow that to happen."

AFTER PRIME SERVICES WERE OVER, Ela asked Bill Talbot to accompany her to the top of the outer walls. She suspected that Deschamps would meet her there once he was alerted to her presence, but she was curious to see how long that would take.

"Where's Safiya?" asked Bill, as they moved past her wagon where it sat in the castle courtyard under the watchful eyes of the sentries. The little donkey had been taken away to a bedded stall along with the castle horses.

"She's settled into a room in the tower. Since someone threatened her life by trying to overturn the wagon earlier, I see no choice but to keep her under guard while she's here."

"She's in a precarious position, with a wagon full of valuables."

"And she's a young and beautiful woman with no husband to protect her."

"Indeed. It's not easy to imagine how she can obtain passage back to her homeland safely."

"I'm not even sure she has a homeland she wants to return to," said Ela. "Her father sounds like a cruel man."

"Yet she can hardly live in England as an infidel woman, can she? Where would she find a new husband?"

Ela arched a brow. "Not every woman needs a husband."

Was he about to protest that someone as young and beautiful as Safiya did need a husband? Or that every woman needed a husband for protection?

"Not every woman is a countess with an array of manors and attendants at her disposal," he muttered. He looked at her with a twinkle of amusement in his eye, but as if he was also ready for a swift tongue lashing.

"I realized my circumstances are unique, but so are Safiya's. The goods she carries must be worth a great deal. Perhaps enough to set her up safely somewhere that she can live in peace."

"If they don't get stolen out from under the noses of our castle guards." Bill glanced at a huddle of them loafing about, unaware that their countess was passing them as dusk became darkness.

"There's a valuable ruby among them, a very great prize of superior color and size, or at least that's what Ziyad told Bishop Poore. Did you find it?"

"No." Bill frowned. "I hope the killer didn't steal it."

Such a valuable gem was certainly a motive for murder. She lowered her voice. "Do you have reason to suspect any of the castle guards?"

"I'd say that a merchant being murdered and thrown from

the walls of the king's garrison is reason to suspect the guards. Keeping this space safe is their responsibility. How would anyone gain entry to the top of the wall without being seen by the sentries?"

They walked past a silent sentry and into the tower room that held the stairs up to the top of the wall.

"It's a long time since I've been up here," said Bill, as they climbed the narrow stone stairs.

"Me too. I went through a phase of coming up here every day when I was pregnant with Nicholas. I was so restless but too big with child to ride abroad. I used to climb up and walk around the length of the entire wall, taking in views of the countryside."

"So you're familiar with the wall." Bill opened the scuffed wood door at the top of the stairs.

"I can't say I've been up here in the dark before, though." They stepped outside, where there was a walk wide enough for two men to pass easily, and a crenelated wall about waist high, just tall enough for archers to hide behind.

Silver moonlight picked out edges of the wall and the familiar contours of the landscape. Ela could smell the smoke rising from cooking fires and hear the evening chorus of dogs barking goodbye to another day.

Two men rode away from the castle and into the darkening countryside. She peered at them. "Who'd be riding out so late?"

"Probably someone going to new Salisbury," said Bill. "The traffic between there and the castle is almost nonstop these days. They must have left just before the gate closed at dusk."

"Does the gate ever open at night?" asked Ela. "I know it isn't supposed to, but does it?"

Bill shrugged. "Gerald Deschamps would be the authority on that."

They walked along the castle wall to about the point where Ziyad's body would have fallen. The featureless stone walls and flagged floor showed no signs of a struggle.

"There's no way to get up on the wall except by the stairs in the towers, so he must have come up the same stairs we used, or the next tower along." There were few stairs up to the top of the wall, and the area was supposed to be off-limits to anyone not employed in guarding the castle. Ela had never seen anyone but guards up here on her own perambulations.

A scuffling noise ahead of them drew her attention. "What was that?"

"I don't know." Bill's hand flew to the handle of his sword. It was now too dark to make out much more than basic shapes, but Ela could see the outline of two men running along the top of the wall toward them.

"Who goes there?" called out Bill.

The men didn't answer but pounded toward them, cloaks flying out behind them.

"This is your countess, Ela of Salisbury!" Bill's cry pierced the darkness. She could hear the edge of alarm in his voice.

The footsteps slowed. Ela heard the swish of Bill unsheathing his sword. "Announce yourselves," he called.

"At your service, my lady," said a gruff male voice. Neither man had a lantern so she wondered how they could see her in the dark. They must have believed Bill's announcement, and maybe recognized his voice. "What are you doing up here in the dark?"

"What's your name?" asked Ela. Her movements were not the business of any common soldier.

"Roger Wilks, my lady. And this is Thomas Belcher. We're members of the king's garrison and charged with patrolling the wall."

"Were you on watch when Ziyad the merchant was killed?"

There was a brief pause. "Aye. We were on watch. But we didn't see or hear anyone."

"How is that possible?"

A longer pause. "We can only be in one place at a time, my lady."

"Where's Gerald Deschamps? I'd like to speak to him up here."

"I'll go find him," said the second man. He bowed slightly, then moved past them toward the tower where they'd climbed the stairs, which was closer than the one they must have come from.

Ela tried to make out Roger Wilks's face in the dark. He looked to be an older man, with silver in his hair. "Do you feel that the wall is adequately guarded?"

"I would have said so, but if someone was murdered up here, then it can't be, can it?"

"The merchant was murdered by someone, then possibly thrown off the wall by two people. So there wasn't just one man trespassing up here but two or even three. And the others must have come down via the stairs in one of the towers. And this all in the wee hours of the early morning, before Matins, because his wife and I both heard him cry out. How is that possible?"

"There was a disturbance at the time, my lady. A female... I'm sorry to say it, but a prostitute was found pestering the soldiers on watch and she was forcibly removed from the castle. It might have been her cry of protest that you heard."

Ela frowned. "This is the first mention I've heard of this woman. Was she known to you?"

"No, my lady."

Ela wondered if he was lying. Would a man really admit to knowing a prostitute? Perhaps Bill would get a better answer if she wasn't here.

Was Ziyad meeting with the prostitute when he was

murdered? Safiya would protest that it was impossible, but Ela knew the wife was often the last to suspect her husband's infidelities.

"Do prostitutes often come to the walls to look for customers?"

He hesitated. "It's not uncommon, my lady. They know the soldiers are far from their homes and families."

"I see. So she came here often?"

"I couldn't say. I didn't talk to her myself."

"Who did?"

"I'm not sure."

Ela thought him a liar. Either way, the castle wall seemed to be poorly managed at best and a magnet for sin and crime at worst.

Gerald Deschamps arrived a few moments later, summoned from his rooms in the castle. "My lady, you should have told me you wanted to see the wall again."

"I wanted to see what it was like to come here with no warning. Sir William and I were able to climb to the wall without being noticed. No one even stopped us."

"But the soldiers know you as their countess, my lady," he protested, with an oily smile. "I'd be mortified if they stopped you and asked you to identify yourself."

"They didn't exactly offer me greetings and flatteries, either. They seemed busy with their own affairs. They should be more alert for the arrival of strangers, and there should be more than three of them patrolling the walls at any one time in the dead of night."

Again, the fake smile. "Normally in peacetime, there's no threat of invasion so it's simply a formality to have the walls patrolled."

"If a man can be murdered and thrown into the ditch from our castle walls, I'd say that's a problem. As castellan of Salisbury Castle, I insist upon two alert guards per watch for each quadrant of the wall. That is eight in total. They can survey the lands outside the wall and the activities in the village and other areas inside the wall."

"But the area where the old bishop's palace and the former cathedral lay is now empty," he protested. They'd both been dismantled, ostensibly so their stones could be used in building the new structures down the road in new Salisbury, but Ela suspected it was so Bishop Poore wouldn't find himself competing with a rival who might be installed in the old buildings within the walls in his absence. Destroying the buildings had assured his dominance over the ecclesiastical domain of Salisbury.

"An empty wasteland is an attractive nuisance." Ela resolved to put the land to some use. Another orchard, perhaps. Right now sheep grazed among the rubbled remains of the venerable old walls. "Place extra guards starting tonight."

"Yes, my lady." His smile congealed into a grimace.

"Your guard Roger Wilks tells me there are prostitutes who frequent the area around the walls and that one was removed from this area last night."

"Well, my lady, men will be men."

"Not while they're on duty, I hope," she said coldly.

"Of course not."

"But any person in the vicinity of the wall at the time of the murder is a potential suspect. I need you to find the woman and bring her to the castle for questioning."

"I hardly think a woman could have strangled the merchant."

"You'd be surprised what women can do if they're well enough motivated." Her voice could probably freeze water. "Which of your men spoke to her?"

Deschamps looked at Wilks, who shuffled awkwardly. "Well, man, who was it?"

"I didn't see, sir. I was up the other end. Might have been Lassiter."

"I shall speak with the men in question, my lady."

"I'd like to speak with them as well. Arrange for the guards who were present and for the woman herself to be brought to the great hall for questioning in front of a jury."

CHAPTER 6

*B*ack at the castle, Ela whiled away the evening watching her sons Richard and Stephen play chess against each other. Stephen, despite being two years younger, was gaining the upper hand when she excused herself to go to bed. She wanted a chance to pray and contemplate before bed, since tomorrow promised to be a hectic day.

Elsie brought fresh water to wash her face and unpinned her barbette and fillet. She'd been wondering something all day. "Elsie, did you know that Ziyad the merchant had a wife in his wagon?"

"No, my lady."

"But someone must have. How did she cook food or even relieve herself? She must have left the wagon sometimes."

"I'm not sure, my lady. I didn't see her come out while they were in the castle. I had no idea anyone was in there at all. Downright odd and creepy if you ask me."

"What is odd and creepy?"

"To keep a woman hidden away like that. It's not natural."

"I suspect it was for her protection."

"I don't much like foreigners," said Elsie, pulling stray hairs from Ela's comb. "With their odd ways."

"Elsie, I'm surprised at you. The Lord created all humans in his likeness, and you must remember that."

"But aren't they heathen infidels? That's what they were saying downstairs."

"Who said that?"

Elsie hesitated. "I don't remember exactly." She placed the comb back on the table next to the pins for Ela's veil. "But aren't they?"

Ela didn't know quite what to say. "Their holy book is much the same as ours." She knew, because she'd read parts of it, translated into Latin, that her husband had brought home from the crusades as a curiosity. "Many of them are devout and worship God, and as you know there's only one God."

She hoped Elsie wouldn't ask more questions as she didn't have answers. Did the Muslims think their God was the same as hers? Ela was fairly sure they did, despite the different name they called him. They did believe that their prophet Mohammed was equal to Jesus, which was sinful blasphemy, of course.

"The merchant and his wife will go to hell on Judgment Day." Elsie said it with confidence that rubbed Ela the wrong way. Sometimes she was almost sure the girl was simple. Other times she just seemed obtuse.

"If they're good people I'm sure they'll know God's mercy." Ela picked up her prayer book from her prie-dieu. The weight of it and the smooth softness of the worn leather cover reassured her. Surely God was just and merciful with good-hearted heathens as he was with unbaptized babes and those who died suddenly without a priest's blessing?

"They'll be in hell with my mother and father." Suddenly

Elsie's lip quivered. Her round child's face reddened and her freckled nose scrunched up.

Elsie looked at Ela as if challenging her to argue.

Which she couldn't. Elsie's father was an adulterer and her mother his murderer.

"We must pray for their souls," was the best she could come up with. "None of us really knows what happens after death."

She'd never make such a blasphemous statement within earshot of Bishop Poore or even another adult. But poor Elsie didn't need her nights tormented by visions of her dead parents writhing in the flames of hell. "We must trust in the Lord and his mercy and do our best to live righteous lives."

Elsie blinked away her tears and swiped a hand across her face. "She shouldn't be in the castle."

"Safiya? Why not?" Ela couldn't hide her surprise at Elsie's statement. The girl was usually taciturn almost to the point of muteness.

"You should send her away. The Saracens are our enemies. She could slit our throats while we sleep."

Ela frowned at her maid. She'd taken pity on the poor orphan who'd been sold into child slavery by her own family. It surprised her that someone with such an unfortunate past could be so unforgiving, hateful even, toward another in a difficult position.

But she raised a provoking point. Ela knew nothing about Safiya other than that she was a woman—newly widowed— in need of protection. Did she, or her husband, have alliances and agendas that went beyond the buying and selling of goods? Elsie's unkind words had planted the seed of doubt in her heart. But she didn't want Elsie to know that.

"Safiya needs our protection and our Lord told us to look kindly on foreigners living among us. Run along to bed now and don't spread any wild stories about murderers in our midst."

"Yes, my lady."

~

A BLOOD-CHILLING SCREAM jerked Ela from her sleep. She sat up and pulled her bed curtains aside. The room was pitch dark. The night was too warm for a fire and clouds blocked the moon.

Had she imagined it? Was she dreaming of Ziyad's murder?

She walked across the rush mat to the door and held her ear to it. No feet scurried outside. She opened the door carefully, trying not to make a sound and wake anyone else.

The guard stationed outside her door startled to attention —revealing that he'd been dozing at his post, even while standing. "What's amiss, my lady?" he managed.

Ela hesitated. She didn't want to cause alarm if the scream had emerged from her own mind. "Did you hear anything out of the ordinary?"

"Um," he pondered, no doubt wondering what to say that would hide the fact that he'd been asleep. "Can't say I did, my lady." He was an older man with a trim gray beard.

Ela peered past him down the hallway. No other doors had opened, and there were no signs of people stirring from their beds. "I'm sure everything's fine. But do wake me if you hear anything unusual."

She closed the door and made her way back to her bed, frowning. How had she heard a shrill scream, piercing enough to jolt her from her slumbers, and no one else heard it? Her mind didn't usually play tricks on her.

Right now she felt like one of her young children, complaining of night terrors and needing to be shown that there was no wolf lurking in the blanket chest or long-taloned falcon among the fire tongs.

She hadn't imagined the last cry in the night. Safiya had heard it, too. And it was either her now-dead husband or the mysterious woman he might have had a tryst with.

Ela climbed back into bed with a deep sense of unease. Even her soft mattress provided no comfort and she soon rose again to seek refuge in prayer at her prie-dieu. She remained there until dawn brightened the room, and she rose with relief to go about her morning errands.

ELA DRESSED HERSELF, as she often did when she rose in the early hours of a summer morning. Her former maid Sibel could hear her take her first breath and would have shot into the room to pin her fillet and barbette without a word. But since Sibel had left to be married, Ela had grown used to the sleepyhead lassitude of younger, less seasoned girls.

The guard outside the door murmured a polite greeting, saying nothing of the nighttime interruption. He followed her down the hall to the room where Safiya slept. Ela knocked quietly until she heard a hesitant greeting.

"It's me, Ela, may I come in?"

She heard rusting and fumbling before Safiya invited her in, and she went in to find Safiya hastily wrapped in her black cloak and blinking red-rimmed eyes.

"Did you hear a scream last night?"

Safiya nodded. "I'm sure it was my husband's ghost. I heard it right by my door. It shivered through my bones. He's lost and wandering in some dark underworld, unable to find his way to paradise." Her lip quivered, and tears fell from her eyes.

"I heard it, too" Ela protested. "It was a real person." She stroked Safiya's arm. "It's not your husband, I assure you of that."

Who would cry out? Especially if nothing was amiss. Unless it was someone looking to cause trouble. "Get some rest, I'll let you know if I find out more."

~

ELA'S GUARD followed her silently down the stairs and into the hall.

No family members had yet awakened, and the dogs barely cocked an ear as she entered. A serving girl and a boy who swept the hearth slept near the fire, which had long ago gone out. Ela frowned to see ale cups from last night's carousing still on the tables. And someone had left the chess set out.

It was too valuable to be left on a table where some drunken soldier might absently knock the delicate carved pieces to the floor with a sweep of his arm. She'd have to speak to Bill or her sons or whoever had left it here, seemingly mid-game.

Some of the pieces had fallen over. She walked over and righted them—then frowned again. There was a stain under one of them.

She lifted the piece—the queen—and called to the sleeping servants by the fire. "Bring a cloth and clean up this spilled wine."

The girl's head rose and, seeing her mistress, she shot to her feet, stammering apologies and darted off to the kitchen to get a rag.

Ela set the piece upright. One of the carved horses that represented the knights had also been knocked over and as she picked it up she saw that it was cracked across the base. A hairline crack but one that could widen and possibly split the piece in two.

It could likely be repaired—perhaps with hide glue— and that should be done before the damage worsened. She'd ask Elsie to send for the silversmith. He'd know the best way to mend it without damaging the delicate structure.

The girl came back with a damp rag and scrubbed at the stain.

"You could put some salt on it," suggested Ela. "That can help lift wine stains."

"I don't think it's wine, my lady," said the girl, scrubbing away. "It looks more like blood."

"What?" Ela startled, and was surprised and annoyed at herself for doing so. "What makes you say that?"

"The color. My pa is the butcher so I've seen more blood than most. It'll lift though, if it hasn't soaked in too far. Then it turns black and you'll never be rid of it."

"Why would there be blood on the table here?" She asked the question more for herself than the girl.

"It would have to be from raw meat, wouldn't it?" she said, scrubbing away. The stain had soaked in and left a dark outline that resisted her efforts.

Ela examined the chess set, moving the inlaid wood board to the side. There was no blood anywhere else on it, just under the queen.

For some reason that gave her a frisson of unease. Had someone dripped blood there deliberately?

The exterior of the queen piece was now wiped clean but blood had seeped into the middle of it through the delicate filigree carving and the girl's cloth couldn't reach it. "I'll have to go rinse this in water, my lady."

"Do it quick before the blood sets."

She watched the girl hurry away with her bloodied cloth and the stained chess piece. Then she picked up the cracked knight piece and looked closely. Who would have tampered with these and why?

Ela arranged the pieces back on the board, in position as if she were about to start a game. Something in her wanted to see them restored to order. But as she put each piece in its place she realized that the white king was missing.

She peered under the table to see if it had rolled off onto the floor. The entire hall had recently been swept clean and strewn with fresh summer herbs. There was no sign of the piece.

Just then the girl came back with the freshly washed queen piece, drying it on a cloth in her hands. "No more blood. Right as rain." She put the piece down on the table."

"There's one missing," said Ela. "Please help me look for it."

"Is it a big one or a small one?" The girl got down on her knees under the table.

"A big one. The biggest."

"I don't see anything down here. Me and Becca spent days getting this floor as clean as the cook's favorite pot. We even swabbed it with water."

"You did a good job. The hall has a fresher atmosphere. Did it roll under a bench?"

The girl climbed around under the table, searching in the nooks of the trestles. "I don't see any sign of it."

"Do keep your eyes peeled and tell the others to look out for it. Hopefully it will turn up before someone steps on it. In the meantime I'd like the chess set locked away when it's not in use. I'll speak to my sons about it." She hesitated. "Did you by any chance hear a cry in in the night?"

The girl shook her head.

ELA SET out on her morning rounds still discomfited by the disturbance in the chess set. Why had only the queen piece been stained with blood? Who'd taken the king?

She soon got lost in the minutiae of her daily routine. She walked through the castle's kitchen garden, assessing the state of the herbs and salad vegetables and testing the growing fruit on the espaliered trees.

She passed by the chicken coops, where fat and contented hens laid their daily eggs, then by the pig sties where the boys were feeding their charges scraps from the kitchen.

The sentries watched her, seemingly more alert than usual. Perhaps they'd been told to be on their guard after the murder. Satisfied that everything was in order, she headed back into the hall to break her fast.

Bill Talbot now sat at the table near the chess set, eating a pastry with berries and soft cheese.

"Good morrow, my lady."

"Ah Bill, I'm glad to see you. I had a restless night and an unsettling sight greeted me when I came down this morning." She told him about the mysterious scream—which only she and Safiya had heard—and the disordered chess set. "Who was playing chess late last night after my sons went to bed? Do you know?"

"Last I saw it was John Dacus and Noel Bazin, but the game drew rapidly to a close, with Bazin as the victor."

"They must have played after my sons finished their game. I wonder if anyone played after them?"

"I don't know. I confess I sat drinking with Deschamps and two others and talking about the old days and sharing fond memories of your husband and quite forgot the time." His rueful expression touched her. "And I slept like a stone so someone might have shrieked right outside my window without my noticing." He paused. "Unless it was you. A whisper from you and I'd fly from my bed like a man struck by lightning."

"I'm sure you would, Bill. It's just so odd. And how would blood get on the table?"

"Perhaps someone cut themselves. Some young fool paring his nails while in his cups might take a fingertip off if he's not careful."

Ela recoiled from the picture he painted. "I suppose you're right." Everyone in the castle except the youngest children carried sharp knives on them for one reason or another. She wore one herself. Her knife was a gift from her husband with a beautiful carved handle and sat in a tooled leather sheath on her belt. She hadn't worn it consistently when her husband was alive since there was always someone at hand to wield one for her. But after a surprise attempt on her life she made sure to carry a knife at all times.

She could still see the shadow of the bloodstain on the table, near where she'd rearranged the chessboard. "I do hope the king can be found. It would be hard to find a sculptor with the skill required to re-create a matching piece."

"Hard? It would be well-nigh impossible. I still don't know how they hollowed out something so hard. Perhaps Safiya would know where her husband bought it and another could be found at the same source?"

"I don't think she knows that much about her husband's business. Unless you got a different impression when you were with her in the wagon yesterday."

"No. She barely said a word. I think she was horrified at being in close quarters with a strange man and suspicious of my every move."

"Perhaps she's more comfortable talking to a woman. I'll ask her more about his business when she comes downstairs."

WHEN THE BELLS rang for Sext, with still no sign of the castle guards or the prostitute she wanted to interview, Ela sent for Gerald Deschamps. "Have you forgotten that I wish to speak to the men who guarded the wall while Ziyad al Wahid was killed?"

"I've already interviewed them all, my lady, and they say they saw nothing."

"You spoke to the prostitute?"

"Well, no, but no one knows who she was."

Nonsense. And provoking that he should defy her orders. "Bring the men—all of them—to see me at once. I shall discover her identity myself." She didn't hide the irritation in her voice. Deschamps had served under her husband and served him far better.

Perhaps he felt he owed his allegiance only to the king, and not to her, even though his garrison was stationed in her castle, which she presided over as castellan with the king's blessing.

She'd paid handsomely for that blessing—five hundred pounds, to be precise.

"I shall fetch them at once, my lady." His expressionless face revealed nothing of his emotions, but she knew he must be furious at her ordering him to do something he'd told her was unnecessary. Clearly he needed to be reminded that she was in command of the castle and everyone in it.

"Did any of your men play chess using the new carved set?"

Deschamps frowned. "The common men know better than to avail themselves of your amusements."

"Someone tampered with it and left it damaged. It will be locked away in future, but do speak to your men about minding their manners and avoiding public drunkenness."

"Yes, my lady."

~

Next Ela summoned her steward, Noel Bazin. He wore an ensemble of blue and yellow that might go unnoticed in the French court but looked rather outlandish in her great hall.

"Did you see who played chess after you last night?"

"I confess that I played another game myself, with Gerald Deschamps." He smiled, and his hazel eyes twinkled with amusement. "I don't flatter myself if I say that I left him a sadder and wiser man."

"You played a full game with him?"

"It didn't take long." His arch expression amused her. Deschamps hadn't mentioned this.

"Do you know how the knight piece was cracked?"

"No. I put all the pieces back in the lined box and closed the lid. As steward I know the great value of this chess set."

"Have we paid Safiya for it yet?"

"Not yet."

Ela decided to ask Safiya to tell her when payment was received. She still didn't entirely trust her new steward not to put the money in his own purse under the circumstances. "So the box with the pieces was left sitting here on the table."

"That's where I left it, my lady. Should it be put away in a storeroom?"

"I think it should. See if you can determine a good place where it can be retrieved when someone wants to play it but isn't in danger from passing soldiers." She peered at the table where the shadow of the stain still lay. "The maid cleaned up a stain that had leaked onto one of the pieces. She said it was blood."

"Blood?" His eyebrows shot up. "I've never heard of blood being drawn over a chess game, but I suppose if there's a wager and the stakes are high enough..." He trailed off. "Someone played a game after I left?"

"It appears that way. I'd like to determine who. And the white king has gone missing. Please keep a look out for it and tell others to do the same. Losing that piece dramatically diminishes the value of the set."

"Indeed it does, my lady. What use is a chess set without a king to capture?"

The loss of the king unsettled Ela the most. Someone must have slipped it into their clothing and taken it, but why?

And why did the queen have blood on her? And whose blood was it?

"What did you learn at the Bull and Bear last night?"

"No one knew anything." Bazin held up his hands in a Gallic gesture. "I tried to press them for information but they were as ignorant as myself."

At that moment Deschamps returned with three guards leading an angry, red-faced woman.

CHAPTER 7

$\mathcal{E}$la walked to her dais, the raised platform where she conducted her official business in the great hall, and sat in her chair. She knew they would follow her. For a moment she wondered if she should call for at least two jurors to witness her talk with them, but instead she had a servant go to find John Dacus. The jurors had seen the body and could be filled in on these details later.

Deschamps approached her and tilted his chin at the woman. "This is the female who was found near the castle wall that night."

The woman glared at Ela. Eyes darted to her from all around the hall and whispers rustled in the corners.

Ela decided to get right down to business. "Why were you near the tower stairs two nights ago?"

"I don't remember." On closer inspection Ela could see that the woman was at least thirty, maybe older. Her hair had been lightened with some substance that gave it an orangey tint that contrasted harshly with her florid skin. Her lips were reddened and her eyes outlined with some black stuff, which gave her a ghoulish appearance. Nearly all prostitutes seemed to put such paint on their faces, perhaps to signal to men that they were available for purchase. Her red dress had grown somewhat faded and worn where it stretched over her ample breasts. Her garish hair straggled over her shoulders, with no covering to contain it.

Ela had never been close enough to such a woman to have to peer into her hard eyes. Which was odd, when she thought about it. Surely her type were engaged in their sinful business while her husband was sheriff? She couldn't remember seeing one in her hall before. Either such women had stayed out of trouble or her husband and his men had deliberately overlooked them when he was sheriff.

"A man has been murdered so this is a very serious matter. Don't think you can't be imprisoned until your memory improves." She didn't like the woman's attitude. "Did you meet with Ziyad the merchant that night?"

"I've never heard of him. I was there doing my usual business with the garrison soldiers."

Ela glanced at Deschamps, who seemed fascinated by the trestles of a nearby table.

"And what, pray, is your usual business?"

"Not starving," said the woman, with a defiant jut of her chin.

Ela was fairly sure she'd rather starve than sell her body to strangers. She'd been fortunate enough never to have been tested, though. Oddly the woman's blunt honesty softened her a bit. "And these men regularly pay you money to…spend time with them?"

"Yes." The woman peered at Ela. Her eyes were a sharp blue at odds with the crude dark paint around them. "Some would say I fulfill a need that keeps these men focused on their work and not groping at the young girls around town."

She made a good point. The soldiers were away from their homes and deprived of female companionship. Still…

"Surely most of these men are married and you're breaking one of God's Commandments by committing adultery with them."

"I suppose I shall burn in hell for it," said the woman, with little concern. "It was that or starve and I made my choice."

Ela frowned. This interview was not going as planned. "What's your name?"

"Rosie."

"Your last name?"

"Which one? I was married twice before so there's three to choose from."

Ela suddenly felt very tired, despite it still being early. "Did your husbands die?"

"Men do, don't they? Fragile things." She looked curiously at Ela, like she was trying to read her mind. "And leave us behind to fend for ourselves."

Indeed they do. Ela had never been more grateful for her large inheritance and the protections it afforded.

"Where do you live?"

Rosie hesitated for a moment. "I have a room above the Bull and Bear."

Ela startled. It was the place her steward had gone yesterday to gather information. He'd reported back that he'd learned nothing of the matter. How was that possible when this witness lived above the place? Giles Haughton, the coroner, went there too, she knew. He'd probably recognize this woman. She made a mental note to ask him about her.

"Does the innkeeper know your profession?"

She laughed, a disconcerting sound that made Ela's hair stand on end. "He'd be a fool if he didn't, now, wouldn't he?"

Ela thought about chastising the woman for her insolence —and half wondered if Deschamps would do it for her—but she didn't, and Deschamps just stood there.

"Who did you meet by the castle walls?"

"No one special. I walk this way regular, like. Always soldiers here needing a little companionship."

Ela didn't believe her. "Did you go up to the top of the wall?"

"Why would I go up there?" Rosie had rotten teeth.

Ela worked to contain her irritation. "For some privacy with your customer, I'd assume. Were you up there, or on the ground?"

"On the ground, as you say." She released a grim cackle. "Though not as much as I'd have liked."

Ela blinked, getting flustered. This woman's brazen sinfulness was enough of an affront without additional rudeness. "So you were…with…a customer that night?"

"Thought I had a live one, seemed ready enough to grope me, but balked at the price, didn't he?"

"What was the price?" For what pittance did a woman sell her dignity in this cruel age?

"A penny." Rosie didn't seem proud of it. "Used to get fourpence back in my day but needs must."

Ela shuddered. Surely there must be some other way this poor woman could keep body and soul together? But that wasn't the immediate issue. "The soldiers said you cried out, and it was your scream that I heard from my bedroom window on that night."

"Couldn't say if I did or didn't."

Ela looked at Deschamps. Who looked at the two guards —Roger Wilks and Thomas Belcher—she'd seen when she went up to the wall the previous night.

"She was in her cups, my lady," said the third guard in a gruff voice. "Pardon me for being blunt, but none of the men was interested in her…wares…and she wouldn't take no for an answer."

"What's your name?"

"Myles Lassiter, my lady."

"And you're the one who confronted her?"

"I was, my lady. I told her to move along and leave the soldiers alone."

"Had you ever seen her before?"

"Indeed I had, my lady."

"Did you see the merchant, Ziyad al Wahid, on that same night."

His eyes darted oddly about. "Nay, my lady."

Ela felt a heavy sigh swell in her chest. "You were here at the base of the wall when you removed her. Did you go up on the wall at any point?"

"No. My job is to guard the stairs in the tower that lead up the wall."

Ela recalled that there was no one stationed there to question her and Bill when they ascended. "Did you leave your post at any point?"

Now his gaze shot to Deschamps, then back to her again. "No. I take my job very seriously."

"Then how, pray tell me," she heard the steely edge in her voice, "did a foreign merchant—one much favored and valued by my own household—climb to the top of the wall in order to fall to his death?"

He had the decency to look flustered. "Perhaps he came up through another tower, my lady?"

It was a long walk to the next tower, and Ela thought it unlikely that he would have walked that distance when he could have climbed up the tower only a few yards from where he died.

"Who else went up on the wall that night?"

She saw Lassiter swallow. "No one but the guards, my lady."

"Are you trying to tell me that the merchant flew up there, perhaps on feathered wings?" She peered at Deschamps. His men were clearly not telling the whole truth.

"That's what it seems like, my lady," said Lassiter, with the beginning of a smile.

"Ziyad al Wahid was murdered and thrown from the wall into the defensive ditch of *my* castle. You"—she looked in turn at each of the men, including Deschamps—"were responsible for the security of both the wall and the ditch and saw nothing? This seems a gross dereliction of duty."

She realized that a hush had fallen over the great hall as most people in it turned to stare in her direction. She must have raised her voice more than she intended.

"My lady, it is indeed a great mystery," said Deschamps in a syrupy voice she hadn't heard before. "And I'm sure we shall get to the bottom of it."

"How? When no one responsible has seen or heard anything?"

"I heard something," said Rosie suddenly. "Saw it, too." She pressed her thin painted lips together.

"What?" said Ela impatiently.

"I saw two men go up the tower together. Both of them wearing long robes, not short ones like the guards."

"Did you see their faces?"

"The first one might have been your merchant. He had a big black beard. That's all I noticed. The other one had a hood pulled over his head so I couldn't see his face."

"She was addled from ale, my lady," interrupted Deschamps. "This might be a fantasy."

Ela ignored him. "They went up to the top of the wall?"

"I didn't see that. I just saw them go in the tower."

"And did you see either of them come down?"

"No, I didn't but I was dragged away rudely right afterward so I don't know what happened. They were most unnecessarily rough if you ask me, which no one ever does."

Ela blinked. So—at least if her account was correct—the

woman had been dragged away right at the moment that Ziyad was likely strangled and thrown from the tower.

Almost as if someone had wanted to deliberately create a disturbance to cover up his murder.

Ela turned to Lassiter again. "It was your job to guard the stairs leading up to the top of the wall, but this woman says she saw two people pass up there. Where were you when this happened?"

"She's imagining things."

"You saw her and took pains to remove her from the area. I'm inclined to believe her account. What would she have to gain by lying?"

"I'm not lying. I saw them plain as day," spat Rosie at Lassiter.

"I didn't accuse the...ah...woman of lying, just of being too drunk to know what she saw."

"If only I could get that drunk," said Rosie. "Sometimes I wish I didn't see what I see. But I saw those two men go up to the tower and if one of them was murdered then the sheriff here needs to know." She lifted her chin high in the air.

All the men blinked at Ela as if they still couldn't believe she was the sheriff. "Thank you, Mistress..." Ela remembered that she'd never revealed her last name. "Rosie. I'd like you to speak with Giles Haughton, the coroner, to see if you can help him with some details about the death."

"I'd be happy to," she said defiantly. "Anything I can do to help solve a murder, even if it was of a foreigner."

Ela sighed inwardly. She wasn't sure Giles Haughton would have any use for Rosie—though if he knew her from the Bull and Bear he might have an opinion about whether she was a reliable witness. Mostly she wanted these men to know that she didn't discount Rosie's testimony, and that this wasn't the end of her investigation into the matter.

"Do any of you have anything to say about the fact that it

appears two men—unauthorized and unsupervised—mounted the outer walls of my castle and breached the king's garrison?

"It's impossible, my lady," said Deschamps. "Would you believe the rantings of a drunken strumpet over the testimony of three trusted men?"

Absolutely.

Ela didn't trust anyone these days. She'd been thrown out of her own castle and forced to buy back her position and her ancestral home by bribing the king, after all.

She looked at Deschamps. "There is ample evidence—witnessed by yourself, your guards, and the jurors, that a man was indeed thrown or pushed from the top of the wall. You cannot possibly seek to deny that he was indeed on top of the wall. It seems most likely that he ascended the wall through the nearby tower, and now we have a witness to that event." She let that sink in. She really wanted to accuse him of denying the facts they could all see, but she knew that to accuse him in front of his men would be a grave insult that might have unpleasant repercussions.

He was the garrison commander, after all. He had access to the king's ear. And already the king's closest confidant was her mortal enemy, Hubert de Burgh.

She'd be wise to marshal her troops and save her attack for another day.

"Two men went up on that wall," she said. "One of them was found dead in the ditch. The most urgent question is the identity of the second man. He is our murderer."

At that moment a hush fell over the hall. The drop in the usual din was dramatic enough to draw her attention from Deschamps, and she soon saw that all eyes were turned in the same direction.

CHAPTER 8

*S*afiya was the object of everyone's gaze. And the reason for their staring was that instead of her usual voluminous dark robes she now wore a bright blue dress that Ela recognized as one her eldest daughter had left behind for Petronella to grow into. Instead of being hidden under a loose scarf her hair had been pulled back into a bun and secured with a crisp white barbette and fillet that stood in stark contrast to her glowing golden skin.

Ela almost gasped to see the transformation. Safiya looked like she wished she could vanish into the rushes on the floor.

"Doesn't she look so much better, Mama?" exclaimed Petronella. "She looks almost Christian now. We thought it would cheer her up. We did let her change in private."

Elsie stood behind Safiya, a shy smile on her face.

Ela's initial instinct was to scold these foolish girls for hounding a freshly widowed woman into dressing up in unfamiliar garments. But poor Elsie was only just starting to come out of her shell after all she'd suffered, and perhaps she did mean well.

"Thank you, girls. Safiya, I do hope their ministrations haven't been too hard to bear in your grief."

"I think they were trying to lift my spirits," she said flatly. Her dark eyes glittered as if tears hovered just behind the surface. The fitted linen headwear framed her striking beauty. Her dark, shiny, and abundant hair made a thick heavy bun that would be the envy of any lady at court.

"I wanted to help her fit in, Mama," said Petronella. She could probably tell Ela was less than thrilled.

"I'm sure that was very thoughtful of you. Please make sure Safiya has food to eat that suits her customs."

Again Safiya looked as if she wished she were dead alongside her husband in the mortuary. Ela vowed to take her aside and offer words of encouragement as soon as she could.

She returned to Deschamps and the guards. "It's unfortunate that the dead man's wife doesn't know who her husband went to meet on the wall that fatal evening. Do you have any idea who that might be?"

"No one except the guards should be up on the wall at any time, day or night," said Deschamps. "But since this person was clearly a killer, he was not likely to obey the rules."

"Why would the murderer go up on the wall to kill someone? Why not do it outside the walls in the dark countryside where no one is likely to see him?"

"If he was inside the walls at nightfall he wouldn't have been able to leave. The gates are closed and guarded until dawn."

"And no one can come in or out for any reason?"

"Not without special permission, and none was given that night."

"So we're looking for someone who was inside the castle walls that evening." That didn't narrow it down by much. "And who had the cunning to get past your guards and climb to the top of the wall unnoticed except by Rosie here."

She turned to Rosie. "Do you think either of the two men saw you as they passed?"

"No." Rosie looked hard at her. "They didn't see me. I was tucked into the shadows."

Her memory had apparently returned. "Why?"

"Because I ain't supposed to be there, am I?" Rosie looked bemused. "So I hide until someone likely comes along and then I pop out and charm him."

Deschamps shifted his weight.

Ela looked at him. "How was this woman allowed to linger unnoticed so near a guard post?"

"Such women are a part of the fabric of a garrison, my lady. Their presence can go unremarked as a stone in the wall as long as they're not causing any trouble beyond plying their trade."

Ela blinked. She could hardly believe what she was hearing. "Sinful and criminal behavior is permitted and excused inside my castle?"

"Men will be men, my lady."

"No doubt murderers will be murderers. Do we just excuse their crimes because it's in their nature?" She wasn't sure if his guards' laxity or Deschamps's bold defense of it appalled her more.

"Indeed not, my lady. And my men did drive her from the spot not long afterward."

She should have been arrested. The only way to stamp out such behavior was to crack down on it. But she didn't want Rosie to become the scapegoat here. That would let these men off the hook far too easily.

"Rosie, would you be able to recognize either of the men again?"

"I didn't see their faces."

"Was there anything distinctive about them?"

Rosie frowned. "Well, the one in the black cloak was tall and might have had a slight limp. Very slight, mind you. Just a hitch to his stride if you know what I mean."

Ela nodded. "Does this sound like anyone you know?"

Deschamps emitted a small, tinny laugh. "Half the men in the garrison have a slight limp. It's the price of doing battle for our king. I have a limp myself if the weather's damp enough."

Ela stared at him. Deschamps had every right to be up on the wall. No one would question him climbing the tower stairs. And if he wanted to go up there unobserved he could easily assign his men to other parts of the wall.

A chill trickled down her spine.

But why would Deschamps want to kill Ziyad the merchant? It made no sense. Still, she'd raise the matter with Bill Talbot. He could be trusted to keep even the darkest secret.

AFTER A LIGHT MEAL Ela set out for a ride. She needed to get away from the castle and clear her head. She decided to ride out to the manor of Fernlees and visit her former lady's maid Hilda, whose marriage she'd recently arranged.

She convinced her daughter Petronella to accompany her so the girl, fast approaching her majority and desperate to take the veil and lock herself away in a cloister, could take a peek into the pleasures of married life.

Petronella flopped onto the saddle of her horse. "I don't know why you're making me come."

"You should seat yourself more gently, my dear. The horse's back is as sensitive as yours. And fresh air is good for your health."

"I get plenty of fresh air as it blows in through all the cracks and crevices in the castle walls," protested Petronella. "I think our castle must be the windiest spot in England." A stiff breeze blasted them in the face as they rode out over the moat toward the open countryside. Two guards followed behind them for protection but kept a discreet distance. "I still don't see why we're riding all the way to Fernlees."

"I wish to offer support and encouragement to Hilda," said Ela. "She's still new to married life and running a manor."

"Only in England could a peasant inherit a manor."

"Her son inherited the manor, and his father was a brave knight." Hilda's swain had been brutally murdered, leaving Hilda alone and pregnant. "Chance plays a great role in human destiny—or some might say it's the will of God."

"You think God wanted Hilda to be a lady of the manor?"

"I do."

"It's entirely your doing. She'd be alone and starving somewhere with her fatherless babe if you hadn't hired expensive lawyers to secure the property for her."

"God put upon my heart the desire to see her safely settled in life."

"Even though she's wilful and fickle and almost killed two of your sons by making them steal a poisoned pie for her?"

"She's kind-hearted and means no harm, though she is spirited," admitted Ela. They turned off the road and onto a narrow track through the fields that led in the direction of Fernlees. Summer wildflowers shone like jewels in the lush grass.

"The only spirit I want growing inside me is the Holy Spirit," said Petronella. "I think that an excess of spirit is likely to lead a woman to stray from the path of duty to God and her husband."

"Quite possibly."

They rode up a hill through a copse of trees. Ela let her horse break into a canter up the hill and enjoyed its steady rhythm. She reined her horse back to a walk at the top of the hill and they rode out into an open field with a flock of sheep clustered up at the far end.

Petronella turned to her. "Why do you persist in wanting to be sheriff?"

Ela fought the urge to sigh. None of her children was enthusiastic about her insistence on holding her late husband's role. "Salisbury castle is the home of our forefathers, and I intend to hold it in trust for the next generation. Being castellan and sheriff is part of that duty."

"But it brings all sorts of dangerous people into our hall. How was a man murdered on the walls of our castle with soldiers all around?"

"That is indeed a strange and perplexing mystery," said Ela. She glanced back at the two guards escorting them, who were far enough behind that they probably couldn't hear. "My being sheriff didn't cause the murder. It does, however, give me the opportunity to solve it. And to tackle other crimes in our community." She hesitated for a moment, not sure whether to confide in Petronella. "Did you know that women sell their virtue to men inside the castle walls without any censure or punishment?"

Petronella put her reins in one hand and crossed herself. "Surely not."

"I'm as shocked as you are. A prostitute was the only witness to the man who murdered Ziyad."

"Will she be hanged for her crimes?"

"Hanged? No!" Ela shook her head. "She's the only person so far who might stand as a witness." Ela wondered what the usual punishment was for a fallen woman. Again, to her surprise, she couldn't remember seeing such a case tried in all her years sitting at her husband's side. "But I can't allow such women to ply their trade in our town."

"Indeed not," Petronella scowled. "They should all be flogged."

"That's a bit cruel. I'm sure most of them found themselves in desperate need. The woman I spoke to this morning had been twice widowed."

"Maybe she killed them both and then murdered Ziyad the merchant," said Petronella dryly.

"Oh, stop. How about a gallop?" The grass plain stretched before them like an invitation.

"Why not?"

ELA ARRIVED at Fernlees with some trepidation. It had been a few weeks since she visited Hilda. She wanted to give the girl time to settle into her new marriage and household without undue interference. Hilda was young and wilful and not one who responded well to excess instruction.

As she and Petronella and their escorts rode up the lane to Fernlees she was a little afraid she'd find the manor halfway to rack and ruin and the air rent with the cries of Hilda's baby or the sound of her parents' yelling.

Instead they were greeted by the quiet chirping of birds and the swish of a scythe. Ela soon found the source of the second sound, when she spied the strong back of Hilda's young husband bent over the tool.

"God be with you, Dunstan."

The lad looked up from the task of cutting back the weeds near the front door of their tidy manor house.

He put the scythe aside, leaning it against the plastered wall. "Good morrow, my lady." He looked a little nervous at the sight of her. As well he might be. She'd entrusted him—a miller's son—with the running of an entire manor and the managing of her headstrong but beloved lady's maid.

Ela looked around. Fine fat hens pecked in the courtyard, guarded by a proud rooster. A newly made fence of woven willow contained a few sturdy brown piglets. Two freshly woven bee skeps stood on a low wood bench nearby and a pretty black cat presided over all from the sill of one of the small, leaded glass windows. "All seems to be in good order, Dunstan. Is the workload manageable?"

Hilda had inherited the land and house with no funds to hire labor to work it. The success or failure of the manor rested entirely in their hands.

"It's the kind of work I enjoy, my lady. Taxes the mind as well as the muscles. The challenge is to decide what must be done today and what can wait until tomorrow." His bright handsome face glowed, tanned by the sun and rosy cheeked from fresh air and good health.

"I'm glad that the work seems to suit you. How are Hilda and the baby?" She didn't yet feel bold enough to say "your baby," when everyone in this part of Wiltshire knew that the baby was sired by another.

"You must ask her yourself." He gestured to the door. Ela dismounted her horse and one of the guards rushed forward to hold it. She and Petronella walked up the scrubbed stone path and into the dark rectangle of the doorway. Before they even entered she could smell freshly baked cakes, and the smell filled her heart with joy. Hilda was clearly mistress of her own kitchen.

The red clay floor tiles weren't the cleanest she'd ever seen, but such tasks weren't easily accomplished with a baby on one hip.

"Hilda!" called Dunstan. "My lady the countess is here to visit."

"Oh!" came a cry from upstairs. "I'll be right down. I'm just cleaning up a mess made by little Thomas."

The house had little furniture as yet, just some surplus odds and ends that Ela had found in her manors. Three mismatched chairs sat around a table near the unlit fireplace.

Hilda came flying down the stairs, carrying her baby under one arm and a bucket in the other. "Babies do make a lot of work, my lady. Especially when there's no servants to clean it up for you."

"Wait until they start running around and leaving little puddles here and there to surprise you," said Ela. "Oh, isn't he so healthy and bonny."

Hilda offered the baby and Ela took him in her arms. "A new baby's smell is the best scent in the world," exclaimed Ela. "There's nothing like it." She pressed her nose into the pretty curls of his fine hair. His eyes had turned a lovely hazel, like oak leaves in the autumn.

"He's started to smile at us! Especially at Dunstan. He knows his daddy already." Ela's heart surged, especially when she glanced at Dunstan's proud face. She'd been worried there might be tension over this little cuckoo in the nest. But who could do anything but love such a sweet creature? "Does he keep you awake all night with his fussing?"

"Nay. I let him sleep with us in the bed so I can nurse him any time he awakes."

"I did that myself more than I care to admit." Ela's husband was away from home much of the time when the children were little. When he'd been home she'd often forced herself to leave her beloved babes with a nurse overnight so she could devote herself utterly to her husband's needs. Of course Hilda didn't have such a choice.

"They're babes for such a short time," said Hilda. "I don't like to let him cry."

"Very sensible. And soon enough he'll be helping you collect the eggs and scatter grain for the hens."

"And I'll teach him to gather kindling and carry wood for the fires," said Dunstan cheerfully.

"Dunstan is very clever. He wove us our bee skeps and all of the fencing for the pigs, and his father has given us three sacks of flour as a gift so we have plenty of food already. Come see my garden!"

Hilda led them back outside again, to where her rather untidy kitchen garden already bristled with salad greens and herbs and buzzed with bees from the nearby skeps. "And we're growing carrots and parsnips for the winter. And there's already a whole orchard of apple trees that must have been here forever—the sour ones that keep well over the winter. We'll be eating like kings even during Lent."

"I'm proud of you and Dunstan for all you've accomplished so far. I know it's been a lot of hard work."

"Hard work is easy when you're your own mistress," said Hilda with a grin.

Ela had to laugh. "That makes sense, when the rewards are all yours to keep."

THEY WALKED around the manor and Dunstan proudly showed off their small flock of brown and white sheep. "I've made an arrangement with a neighbor that he'll lend me his best ram for breeding in exchange for help with his harvest. Soon we'll have a flock of good wool-producing sheep and we'll eat the ones with rough coats."

Ela nodded in approval. She was introduced to their rather scraggly yellow cow, who looked on placidly as Hilda exclaimed over her superior milk-producing capabilities. Their horse was a rugged bay beast with a stoic expression, who barely lifted his head from the tufts of grass when they approached. Dunstan told them his father had gifted them one of his best cart horses, so they'd be able to take their goods to market.

"And he's also safe to ride, even for me," exclaimed Hilda, who—Ela knew—had barely sat on a horse three times in her life. "So as you can see we have almost everything you have up at the castle, now, don't we?"

Ela laughed again. She could feel Petronella bristling with indignation over Hilda's pride and excess of enthusiasm. Her daughter had been silent this entire time, except for cooing and smiling when Hilda let her hold her precious baby.

"You don't have a bone chess set," said Petronella.

"Why would anyone want a bone chess set?" asked Hilda.

Ela laughed again. "Why indeed? Such things are nothing but a waste of time."

"And money that could be donated to the poor," said Petronella stiffly. "And already the white king's been lost. Richard and Stephen were looking all over for it this morning."

Ela sighed. "I know. I'm sure it will turn up." She didn't mention the mysterious blood stains on the queen or the crack in the knight. She was beginning to curse the day she'd seen that bone chess set.

"What kind of bone is it made from?" asked Hilda curiously.

"Ox, probably," said Petronella. "They have big bones."

"Or camel," said Ela. "It's from the East and I believe they use camel bones for a lot of their carvings."

"Maybe it's made from human bones," said Hilda with a grin. "You never know what foreigners will get up to."

Ela felt an odd shiver creep up her spine. It had never crossed her mind to ask what kind of bones the chess set had been carved from. Certainly something larger than a human, though, so why her reaction?

"Foreigners are like us," she protested. "With different customs."

"They're not like us," protested Petronella. "They won't eat pigs, which is just wasteful when pigs are so abundant."

"And so tasty," said Hilda cheerfully. "I'd be sad not to eat them."

"We don't eat pigs during Lent," said Ela. "It's like that."

"They worship the wrong God, too," said Petronella reflectively. "So they're all going to hell on Judgment Day."

"That's not true," said Ela.

"Then where do they go?"

Ela hesitated. "Purgatory, I believe. Along with unbaptized babies and others who weren't fortunate enough to receive the Lord's blessings in life but who haven't committed great wrongs."

"Some of them go to hell," said Petronella with conviction. "And we have one living in our castle right now who killed her husband."

CHAPTER 9

"What on earth makes you think that Safiya killed her husband?" Ela was too shocked to be circumspect.

"Killed? Who's been killed?" Hilda looked alarmed.

"Um, it's a case up in the town that I'm looking into as sheriff," explained Ela as drily as possible. She didn't want to discuss the matter here. "We must be going."

She said hasty goodbyes to Hilda and Dunstan, then she and Petronella mounted their horses and set out for the castle with the guards in tow.

Once they were out of earshot of Fernlees, and of the guards, Ela turned to Petronella with fury in her heart. "Why would you publicly accuse Safiya of murder? You don't even know the facts of the case."

Petronella looked at her blankly. "Everyone says she did it."

"Apparently there were people who dared to accuse me of killing your father. Would you believe them, too?"

"Who said that?" Petronella accidentally tugged on her horse's reins and its head shot up.

"It doesn't matter. They were wrong and you know it. Idle gossips seek to stir up trouble. What motive would Safiya have for killing her husband?"

"I don't know. Maybe he beat her?"

Ela reflected that when Safiya had said she loved and missed her husband, she'd taken her word for it. "Her grief seems genuine."

"*Seems* is the telling word in that sentence. You don't know this woman. Perhaps you should look beneath the surface."

"Well, you and Elsie certainly exposed her surface."

"She might as well look like a good Christian, even if she isn't one."

Ela had impressed the importance of conventional dress and deportment on her children, so it felt churlish to argue against it now. "Tell me who accused her of murdering her husband."

"Well, Cook, for one."

"Is she on the jury of the hundred?"

"She would be if she were a man."

True, reflected Ela.

"And the new steward was saying snide things about her. He thinks it's foolish to pay our debts to her now her husband is dead." Now Ela was shocked since she'd already made her views on the matter clear to Bazin, and—even if she hadn't—he should not be discussing such matters in public. She'd have sharp words with him on her return.

"And Bill Talbot thinks she could have done it."

"Never!" Ela couldn't believe Bill Talbot would gossip like a washerwoman. Not when he was her closest confidant. "What exactly did he say?"

"Well, maybe he didn't exactly come out and accuse her. But he did say she was odd. And that their wagon had all kinds of things secreted away in little drawers. And that he found the whole situation most mysterious."

They trotted up a hill. Dark storm clouds gathered in the distance behind the castle. "You must be kind to Safiya. She's all alone in a strange country with no one to protect her."

"Except you."

"Indeed, and I shall defend her from those who wish her harm."

"Even if she's a murderer?"

BACK AT THE castle Ela looked around for Safiya. Not finding her, she sent Bill Talbot to look for her, and he soon found her tucked into the depths of her wagon. Ela climbed up onto the platform above the wheels and entered in past the curtains.

Safiya still wore the barbette and fillet that the girls had pinned on her, but her eyes were red with weeping and she'd draped a black robe over herself.

"Are all your goods still in here?" Ela wasn't sure whether to trust the guards to look after the stores of exotic goods, especially when no one seemed to respect their owner.

"I don't know," said Safiya. "They were my husband's business."

"How is it that you had nothing to do with his goods and business when you lived day and night in this tiny space with them?" Perhaps Safiya's marriage kept her powerless and penniless to the point of wanting freedom from it? "Did you wish you were more involved?"

"No." Safiya blinked and tears glittered in her long eyelashes.

Was she telling the truth? How could a woman be so totally uninterested in the affairs of business that occupied her husband's time? "Did he ever speak to you about the men he did business with?"

"Never. And when I asked he told me to leave it alone. That it was safer for me not to know."

Is she toying with me? For the first time Ela felt a slight tug of doubt about Safiya and her innocent guise of bereaved widow. She'd alerted them to her husband's disappearance and sent them all scurrying around looking for him. Was it a clever ruse to divert suspicion from herself?

She looked at Safiya's black wrapper. Which could easily appear to be a black cloak to a casual observer. When a person was wrapped in a cloak it could be hard to tell if they were male or female.

"Have you ever been up onto the castle's outer walls?"

Safiya blinked again. "I don't know."

"What do you mean you don't know?" Unease curled in Ela's stomach. "Either you have or you haven't."

"I've been to Salisbury many times. It's a lot like other fortified towns. Whether I've been on this wall or not I can't remember."

"Were you on it in the last few days, since you and your husband arrived in Salisbury? Surely you can remember that."

She peered at Safiya, who gazed at the floor. "No."

"Why would you go up on the walls of a city? Or why would your husband?" She didn't understand why he would have climbed up there in the first place.

"My husband liked to be up above the city and able to conduct discussion where no one could overhear it."

So he'd done it before. "Why?" Ela's sense of misgivings deepened. "What was so secret?"

Safiya shrugged. "Like I said, he didn't tell me."

Suddenly Ela wanted to ask Rosie the prostitute if Safiya —in her black cloak—might be the second man she saw.

Safiya burst into tears. "What am I going to do without him? I know nothing about business." She choked out the words between sobs that racked her body. "I have no family. I have nowhere to go. I should go throw myself from the top of the wall so I can go to paradise with him."

Guilt swept over Ela for her uncharitable thoughts. Had she let Petronella—and by extension the doubters around her —sow seeds of mistrust that made her doubt a grieving widow?

"You must never think of killing yourself. I don't know the teachings of your religion well, but in mine the taking of a life—including your own—is a mortal sin."

"I can't survive without him," cried Safiya. "I might as well be dead."

"You can and you will," said Ela as calmly as she could. "I can help you find a buyer for all the goods you have left, and for the wagon, and help you find passage back to your country."

Horror flickered in Safiya's dark eyes. "I have nothing to return home to. My father sold me like a fatted calf."

"But you must have friends? Other family?"

Tears pooled in her eyes and she blinked, which sent them cascading down her already tear-streaked cheeks. "No one. I had one friend who I used to play with as a child, but she got married and then died in childbirth within the year. Since then my husband has been my only friend."

Ela couldn't imagine having no family to turn to. Her mother could sometimes be provokingly traditional, but she was still Ela's closest female confidant. And Bill Talbot wasn't a blood relative but he served the role of one in her life. And then there were her children—they needed her to be strong and that had helped her drag herself out of her grief.

"Don't worry. I'll help you make a plan. But our most important goal right now is to find out who killed your husband." She took Safiya's hands in hers. "Think hard. Think about anyone you saw or heard him with. Even people who seemed utterly normal and harmless at the time. Who did he do business with that might have wanted him dead?"

"I don't know. But I want to sleep here. It makes me feel close to him."

Ela hesitated. It would make more sense to inventory the goods and store them safely in a room in the castle. The wagon wasn't secure. The walls were only made of canvas and the strange walls of drawers—filled with precious things —could likely be pried off with a chisel and stolen.

"I'm not sure you're safe in here."

"But there are soldiers outside." Safiya looked so tired.

Did Ela dare admit that she didn't entirely trust the soldiers that guarded her own castle? She sighed. "I understand that you need to grieve, so I'll leave you for now. But come to me at once if you need anything or if you think of any clue that might give us insight into your husband's death. Anything, no matter how small."

Safiya nodded mutely.

Ela took her leave and walked back into the great hall, frustrated by the lack of leads. A man in a black cloak. This could be literally anyone in Wiltshire, even a woman, as she'd already pondered.

BACK IN THE castle Ela was easily distracted by the cares and concerns of the townspeople who flooded her hall with complaints about tainted flour, a dispute over a diseased hen, and a man's quarrel with the neighbor who broke his plough. The afternoon and early evening flew by, and she didn't catch her breath until she ran to the chapel for refuge at Vespers.

Ela knelt, deep in prayer, begging the Lord for insight into the wickedness in the heart of whoever had killed Ziyad, when the door to the chapel flew open and Elsie rushed in. Ela opened her mouth to scold the girl for disturbing the peace of the chapel and interrupting the sacred service. But the horrified expression on the girl's face stilled her tongue.

"My lady, it's Sir William. He's badly wounded!"

~

ELA FLEW OUT of the chapel and followed Elsie down a corridor and across the kitchen garden. It had just rained and droplets glistened on the plants. "What happened?" she called after her.

"Something fell on him."

When they reached the arched doorway that led to the back stables, a crowd of guards and servants and townspeople thronged the cobbled courtyard beyond, obscuring her view.

"Let me through," she stammered, her heart pounding. Bill lay sprawled on the hard stones, a trickle of blood at the corner of his mouth. Ela suppressed a scream that rose in her throat.

"Bill," she called, though she could see he was unconscious. She bent over him and pressed her head to his chest.

"He's breathing, my lady," said a man's voice nearby. "I checked him."

The steady thud of Bill's heartbeat reassured her. But he didn't stir. "Did anyone see what happened?"

"I did," said a lad who tended the pigs. "A piece of stone fell on him from the arch." He pointed up at the archway that led toward the stable yard.

Ela peered up and could see a hunk of stone—perhaps the size of a human skull—missing from the arch.

"It must have fallen just as he passed under it."

"Where did it strike him?"

"On his shoulder, I think," said the lad. "Then he fell to the ground and I think he hit his head."

"Fetch smelling salts," Ela called to Elsie. "And ask the cook to brew a tonic. We must wake him as fast as possible."

"Bill," she murmured, her lips almost touching his ear. "It's Ela." Bill would be mortified to know that she was calling for him and he wasn't able to respond.

Her co-sheriff, John Dacus, hurried over. "Should I call for a jury?"

"Has a crime been committed? He was hit by a falling piece of stone from the arch."

"Oh, I assumed someone attacked him." Dacus looked perplexed.

Ela paused and peered up at the arch. "Perhaps they did."

ELSIE BROUGHT a sachet of strong salts. She and Ela held them under his nose and gently slapped his cheeks. To their great relief they managed to awaken Bill before the jurors arrived. He looked dazed at first but soon scrambled to his feet, wanting to know exactly how he'd come to be lying on the ground with half of Salisbury standing over him.

"A stone fell from the archway as you passed under it." Ela pointed to the spot. "This lad saw it all." The boy stood nearby. The stone itself lay a few feet away, now broken into three pieces on the courtyard cobbles.

Stephen Hale, the cordwainer, and Hugh Clifford, the wine seller, were the first jurors on the scene because they both kept shops near the castle. Bill was now on his feet, brushing himself off. "Jurors? Surely it was just an unlucky accident. Praise be to God I'm not badly hurt."

"It seems like an accident, but I've lived most of my life in this castle and never in all my days have I seen a stone come loose from an archway. This arch has stood, unmoving, for a hundred and fifty years. And an archway is typically the strongest part of a wall because the wedge-shaped stones lock each other in place."

"That is indeed true," said Dacus. "I commissioned a new doorway at my manor, and the mason explained it to me in exacting detail."

"Who would tamper with it?" asked Bill. "Do you think someone aimed to hurt me? Surely it was mere chance that I passed under it at the moment that it fell?"

Ela held her tongue. Too many strange things had happened.

The knight in the chess set had inexplicably cracked.

The king was now missing.

And the queen soaked in blood...

She knew better than to ramble about such seemingly fanciful oddities in a crowd of townsmen. "We need a stone-mason to examine the stone and see if it's been tampered with," she said firmly. "Sir John, please fetch Ralph Towney. He's one of the jurors and an expert stonemason employed on the cathedral."

The newly erected cathedral down in the water meadows was already in use, but there was still much decorative work to be done and they could hear the tap of hammers and chisels all the way up here on the castle mound.

Dacus nodded his assent and strode off. Ela appreciated his swift support.

Bill looked bemused. "Who'd want to beat me over the head with a rock?" He cast his glance around the crowd. It was a good question. Naturally thoughtful and kind, Bill had an easy manner that ingratiated him with nobles and commoners alike.

In attacking him, Ela felt it far more likely they were attacking her.

If indeed it was an attack. She couldn't ignore the possibility that the stone might have fallen by itself.

One of the guards moved to pick up a fallen piece of stone, which sent a jolt of alarm through Ela. "No one touch the pieces until Ralph Towney examines them."

The guard jerked back as if she'd slapped his hand. Ela wanted to take Bill inside for some wine. He might still be dizzy and in need of further reviving. But could she trust the guards to leave the scene intact?

They'd been trusted with guarding the castle wall, and a man was murdered on their watch. The only men she truly trusted were Dacus—who'd gone into new Salisbury to find the stonemason—and Bill, who'd been at her side for her entire adult life. The jurors were generally honest and decent, but men often had their own motives in any given situation.

"Elsie, find Stephen and Richard and ask them to hurry here at once."

When her sons arrived, she instructed them to guard the fallen pieces of stone and make sure no one touched them, and to watch the arch in the same manner. Then she ordered the crowd to disperse and go about their business.

THE BELLS WERE CHIMING for Compline by the time the stonemason arrived. The jurors had gone back to their homes and the crowd dispersed. Bill insisted that he was entirely recovered and stood with Ela to greet the mason in the courtyard.

"God be with you, Master Towney."

"His blessings upon you, my lady." The stonemason

doffed his cap. He was a tall, broad-shouldered man who looked as if he could lead an army. In a way he reminded her of her husband.

"A piece of stone fell from this arch, injuring Sir William Talbot. I'd like you to examine the stone and the arch and let me know if you think this was a natural occurrence or if foul play was involved." She was glad the days were long enough that daylight stretched into the evening. She wanted him to examine every detail of the scene.

The mason's brown eyes shone with curiosity, but he didn't ask any further questions. First he examined the shattered fragments of stone. There were three big pieces that fit together to form a whole, and a few smaller bits that had broken off them. He picked each up and turned them over in his hands, frowning.

Then he climbed up a ladder—fetched by servants—and peered at the archway. "I'll need to replace this missing stone as soon as possible. It weakens the arch to have it gone."

"Could it collapse?"

"Not overnight, but eventually it might because the stones around it could work loose. In the meantime I'll put a wood jig in there to hold them in place."

"Did it fall out of its own accord?"

"It did not."

"It's been tampered with?"

"I believe so." He ran his fingers over the adjacent stones. "There are chisel marks here that don't look to be part of the original carving." He touched them and pulled his finger away. "The dust on them is fresh, so it hasn't been rained on."

"How would someone loosen the stone and have it fall at the exact moment that I was passing by?" asked Bill, sounding skeptical.

"I suppose if they tied a cord around it they might have

pulled it. If the cord was fine enough you wouldn't have noticed it."

"But there is no cord," said Ela. "Unless someone removed it from the scene before I got here."

A fine cord. The thought jolted Ela. "A man was strangled using a thin cord earlier this week. We haven't found that either."

"Why would anyone want to drop a stone on me?" asked Bill.

"Perhaps because you're my right-hand man?" It was hard to imagine any other motive. Bill had no enemies that she knew of.

"But why would they want to attack you?" asked Bill, looking at Ela.

Ela drew in a deep breath. "As sheriff I find myself the object of envy and curiosity," she said in a low voice. "There are those who resent my hold on power in the wake of my husband's death."

Bill blinked. She could tell he immediately thought of Hubert de Burgh, the king's justiciar and the man she blamed for the death of her husband.

He knew better than to utter de Burgh's name in front of the stonemason.

The stonemason cleared his throat. Obviously he found the situation awkward. He pulled some scraps of wood from his bag and set at them with a saw and a chisel—also in his bag—and soon was up the ladder tapping them into place.

"I do appreciate your coming so quickly," said Ela. "Send my steward a bill for your work." And she'd have a word with Bazin about adding something extra. She must also ask him whether he'd paid Safiya yet for her husband's wares. And she wanted to ask Haughton about whether the harlot Rosie was a reliable witness.

Ela was heading back into the hall when her son Stephen came running. "Mama, Richard and I found the king!"

Ela had so many thoughts running through her head that it took her a moment to realize that they were talking about the chess piece. "Where was it?"

"In the moat."

CHAPTER 10

"Ohat were you doing out in the moat?" asked Ela, as she fingered the chess piece. Soil now nestled in some of the carved crevices.

"The steward said we should go to the place where the merchant was found and look for clues to who killed him."

How odd. "And you found this in the same spot?"

"Yes, I think so. There were footprints all around. Does it help solve the murder?" Stephen looked at her eagerly.

They walked into the hall. Ela looked around for Bazin. Why would he send her sons out to the moat? For a start he had no business telling them to do something entirely outside his purview.

She'd offered both boys to Bazin to serve as quasi apprentices, partly because she wanted them to learn the financial aspects of running a large estate with multiple manors, and also because she liked to have another set of eyes on her books now that she was too busy to go over them with a fine-tooth comb herself.

"Well, does it?" Stephen asked again.

"I can't say it does. Why would Bazin suggest you go there?"

"I don't know." Stephen shrugged. "Maybe we were bothering him. I wanted to play chess with him again. I've never seen anyone with such a sharp mind for the game."

I wonder what else he has a sharp mind for?

Once again Ela found herself pondering what her steward was up to. She found Bazin in the small room where the books were kept, hunched over a ledger with a quill pen in his hand. "Did you send my sons out to the moat?"

"Did I?" He appeared confused. "I did tell them I needed time to think. I'm calculating the profits and losses from the Notton estate. The wool was of an inferior quality this spring and didn't fetch a good price at market. The farmer says the sheep suffered in the wet winter and—"

Was he trying to distract her? "They found something there."

"Oh?" He looked only mildly interested.

"Stephen said you had told him to look for clues to the merchant's murder. Why would you do such an extraordinary thing?"

"Extraordinary?" Now he looked a little offended. "I simply thought that with their keen youthful senses…. What did they find?"

Was this a rhetorical question? At this moment Ela entirely suspected that Bazin had placed the chess piece there himself. But why?

And had he cracked the knight piece and bloodied the queen?

Ela glanced over her shoulder as if to reassure herself that she was still in the busy castle, surrounded by people. She felt oddly vulnerable.

In a position of power you must always be on your guard. Her husband used to say that. Or was it her father? Sometimes their sayings ran together in her head now they were both gone.

"Do you know how the chess set got damaged?"

"I have no idea, my lady. As I told you I put the set away in the box after we finished. Someone else must have removed it again, then perhaps some soldiers were careless after drinking too much."

"This chess set seems to have sent my household into a frenzy of chess playing. It's clear that you are a formidable opponent."

"I have a head for numbers and calculation." He pointed to the ledger. "Which skills lend themselves well enough to the game of chess."

"Perhaps you could turn your mind to the puzzle of how the king from my new chess set happened to find himself in the ditch, near where the merchant's body was found?" She watched his reaction.

He looked bemused. "Most strange, to be sure."

The lord of this castle was murdered. The thought sliced keenly through Ela's mind. And now its knight—Bill Talbot —has been injured.

Is the queen in danger?

Her fingertips stung with an odd nervous sensation.

"Would you like me to speak to the farmer at Notton about altering the management of the flocks?"

"Not yet." She didn't entirely trust Bazin and his advice.

He looked surprised. "If it pleases you, my lady." He cleared his throat. "I wonder if you might like my assistance in valuing the items that the Moorish woman has in her wagon, and perhaps facilitating their sale?"

"Again, not yet," She answered quickly. "We must find the murderer first."

Ela walked away, closing the door behind her. Right now she didn't even like this new steward being alone with her books. She didn't trust him. Bazin sending her sons to look for clues in the ditch could not be a coincidence.

What was he up to?

Her mother had sent him to her, swearing up and down that he was a treasure. If he was so wonderful, why had she not kept him herself?

Ela decided to pay a visit to her mother.

ELA'S MOTHER, Alianore de Vitre, owned a fine manor a few hours' ride away with her fourth husband, Jean. They spent much of the year in London, where her mother enjoyed the entertainments at court and a busy social life. The summers in London could be unpleasantly malodorous, so Ela knew her mother had retired to her pretty manor in the country.

Ela didn't send a servant to warn Alianore of her impending arrival. She didn't intend to stay more than one night, especially with the strange events unfolding in Salisbury castle.

Bill Talbot pleaded to come with her, but she told him she needed him to stay behind to keep a watchful eye on Bazin and to protect Safiya from the gossips as well as any who might harm her. Truth be told she wasn't sure he'd entirely escaped injury when he was knocked to the ground.

She brought her son Stephen with her. John Dacus could fulfill her role as sheriff, but without Bill Talbot at her side she felt uneasy. The castle guards were all hired men whom she trusted to varying degrees, but she'd witnessed enough betrayal among them that she'd likely never trust one entirely with her life again.

In the aftermath of her husband's death she'd grown used to her son William being her armed deputy. With him now married and living far away, she enjoyed the comfort of another trusty young man well trained in the art of the sword. Although Stephen was yet young, he'd proven steady and brave in the hunting field and his presence reassured her.

While she normally took such a journey in the carriage, to be better prepared for sudden downpours and easy transportation of her servants and children, this time she rode her horse, Freya. The rains of spring had given way to balmy June days, and she craved the beauty of the countryside and the summer breezes against her skin.

THE JOURNEY PASSED SWIFTLY, with Stephen enjoying the athleticism of one of his father's favorite horses, and chattering easily with the guards as they rode. The bells for Nones had just finished ringing out over the countryside when they arrived at the well-tended gates of Alianore's house.

They'd barely dismounted when Alianore rushed out to meet them, exclaiming that if she'd had adequate warning she'd have prepared a proper feast to welcome them.

"Oh Stephen, you do look so fine on that magnificent animal. And I'm glad to see you have a sword worthy of your position."

"It was my father's."

"It's still rather too long for him," said Ela. "But he'll grow into it."

"I'm sure he swings it like William the Conqueror himself," exclaimed Alianore, beaming. She never showed any compunction about letting her nearest and dearest heroically risk their lives by the sword. "We'll have a new suit of armor made for you with your father's coat of arms. I know of an armorer in Naples who produces mail that's so lightweight you'd swear it was made of wool. We can send him your measurements."

She welcomed them into the house, as always beautifully decorated with the finest fabrics, and plied them with wine so smooth and sweet that they all exclaimed over it.

"Ah, it was Noel Bazin who secured this shipment of wine. His knowledge of the vineyards of southern France is unrivaled. And he negotiated an excellent price."

Ela pricked to attention. "If Noel Bazin is such an unparalleled wonder, how did you convince yourself to part with him?"

Her mother swallowed her wine and smiled. "Oh, you know how it is. Sometimes one wants to handle one's own affairs rather than be given excellent advice about them at every moment."

"Does one? That doesn't sound like you. I've never known you to be satisfied with less than the finest of everything. And in all honesty Bazin is part of the reason I'm here."

"Oh?" Eleanor looked a little alarmed.

"He's…odd. He plays chess better than any man in the castle, which is not alarming in itself, but some strange things have happened since he arrived."

"Ela!" Alianore's husband, Jean, strode into the room. "No one told me you were coming."

"She doesn't dare give me warning," said Alianore. "Or she thinks I'll have prospective husbands lined up ready to meet her."

"She knows you too well," said Jean. "But I hope I'm living proof that a remarriage can be satisfactory." He smiled his dimpled smile. A knight in middle age, he was still handsome enough to be a catch for any woman.

"There's only one of you, Jean," said Ela, pretending to be amused. "More's the pity. Meanwhile I have my hands full running Salisbury castle and being sheriff of Wiltshire."

"A burden shared is a burden halved," said her mother in a singsong voice. "Isn't it, darling?"

"I suppose that rather depends on whose burden it was in the first place," said Jean, with a wink at Ela. "But either way it's a delight to see you here." He made some manly banter with Stephen that soon had the youth beaming with pride.

Next they were whisked around the estate on a tour of the flourishing quince and pear orchard and a new herb garden arranged in a pattern like the spokes of a wheel. "Your mother is always full of creative ideas," exclaimed Jean.

"Just trying to keep myself busy when I'm cooped up out here in the wilderness."

"You know London's miserable at this time of year, my love," exclaimed Jean. "The river reeks like a fetid armpit and all courtiers with sense are away for the season." He smiled. "And now Ela's here to keep you entertained. I do hope you're able to stay for a few weeks."

"Weeks? Goodness, no. In fact, I'm intending to head back tomorrow."

Alianore gasped. "Why so soon?"

"Strange things are happening at the castle. A visiting merchant was murdered shortly after I purchased several expensive items from him."

"Before you paid, I hope," teased Jean.

Ela didn't find this funny. "His widow is devastated. And I have no idea what to do with her as she's foreign—a Moor from Tangier—and I fear for her safety. I've given her shelter in the castle for now."

"Harboring foreigners is risky, my dear," said Alianore. "And can bring enemies to your keep."

"She's one lone woman," protested Ela. "I hardly think she'll bring the Saracen armies to Salisbury. Besides, her husband was from Sevilla, not Jerusalem."

"That's close enough. You can send her back there," said Jean.

"I need to find out who killed her husband first. He was strangled with a fine cord, so fine as to barely leave a mark, then pushed off the castle's outer wall into the moat."

"As I said, foreigners attract trouble."

"The merchant visited us every year and brought many fine things. That beautiful carved lute I gave you two years ago is one of the treasures I bought from him."

"That lute sings like a nightingale. If his stock is all so fine you should offer to buy it from his widow and resell it for profit. I'm sure Noel Bazin could manage that for you. He's wily as a fox and drives an excellent bargain."

"Now that you mention it, he did suggest that."

"See? He's full of good ideas."

"Too full sometimes, it seems," said Ela.

"What do you mean?" Her mother brushed at an imaginary piece of lint on her gown.

"Some odd things happened to the chess set I bought from the merchant. The king vanished. Bazin told my sons to go search the moat where the dead merchant's body was found." She paused and sipped her wine. "And there it was."

"How odd," said her mother stiffly.

"So I'm wondering if you know more about Noel Bazin. I know he's from Picardy and that he comes highly recommended by you and others. He claims to have beaten old King Louis himself at chess. But what else is there to know about him?"

Alianore glanced at Jean, and the look that passed between them made Ela's gut tighten.

"I never liked him," said Jean. "Odd man and far too full of himself for a steward if you ask me. A steward should count your sheep and pelts and add up the profits from them but shouldn't be telling which ram to put to your ewes. He told me we should get rid of the perfectly good English cattle we have and replace them with some breed from Burgundy just because he preferred them!"

"Burgundy steers are better marbled," said Alianore.

"That's what he'd have us believe anyway. I put my foot down."

Ela glanced at Jean's foot, handsomely encased in soft tanned leather. "I don't mind advice from my steward and I'm not above taking it if it's good."

"See? I knew you'd appreciate his—" Alianore hesitated.

"Impertinence," said Jean with a laugh.

"Initiative, perhaps," said Ela. "I don't claim to be an expert on everything and with all the pots I have on the fire I value someone who can stir the ones left unattended."

"Then he's perfect for you," said Alianore, clapping her hands together. "I thought he might be."

"I'm happy to listen to his advice on matters involving money and property, though I'd have no compunction in ignoring it should I find it inappropriate. But did he know the missing chess piece would be found at the site of the murder?"

"Who cares, my darling? It's just a chess piece."

It's not just a chess piece. "I know this sounds strange and nonsensical, but somehow that chess piece seems to represent William to me."

"William's enjoying married life with Idonea. I've heard nothing but wonderful reports of them from her dear grandmother."

"Not William my son. William my husband."

Her mother's face fell slightly. "Your husband?"

"There's a strange pattern to the events. The knight piece was cracked, and then a stone fell from an arch and injured Bill Talbot."

"Oh poor Bill. Is he badly hurt?"

"He escaped serious injury, but a stonemason said that the stone had been tampered with and possibly pulled from its place with a cord as Bill walked beneath it."

"How unsettling." Alianore crossed herself, and Ela followed suit.

"And the king piece went missing—like my dead husband." William had disappeared for a year, lost and injured on the Ile de Ré, before returning home—to die suddenly. She'd never told her mother her suspicions that William was poisoned. The knowledge was too dangerous. "And the queen…" She hesitated, not wanting to speak the words aloud. "The queen stood in a pool of blood, as if injured."

Alianore blinked at her. "The queen would be you?"

"Yes." Ela realized how ridiculous this all sounded now that she'd spoken it aloud.

"But you're not injured? Has anyone tried to hurt you?"

"No." *Not yet.* But why did she feel like someone was about to try? "But who would do such a thing?"

"I expect it was an accident. There are always so many strange men in your hall. All those wild soldiers. It's a shame the king can't garrison his soldiers elsewhere."

"The ordinary men aren't banging elbows at my tables, just the knights," protested Ela. "Though I admit they can create a disturbance. But isn't it a bizarre coincidence that the king goes missing and is found on Bazin's advice? And that the knight is cracked and Bill Talbot is struck by a stone?"

"It sounds rather like coincidence to me," said Jean. "But that Bazin fellow always set my teeth on edge. I never trusted him."

"Jean! This is news to me," exclaimed Alianore. "I would never have sent him to mind Ela's books if I thought he was untrustworthy."

"I suppose I thought he'd be too busy to make a nuisance of himself in Ela's household. All those manors to manage and veritable flocks of pheasants and herds of swine to count. He should have his hands far too full for any nonsense about a chess set."

"It's probably all a coincidence my dear. Perhaps he wanted the boys out of his hair and knew that young men would find a murder scene enticing."

"That is what he said when I asked him to explain it. But it doesn't sit right with me." Ela frowned. "Should I dismiss him?"

"Absolutely," said Jean, without a moment's hesitation. "Just the fact that you're having these doubts tells me he doesn't belong in your household."

"But I can't put my finger on actual wrongdoing, so sending him away doesn't seem fair," mused Ela. "What would I even tell him about why he's being dismissed?"

"Well, my dear, the ideal way is to find a wonderful new position for him and tell him he's been graced with a marvelous new opportunity." A slow smile spread across Alianore's mouth.

"And then trouble one of my children with him, like you did?" Ela's brow lifted, though she did feel a smile trying to cross her mouth.

"Three of your babes now have complex households to manage."

"And the last thing they need is chess master Noel Bazin running circles around them. If only I had an enemy to send him to." Silently, she reflected that she had several. De Burgh for one, and Simon de Hal, her predecessor as sheriff, for another. "But I'd hardly want an enemy privy to my private financial details."

"As you suggested, you can always dismiss him," said Alianore.

"But on what grounds?" replied Ela. "He's an exemplary steward and I can't find fault with the work he's done for me."

"Then simply celebrate your good fortune in enjoying his talents."

Ela sighed. "I suppose I should, but don't you think it's odd that he sent my boys right to where the missing chess piece lay?"

"Perhaps he dropped it there himself," suggested Jean.

"Why would he do that?"

"To make mischief. He had an odd sense of humor." He looked at Alianore. "Do you remember the week he kept moving things in the kitchen to convince the cook that it was haunted?"

Alianore rolled her eyes. "Yes, very tiresome."

"The missing piece is valuable. He knew exactly how much it was worth. I can't believe he'd deliberately risk harm to it."

"But what if he did? And perhaps he murdered your merchant as well?" Jean's eyes twinkled with amusement.

"Oh, stop it!" protested Alianore, smacking Jean gently on the arm. "You know I'd hardly send Ela a murderer to manage her household accounts. Though perhaps he is a little more…interesting than one wants one's steward to be. I suggest that you dismiss him, my dear. Clearly I should have done that myself instead of sending him to you."

"I don't know," mused Ela. "He seems the type to make trouble if he feels he's been wronged. And now he knows a lot about how I manage my estates and how much wealth is in them. It's not information I'd like to fall into the wrong hands."

She could easily imagine the king finding new ways to wring funds from her if he knew how profitable her estates were. Kings always needed money to finance some foolhardy foreign campaign or just to fund their lavish lifestyle.

"I suppose you'll have to kill him. If you smother him you can pretend he died in his sleep," said Jean.

"Sometimes I don't know how I put up with him," said her mother.

"Every woman dreams of a husband with a sense of humor," said Jean with a wink. "Don't they, Ela?"

"My dear William did enjoy a jest," said Ela wistfully. "And sometimes he got on my nerves terribly as well. And sadly I can't kill my steward. As sheriff I'm supposed to uphold the law, not bend it to my will."

"Pshaw. Sheriffs all over England bend the law until it snaps almost in half," said Jean.

"I'm painfully aware of that," said Ela. "And I prefer to set a good example rather than join in their misdeeds. Perhaps I'll send Bazin to live on my estate in Notton. It could use an overhaul in how it's managed and should keep him busy until I can think of something else to do with him."

"Or until he kills again, at which time you can hang him and be done with him," said Jean, jovially. "How can you be sure he didn't kill your merchant?"

"He had no motive. As far as I know he never laid eyes on Ziyad al Wahid until he came to the castle selling his wares. Why would he kill him?"

"To save his mistress money, of course," quipped Jean. "It's a simple act of loyalty. You seem most ungrateful."

Ela sighed. "Sorry, Jean, but my sense of humor is not what it used to be. And motives for murder can be most perplexing, but I can't see a single reason why Noel Bazin should be a suspect."

"Who are your suspects?"

"Sadly, I have none. The merchant had no enemies that his wife knows of, and I can think of none in my castle. He was last seen with an unknown man in a black cloak, and the only witness was a prostitute"—Ela inhaled deeply—"who didn't see his face. The case is at an impasse."

"Then I recommend what I do when a chess game is at an impasse," said Jean.

"What's that?"

"Try something bold—and possibly rash—to force your opponent's hand."

CHAPTER 11

*A*fter a brief stay with her mother—and the rather infuriating Jean—Ela returned to Salisbury with a plan. She summoned Giles Haughton to her hall, then walked with him to the herb gardens, where they could talk away from prying ears.

Bees buzzed around the fragrant lavender blossoms and the pink pompoms hovering above the chives. "Did you hear that a prostitute was the last person—that we know of—to see Ziyad the merchant alive?"

"I did hear tell of it."

Ela wondered if he'd heard it from her own lips. "She lives above the Bull and Bear. I know you drink there sometimes. Are you familiar with her?"

"Naturally I don't share a cup with ladies of the night, but I've seen her there." His voice sounded unusually gruff. Ela suspected he'd shared at least a laugh with her at some point.

"Do you think she's a reliable source of information?"

"She seems frank to a fault if that's any guide."

"Has she mentioned the incident since?"

Haughton hesitated and studied at a feathery plume of

fennel before they passed by it. "I believe I did overhear her on the subject." He clearly didn't want to commit himself.

Ela cleared her throat. "I shan't hold your familiarity with her against you. I'd consider it investigation into this heinous murder."

"She said that it was odd how the guards let a stranger go up on the wall without question."

"I thought the same. How did they climb through the tower without being stopped? None of the guards or Deschamps himself has any good answer. It's a clear dereliction of duty."

Haughton frowned. "Do you think it was deliberate?"

Ela tripped on a cobblestone and reached out to grab Haughton's arm for balance before she could catch herself. His arm was as sturdy as a carved pillar, and he immediately stopped walking. "Are you all right, my lady?"

"Yes, I am. I'm sorry, I should look where I'm stepping." She let go of him. And sighed. "Why would it be deliberate? What could any of the guards have to do with a foreign merchant who's just passing through Salisbury for a few days before he goes elsewhere?"

"I suppose that makes people less interested in his death. If he were a Salisbury man, born and bred, the jurors would be up in arms to find out who killed him."

"As it is, he's a foreigner that they don't care two figs about," admitted Ela. "But his wife deserves to know the truth. And I wish to see his murderer punished. A killer still walks among us." She spoke the last part softly, and suddenly looked around, as if the killer might be watching them from behind an espaliered pear tree.

"What of the guards?" asked Haughton.

"They're all longtime employees of the garrison, loyal men according to Deschamps. There's no reason to believe they'd be involved in the murder. Deschamps claims they're guilty of dereliction of duty, nothing more."

"Surely he is responsible for their dereliction?"

"He brushes it off with platitudes about us being at peace." Ela knelt to sniff the first blooms of chamomile. She craved their soothing brew. "And there's some truth to it. We're hardly expecting King Louis's army to march upon our walls this summer."

Haughton looked thoughtful. "Rosie—the woman in question—claims she saw a second man with the merchant before he died. A man in a black cloak."

"She said as much when I interviewed her. Did she talk aloud of this in the Bull and Bear?"

"She did indeed and was canvassing the denizens of that establishment for his identity."

"Perhaps she'd make a better palace guard than Wilks, Belcher, or Lassiter," said Ela wryly.

"A woman in her position learns to be a judge of character. She's plied her profession for long enough to know the darkness in men's hearts."

"And the secrets of half the men in Salisbury, I'd imagine. Did she say anything about knowing the merchant? My first thought was that he'd gone there to meet with her without his wife's knowledge."

"She'd never seen or heard of him before. At least that's what she said."

"She would say that if she'd killed him herself." Ela was joking but didn't entirely rule out the idea either. "Which, though unlikely, is not utterly impossible."

Haughton stopped walking and let out a guffaw. "Rosie Dobson kill a man? She might slide her fingers into his purse —or other places—but I can't see her taking a life. She talks too much for her own good and would have told the whole town about it if she did."

"Rosie Dobson." Ela rolled the name over her tongue. "So she does have a surname. She was sly about it when I asked. Said she'd had too many of them."

"She may have made that one up for all I know. Most women in her position claim to be a soldier's widow or some such." Haughton pursed his lips for a moment. "They're mostly unfortunates who've fallen into that life while trying not to starve. Once they've gone down that road there's no way back as no decent man will have them."

Ela nodded. Haughton's frankness surprised her. "I had the same thought while talking to her. It's shocking that she's breaking the laws of God and man under the noses of the king's garrison here in Salisbury, but Deschamps seems to think that she and her kind are providing a public service to the king's men."

"I daresay they are." Haughton seemed intrigued by a lavender bed at the end of the path.

Ela wondered if Haughton had ever cheated on his wife. Then she banished the thought from her mind. It was none of her business, and it would do her no good to have the knowledge either way.

"Did Rosie Dobson make any further discoveries about the mysterious man in the black cloak from her inquiries in the Bull and Bear?"

"Everyone seemed to think it was the merchant's wife. She's been seen draped all in black and mooning about like a ghost since the murder. And they all thought it odd that no one knew she existed before her husband died. Like he'd kept her imprisoned and finally she broke free by killing her captor."

Irritation rippled through Ela. "I can't imagine how this idea has spread through the town. Safiya keeps wanting to sleep in the wagon, but I insisted that she come back and sleep in a chamber where we can protect her from all this strange hostility. I'm sure it's unnerving her, coming on top of her bereavement. Petronella tells me she won't leave her room now even to eat." Ela had looked in on her, hoping to press her on the matter of what to do with her husband's wagon of goods, which was rather an attractive nuisance in the courtyard, but Safiya simply turned a tear-stained face to her and stared mutely. Ela had resisted the urge to say a quick prayer—wary of offending Safiya since her prayers were different—and made a speedy exit.

"Perhaps she's afraid for her immortal soul if she did indeed kill her husband," said Haughton.

"I can't believe that." Ela tried to recall Safiya's demeanor when she'd first appeared at the castle that night. She seemed worried and desperate. But why was she so worried about her husband if he'd just disappeared? Did she already know he was dead because she'd killed him herself?

"Are you all right?" Haughton's comment made her realize that she'd stopped walking.

"Oh, yes, fine." She frowned. "But why would she kill him if that left her alone in a strange land with no means to support herself?"

"Crimes of passion are rarely committed by someone with a plan." They turned around the bed of herbs and strolled back the other way. A dragonfly lighted on Haughton's shoulder, and he muttered a greeting to it instead of flicking it off with his fingers.

"Do you think she should be brought before a jury for questioning?" Much as Ela despised the idea it would likely be a dereliction of her duties not to suggest it.

"I suspect that you can delve deeper into her motives in a woman-to-woman conversation. It's possible that the jury will find her guilty of being foreign and mysterious and a woman alone."

Again, his frankness surprised her. "That does worry me.

She's already the object of gossip in my own household. You'd think people would be reassured that she speaks our language, instead it makes them more suspicious of her, like she's a spy for the Saracens." Ela shook her head. The intolerance among her staff, even simple Elsie, irritated and alarmed her. "I'll have another talk with her this afternoon, and if I have even the slightest suspicion of guilt I'll have her put under guard and summon a jury."

She sighed. "I just wish we had a real suspect. It's so disconcerting for a man to be murdered for no apparent reason."

"If I were you I'd want to know why the guards weren't minding the wall better," said Haughton in a low voice. He didn't look at her. "When it's their job to do just that."

"True." Ela plucked a few leaves of sage and inhaled their heady fragrance. "I'll speak to Deschamps as well. I thank you for your wise counsel."

ELA WAS HALF TEMPTED to hold Deschamps's feet to the fire in the great hall, in full view of all and sundry. But discretion won out and she summoned him to meet her in the armory, where they could talk in private. Rather than give him the opportunity to let her stand around waiting in there, she asked Elsie to summon her as soon as he arrived.

When Elsie fetched Ela, she found Deschamps pacing impatiently around the long wood table in the center of the room. The walls around him glittered with polished arms—swords, halberds, poleaxes, and lances. The scarred table bore the marks from a century of polishing and grinding to keep the garrison's weapons sharp and battle-ready.

"My lady." The respectful nod of his head was so slight as

to be almost imperceptible. "You requested a word?" He strode toward her as if he had no further time to waste.

"I'd like to know if you've made further progress in determining why our castle wall was so unguarded that a murder could be committed upon it and a body thrown into the moat."

"I believe we discussed that, my lady," he said without missing a beat. "The soldiers were otherwise occupied on a different part of the wall. They've been sternly warned that it must not happen again or there will be dire consequences."

"What consequences?" Genuine curiosity spurred her.

"Termination of their position at the least and prosecution for dereliction of duty if needed."

That satisfied her. "Clearly the killer is still in our midst, so your men must be on guard at all times."

"As they now are, my lady."

"You must also command your men not to consort with prostitutes. As sheriff I serve our God as well as our king and I cannot tolerate such flagrant disregard for his holy laws."

"What laws would those be, my lady?" Deschamps's brow lifted slightly.

Surely Deschamps knew that sex outside of marriage was a sin? However, the Commandments only directly addressed adultery. "I think you will find the writings of St. Augustine very instructive." She didn't want to indulge him with further discussion. "You know right from wrong as well as I do. Ensure that your men are told to set an example for the people of Salisbury with their behavior."

"Men are men, my lady." He lifted his hands in a gesture of mock despair. "Surely their willingness and courage to fight for their king is more important than what they do in the dark hours of the night?"

Anger flashed inside her. "Men are indeed men, not brute beasts. They should not be drinking to excess or creating a disturbance, either. You're well aware that it was the loud and raucous behavior of the garrison troops that allowed Bishop Poore to convince the pope to let him build a new cathedral away from our castle."

"I was not garrison commander at that time, my lady." His smug expression further irked her.

"But from what you're saying you would have shrugged and said, 'Men are men,' when asked to control your troops in order to appease the bishop."

"Bishops and fighting men are not cut from the same cloth."

"I beg to differ. The men of my family have distinguished themselves on the battlefield, then later in life served our Lord from the quiet of the cloister. Our young king is known for his piety, and I feel sure that he would share my view."

This was a bold statement, but Ela felt fairly confident that Deschamps wouldn't ask the king whether he approved of his soldiers consorting with whores. Also, if pressed, she was equally certain that the king would say he disapproved. King Henry III was barely in his majority and didn't have the life experience to become jaded and accepting of other men's moral failings.

"I shall have words with the troops, my lady." His steady gaze challenged her. "Would you like me to tell them to abstain from strong drink and to say a prayer each time the church bells ring?"

Ela felt his mockery as a slap. It shocked her so much that she could barely gather her thoughts to respond. Was Deschamps testing to see if he had power over her?

She was High Sheriff of Wiltshire and in command of the castle here at Salisbury. In that sphere, he served under her. Though he did ultimately report to the king, as did she.

"Yes, you should." Why not call his bluff? "I'm sure the serving girls will appreciate how much better they'll be treated when the men aren't getting tipsy and trying to interfere with them." She spoke coldly. They'd had words on several prior occasions about the misbehavior of certain drunken troops. Just because that nonsense had been tolerated in her husband's time did not mean she had to turn a blind eye.

"As you wish, my lady," he said flatly.

"I intend to find out who murdered Ziyad al Wahid on my castle wall. If it's one of your guards, his position will not spare him the noose."

"Of course not, my lady. You find me in complete agreement on that score."

"I'm glad to hear it."

~

ELA STILL NEEDED to resolve the matter of Safiya's future and the fate of her husband's goods. She also had to deal with Noel Bazin the steward. Against her will, Jean's words had played in her head since her visit: first his jests about how Bazin might be the killer—which she couldn't seriously countenance—and second that he stuck his prominent nose where it didn't belong and might be up to no good.

And then there was Jean's suggestion that she make a bold move to force her steward's hand. Much as the idea rankled her, she had to admit that it held promise. If she gave Bazin free rein to imagine and arrange the disposal of Safiya's goods, she'd soon find out what he was made of.

She summoned both Safiya and Bazin to a small private parlor that she used for reading and writing letters, and asked them both to sit in the chairs near the small, empty fireplace.

Bazin, dressed in a smart blue tunic that emphasized the bony angularity of his form, seated himself gingerly in the chair and eyed Safiya with suspicion. Safiya, now swathed in a black wrap from head to foot so that Ela couldn't even tell if she was wearing the clothes and headdress her daughter had given her, returned his suspicion with interest.

"Master Bazin, your skill in the valuation and disposition of goods was much praised by my dear mother. I thought that perhaps you could be of service to Mistress al Wahid in helping her reap the value of the assets left to her by her husband."

"Are you sure they're hers to sell?" he asked brightly. "Surely a male heir would be a more likely beneficiary?"

"Ziyad al Wahid had no sons," said Ela briskly. She felt Safiya stiffen at the reminder.

"Brothers? Nephews?" pressed Bazin. "I want to make sure that there are no legal ramifications after we sell the goods."

Ela hated his implication that a mere woman shouldn't claim an inheritance, but he made a good point, unfortunately. Ela turned to Safiya. "Do you know of anyone—anyone at all—who might make a claim to your late husband's assets?"

Safiya shook her head mutely. When Ela and Bazin waited for her to speak, she finally cleared her throat. "His father is dead. He has a mother and two sisters in Sevilla, but no brothers."

Ela looked at Bazin. "I believe that answers your question. Now how do we find a buyer and ensure that the best price is paid?"

"I have contacts in London who can price the items and resell them in the markets."

Ela frowned. "Some of them are ordinary things that might be sold at a market stall, others are rare and valuable and demand more careful selling." Was he hoping she'd just let the goods slip through her fingers like so many cheap glass beads?

"Of course, my lady," he replied with a tiny smile. "But you may find that many of the finer items are already sold—to yourself, for example—and that only the more commonplace ones remain."

"Is that true?" asked Ela of Safiya.

"I don't know." Her expression and demeanor suggested that she didn't care if they threw all her husband's goods in the Avon.

"Surely you want the highest possible price?" said Ela, a little irritated by her nonchalance. "To support yourself in widowhood. Did you find anything of great value when you looked through the contents with Sir William Talbot?"

"Yes. I suppose so," she said lifelessly. "There are still some expensive items left. People have approached me about buying them."

"Who?" Ela's ears pricked up. She was fairly sure that someone had killed the merchant to get their hands on something he owned. What other motive would they have?

"I don't know. They all look the same to me."

Ela sighed. Safiya was behaving like a moody child.

"Did you show them any goods?"

"I said nothing was for sale yet and they'd have to wait."

"Very sensible," said Ela.

Safiya looked at Ela directly. "And there are people who still owe for the things they bought but didn't pay for yet."

"Myself included, I suspect. Bazin, did you pay Safiya for the chess set and the other goods we bought?"

"Not yet, my lady, though I will make sure that—"

"Today. There's no excuse for this delay."

"But where will the girl keep the money? She might be robbed of it."

Ela looked at Safiya. She'd made no mention of where her

143

husband kept his profits. It must be somewhere hidden and secure. Probably in the wagon. "Do you know where your husband kept the money?"

"Yes." Safiya's lips pressed together.

Ela waited for her to expound. She didn't. "Where?"

"On me."

CHAPTER 12

*E*la dismissed Bazin with instructions to get in touch with his London connections. Left alone with Safiya, she closed the door. "What do you mean, you have your husband's profits...on you?"

Safiya slowly unwound the black robe that covered her from head to toe. She no longer wore the barbette and fillet that Petronella had found for her, and had tucked her hair into a loose knot at her nape. She unwrapped the robe from her shoulders and draped it over the chair. Underneath she wore the blue gown the girls had given her. She bent to the floor and plucked at the hem, then lifted it up as if she intended to pull the gown over her head. As she raised it past her thighs, Ela gasped. Beneath the ordinary gown she wore an elaborate chain mail of coins laced into a web of woven thread.

The money covered her torso and upper thighs. Many of the coins were gold—foreign coins—but there were also silver pieces. It was easy to see that she wore a hundred pounds worth of coins on her person, maybe more.

Ela blinked. "How do the coins not clink together and make noise?"

"The thread keeps them apart."

Ela peered at the mesh, woven like a spiderweb where each coin slid into place.

"Who made this?"

"I did, based on an older one that my husband showed me, from a trader he once worked with. I hated it at first. I felt like another of his goods, but he told me that it made sense for all his wealth to be worn by the treasure he valued the highest." She said it calmly, with no hint of tears.

"It's…astonishing."

"He said that if anyone tried to take his money he could kill them for assaulting his wife."

"He's right. No court would argue with a man's right to defend his wife."

"He said it was important because sometimes men have no respect for a foreigner, and they'd try to cheat or steal from him."

"And it also explains why he kept you hidden. He wanted to safeguard his treasure, both human and monetary."

Safiya nodded and let her hem fall back to the floor.

"We should put your money somewhere safe."

Safiya stiffened. "It is safe."

"It was safe when your husband was alive to draw his knife to defend you. Things are different now. If word got out about this—and it might now that Bazin knows something—you might find yourself the subject of bawdy gossip at best and robbery at worst."

"I don't know where else to put it."

"It's a great sum. It should be with a banker. You can keep it with my banker, whom I trust with my fortune."

Safiya looked doubtful.

"You're a rich woman. You could buy yourself a house and hire a servant and live quietly."

"Where?"

Ela blinked. "London, perhaps? There are people from many nations there. You wouldn't feel out of place. Or you could return to Sevilla or Tangier."

Tears suddenly welled in Safiya's eyes. "I don't belong anywhere."

"With money you have the power to decide where you belong. My heart lies in Salisbury, and I fought to live here after my husband's death. There were—and still are—plenty of people who think I should retire to a quiet manor and spend my days spinning and weaving, or to a monastery for a life of prayer. I choose to live here and seek justice for the people of Salisbury, including your husband."

Safiya inhaled. "I don't understand the ways and customs of English people."

"You speak English as well as I do. I grew up speaking French and spent a good portion of my childhood in Normandy. I learned English mostly from the servants. This is a land of many cultures. Did you know the Romans once ruled it? The remains of their roads run across our country-side like blood vessels in the body."

"Al Andalus is the same. And they have better food." She looked up, the tiniest hint of amusement in her eyes. "Have the English never heard of olives?"

Ela laughed. "They don't grow here so they have to be imported, usually pressed into oil. We're a land of bread eaters."

"You make me feel like I might have a life without my husband." Safiya looked rather amazed and amused by this. "Though I can't picture it."

"Take your time. You're welcome to stay here in the castle until you decide what to do. I'll contact my banker to secure safe storage for your coins. And I won't rest until I find your husband's killer."

Ela had promised Haughton that she'd ask Safiya again about whether she had killed her husband, but—face-to-face with the grieving widow—she just couldn't bring herself to do it.

~

Ela retired to her room to spend a few moments in prayer. She asked Elsie to unpin her fillet as she had a headache, caused no doubt by the tumultuous events of the last few days.

Elsie pulled the pins out, one by one. Her breathing sounded a little odd. Or maybe it was just odd that Ela could hear her breathing at all. "What's amiss, Elsie?"

"I don't like to say, my lady, but I'm worried that you're in danger."

Ela spun to face her. "What do you mean?"

"It's that Safiya, my lady. Everyone's talking about her."

Ela sighed. "I've already told you that's just idle gossip. People are suspicious of foreigners and they—"

"Someone saw her kill her husband."

Ela froze. "Who?"

"I don't know."

Now Ela grew impatient. "Then how did you hear it?"

"I just heard it repeated. People were talking in the hall. The soldiers, I think it was. They said that fancy chess set is made from human bone. With bones from the people they've killed and—"

"That's quite enough, Elsie. The soldiers are brave fighting men, but some of them don't have the sense of a doorpost. Don't listen to their nonsense. The chess set is made from either ox bone or ivory. No other creature has large enough pieces of bone to carve such grand figures. Certainly not a human."

"Oh." Elsie's round eyes looked up at her.

"And regarding the murder, I've already spoken to the sentries who were on the wall when he was murdered and they swear up and down that they saw nothing. Whoever said they did see it is lying, or else why wouldn't they come to me with the truth?"

Elsie considered this for a moment. "I suppose you're right, my lady."

"I would like to know who's spreading these rumors, though. I daresay they aren't rising out of thin air. If you know who the source of them is, I'd be very interested to know."

Elsie blinked, dumbly. Ela wondered if she knew but was afraid to say for fear of being scolded for listening to gossip again. "Would it be all right if I used your garderobe, my lady? My stomach's in a knot all of a sudden."

"Yes, you may." That explained her odd expression. She wasn't supposed to use Ela's private garderobe, which adjoined her solar, but to take care of her personal business downstairs where the other servants did.

"Thank you, my lady." Elsie looked fit to burst.

"Go on, then. What are you waiting for?"

Elsie rushed into the tiny antechamber that held the garderobe. She'd cleaned it, of course. And probably used it before, unbeknownst to Ela. She closed the door behind her and Ela removed the last pins from her headwear, shaking her head with a smile. She was glad Elsie had the spirit to ask such a favor of her. Last year the poor girl had been like a whipped dog, expecting punishment at every turn.

Ela rose to retrieve her prayer book, but a strange noise from the garderobe stopped her cold.

"Are you all right in there, Elsie?"

"No, my lady," came the strangled response.

Ela hurried to the door and pulled on the handle, expecting to find Elsie struggling with a turned stomach. But there was no sign of the girl at all. Or the carved wooden seat.

"Elsie, where are you?" Panic rushed her chest. She glanced up at the ceiling as if the girl might have been suddenly hoisted there. Nothing greeted her gaze but a few cobwebs.

"I fell in." The voice came from below her feet.

Ela heard a small cry escape her throat as she rushed to the hole, where the effluent rushed down a long, narrow channel to the moat below. She peered in and, to her horror, saw Elsie about eight feet down in the narrow shaft, clinging to the side walls with her fingertips, elbows, knees, and feet —like a great spider—for dear life.

"Dear God, hold on! The drop is thirty feet or more. I'll fetch help."

Ela shot through her solar and out into the hallway. "Help! Bring a rope and a ladder!" she cried to the guards who hovered around the doorway like shadows. She ran down the passage to Bill Talbot's room and pounded on the door. No answer—it was the middle of the day, and he was probably downstairs in the hall or attending to some business or other.

"Help!" she cried again, to no one in particular.

A servant girl poked her head out of Nicky's room. "Fetch someone with a rope," called Ela. The girl looked at her for a moment like she was mad, then nodded and darted for the stairs.

Ela ran back to the garderobe, heart thudding. What if Elsie got too scared to keep her grip on the walls? "Help is on its way," she called, before she even got there.

Inside the garderobe Elsie was now in a slightly different

position in the tight shaft, her legs now almost higher than her head and arms, as if she'd lost her footing on the wall. Her face had turned white and her mouth shrunk to a terrified line.

"Have courage. Try not to move at all. We can pull you up from where you are." She'd be hard to reach if she fell much lower. If she lost her grip and plunged all the way down, she'd endure a terrible battering and scraping on the walls as well as the precipitous fall to the moat far below. It was unlikely that she'd survive.

Ela found her breath coming in unsteady gasps, and she struggled to get a hold of herself. Where was the help she'd called for? Would the guards or the young maid come back with a rope? She ran out of the room again in a panic. As she neared the stairs, Bill pounded up them, Richard and Stephen hot on his heels.

"Elsie fell into the garderobe and is down several feet. We need a rope for her to grab."

"Boys, follow me." He looked at Ela. "There's no time to hunt for rope. We can improvise." He rushed past Ela and into her private chamber. In the garderobe he stopped at the top of the hole and peered down. "Don't worry, Elsie, we'll have you out of there in no time."

He turned back into Ela's room and—with a swift motion of his arm—pulled one of her bed curtains from the bed. He drew his knife and slashed the sturdy fabric—rich blue damask from Venice—which rent with a ferocious ripping sound that made Ela flinch as he tore it in half. Bill quickly tied the two halves together and made a knot at one end, then hurried back to the garderobe entrance.

Ela watched as he lowered her knotted curtain into the hole. "Don't move now, Elsie, even when it reaches you. Every move must be made with great care."

Ela knew that if Elsie let go of the wall and didn't grasp

the curtain right, she'd lose her chance and fall to her death and there would be no way they could stop her.

A shriek pierced the air as a stone shifted in the garderobe shaft and Elsie lost her grip with one hand and tilted further upside down. A stone banged and bounced on the walls on its way down the hole before it thudded to the dry earth of the moat.

Ela crossed herself.

"Don't move a hair, dear Elsie. I'm coming down to hold you tight and bring you back up." Bill handed the end of the curtain to Stephen and told him to hold onto it for dear life. "And Richard, you hold onto Stephen. Elsie's a slip of a girl, but I weigh as much as a horse so you need to be steady."

Ela wanted to laugh at his kindness. Elsie was quite stout for a girl her age, and Bill Talbot was honed like a fine broadsword. She held her breath as Bill climbed up onto the part of the garderobe that normally held the wooden seat, and lowered himself in, one foot at a time.

The shaft was so narrow that for a moment Ela wondered if his broad shoulders would even fit into the hole. "Don't get stuck," she breathed. That would make things far worse. "Are you sure you're recovered enough to do this?" Even if he hadn't just been injured with a blow to the head, Bill Talbot was nearly twenty years older than herself and not exactly a nimble youth, much though he tried to act like one.

But she watched Bill's head disappear into the shaft as he shinned himself down the curtain. "Hold steady, Elsie, I'm almost there."

"I can't hold on." Her voice came in a tiny quaver. "My fingers and toes are going numb."

"Just another moment while I get close. I've almost got you."

Ela held her breath. More people had rushed into the

room, now. Servants, guards and her younger children with their tutors in tow.

"There we go." Bill's deep voice carried up the shaft. "I've got my arm under you now. I'm going to tug you toward me and you're to take hold of me and hang on."

Elsie let out a small cry, and Ela bit her lip and held her breath.

"Now, boys," called Bill up the shaft. "Give it everything you've got and pull us up."

Ela urged servants to help Richard and Stephen as they turned their backs to the opening and pulled like a hitched team of oxen.

"There we go. We're almost up."

Bill's hand grasped at the lip of the hole. "Stephen, you come forward. I'm going to push Elsie up to you so you can grab her and pull her free."

Ela muttered a prayer under her breath during this delicate operation, which involved Bill jamming himself hard against the wall and sliding Elsie past him in the narrow space, but soon Elsie lay in a crumpled heap on the floor, sobbing and gasping for air.

"Praise be to God!" Ela exclaimed. She helped Elsie to her feet and examined her for scrapes. The poor girl had angry red marks on her knuckles from where they'd pressed into the rough stone wall.

"Come on, Bill, I'm pulling." Stephen had hold of Bill's wrist, but his head hadn't yet emerged from the opening.

"My shoulders are stuck against the wall. I always said they were too big. I'm going to have to shift myself around sideways."

Ela heard a scrabbling sound and then another rumble as rock cascaded down through the opening. Stephen gave a gasp, and Ela saw that he'd lost hold of Bill's hand.

"No!" she cried, and rushed back to the hole. Bill was now

even further down the shaft than Elsie had been. His body was too big for the space, and he couldn't extend his arms and legs enough to get a good grip.

"I don't think the curtain will reach down that far," said Richard, with a tremor to his voice.

"I think I can shin my way down to the bottom of the shaft," called Bill.

"Don't!" cried Ela. "You'll get stuck halfway down, or even down near the bottom, and we won't be able to get you out. We can tie more curtains together."

Richard had already had the same idea, and soon her sons were knotting another of her expensive silk curtains to the first and lowering the rich fabric down into the garderobe opening.

"I'm so sorry," whimpered Elsie. "I broke the seat! I know I'm too heavy and it's all my fault that he's going to die!"

"Don't talk nonsense, Elsie," said Ela. "It wasn't your fault at all. That seat was carved from a single piece of oak and there's no way it could break. It was stout enough to yoke an ox." She wished they had an ox up here right now, as her sons fought, with the help of guards and servants, to heave Bill farther up the long, narrow shaft.

It seemed an eternity of struggling, but eventually they managed to pull him out. Bill eased himself up out of the hole by his arms—with considerable difficulty that he tried his best to conceal.

"You're a hero, as always, Bill," said Ela as casually as she could manage.

"Nonsense. It's your fine young sons that are the heroes." He looked at Elsie, who was now shaking like a willow in a stiff breeze. "What's amiss, girl? You've lived to tell the tale."

"I shall never tell this tale," she said in a rush. "I'm so ashamed. Who would fall in a garderobe but me?"

"Did the seat break in pieces?" asked Ela. She couldn't

imagine how the entire seat had fallen in. It was larger than the hole, for obvious reasons.

"Yes, it just crumbled underneath me." Elsie looked at her with big, scared eyes.

"We must find the pieces at once and examine them," said Ela. "Someone might have tampered with the seat like the mason said they did with the stone that fell on Bill."

"They wanted you to fall down the hole," said Bill to Ela.

"Indeed they did. They may not even have intended to kill me but just to humiliate me." She glanced at Elsie. "Not that there's anything to be embarrassed about. It's not your fault at all."

A crowd of palace staff and guards now filled her solar and the hallway outside and suddenly Ela wanted them gone from her private space. No doubt they were all ogling her now-exposed bed and her prie-dieu with its gorgeously illustrated prayer book and maybe even looking at her comb and hairpins and the spare veil that Elsie had hung up to air.

"Everyone is fine, and I'll thank you all to return to your duties," she said briskly. Once they'd all filed out, including her younger children and their tutors, she closed the door behind them. Bill, Richard, Stephen, and Elsie were all who remained. "I suspect someone of deliberately trying to frighten me."

"They obviously don't know you very well, then, do they?" said Bill with a wry grin. Stephen laughed.

Richard looked grim. "Why would someone want to do that, Mama?"

"To undermine my authority," she said slowly. "To cast doubt on my ability to rule this castle and preside over justice in Wiltshire."

"Well, they've failed, then, haven't they," said Stephen with conviction. "Even though poor Elsie and Bill are rather the worse for wear."

"I hope they haven't got something else up their sleeve," said Ela. She frowned and looked back into the now-empty garderobe hole. She'd need to commission a carpenter to make a new seat. "There's far too much mischief afoot."

"Do you have any suspects, Mama?" asked Richard.

"I wish I did."

"Some people think Safiya is wicked," said Richard. "But I think she's just shy and sad."

"I do as well, my love. And she wouldn't have a key to get in here. You can be sure that my room is kept locked unless I'm in it."

"Who else has the key?" asked Bill.

"Well, Albert the porter. He's guardian of all the castle keys. Elsie has a key." She looked at the girl. "Did anyone ask to gain entry or could anyone have stolen your key?"

Elsie's face grew white and her lip trembled.

Ela's nerves jangled. Had Elsie let someone into her room? "Well, who?"

"I lost my key yesterday," she admitted. "I locked your room up as I always do, after you went down to break your fast. Then I went to the kitchen and ate something, and when I came back up with some lavender for your sheets I found I'd misplaced my key."

"But you had it last night."

"Albert the porter found it. He knew it was mine as it's on a green ribbon."

"Where did he find it?"

"I don't know. I didn't ask."

Ela decided that she'd ask him. Someone must have stolen it from Elsie, then used it to sneak into her room and tamper with the garderobe. "We need to find the broken pieces of the garderobe seat. They may lend clues as to who tampered with it."

"I'll go right down to look for it," said Richard.

Ela wondered if this was a serious enough matter to warrant calling a jury. The prospect of several gruff male jurors traipsing through her private chamber and peering into her garderobe convinced her that it wasn't.

Still, someone had bloodied the queen in the chess set, and now their ill intentions had settled on her.

CHAPTER 13

*D*own in the hall, they ate trout roasted with figs for supper. Richard had searched for the broken pieces of the wooden seat at the bottom of the chute where the garderobe emptied, but found no sign of them.

"They might still be stuck in the channel."

"Surely we'd be able to see them by peering down the hole? It's long but it's not that long," said Petronella, who'd missed all the excitement since she's spent the afternoon repenting her sins in the chapel.

"It will be easier to look in daylight," said Richard. "Right now it's too dark."

"I bet they fell all the way down right away and someone took them," said Stephen. He looked at Elsie. "Did it break into big pieces or small pieces?"

"I'm not sure," said Elsie, looking embarrassed. She was the age when the idea of someone picturing her in such a position was mortifying. "It broke as soon as I sat on it and the pieces all fell in right away. Almost like that carved puzzle box thing that little Nicky loves so."

Ela frowned. Nicky had a wooden toy that they'd bought

158

from a traveling merchant a year ago. The wood was carved so that the pieces fit tightly together when arranged right, and looked like a single, solid piece of wood, but when someone tried to lift it up it broke back into its pieces. Her older boys had played a joke on her mother by exclaiming over the beauty of the carving, then pretending to break it.

"If the pieces are gone, no doubt they were retrieved by the person who carved up the seat."

"Who must have grabbed them while we were all up in your chamber," said Bill Talbot. "So the culprit is someone who wasn't there."

"That's most people in the castle unfortunately. I hardly suspected my children of trying to tip me down the garderobe."

Nicky giggled. "I wouldn't do that, Mama. I promise."

She pretended to look alarmed. "I'm relieved to hear that." It was disturbing that someone had put so much energy into cutting her seat to pieces. Also that they'd managed to gain entrance to her private chamber by stealing the key. Whoever was behind this showed considerable cunning.

Could it be Bazin?

She didn't dare raise her suspicions in front of the family when she had nothing whatsoever to back them up. And why would Bazin want her to fall down the garderobe shaft? Such a plunge could kill someone. If she died he'd be out of a job as steward so it didn't serve his interests to fatally injure her.

Still, doubts lingered and she resolved to rid herself of him as quickly as possible.

AT NIGHT, alone in her chamber, Ela prayed for peace and healing for Safiya. And she prayed harder that she might have insight into the identity of her husband's killer. The person—man or woman—in the black cloak was the last one seen with Ziyad before his death, but who was it?

She climbed under her padded coverlet thinking again about Bazin. There was clearly more to the steward than met the eye. His thought process was complex, as evidenced by his mastery of chess.

As steward, Bazin was handsomely paid and had coin at his disposal. Any man who earned his living handling another's assets was sure to pay attention to growing his own. If he knew how to buy and sell goods in select markets, he might have motive for making a deal of some kind with Ziyad al Wahid.

Still, that was no motive for murder...

She drifted off into a fitful sleep. In her dream she paced the stone corridors of a cloister around a bare stone courtyard. No singing, no procession of nuns or holy brothers, just her, alone, passing by the arches and columns again and again. The strong smell of a censer filled with smoking incense stung her nostrils.

Then she saw a tall pair of wood doors—the entrance to a chapel? She approached the doors, the smell of censer smoke growing stronger and stronger—

"Fire!" The shout woke her with a start. Her feet hit the cold floor before her eyes opened. "Fire! Fire! Rouse yourselves!" Ela flew out of her room, heading for the chambers of her littlest ones. She couldn't see the smoke, but she could smell it, like in her dream but not the smoke of precious incense. Now her nostrils stung with the acrid smell of burning timber.

She shoved open Elsie's door to find her already out of bed and frightened, then she swept Nicky from his room.

"Run downstairs! Don't delay! No need for a wrap, it's not cold out."

Only one door in the passage remained closed, Safiya's.

Ela banged on it. "Wake up! The castle's on fire!" She tried the handle and found the door locked from the inside. She'd removed the keys from all the children's bedrooms so they couldn't make the mistake of locking themselves in by accident, but she'd left Safiya the key to her chamber so she could be assured of solitude in her grief. "Safiya! It's Ela! Wake up!" She pounded on the door. She watched as her children were herded downstairs by the eldest two, coughing in the smoke.

"My lady, you must come downstairs," said a guard. "It's not safe here. You could be overcome by the smoke."

"Safiya's locked inside. She must be asleep, and I can't rouse her."

"Perhaps she's already escaped through the window?"

Ela knew that was impossible. It would be a leap to her death on the cobbles outside. She banged on the door with her fist. "Safiya! Come to the door at once!" Just as she began to despair, she heard the scritch of the old iron bolt moving in the lock, and the door cracked open.

"Safiya! Thanks be to God, the castle's on fire and we must run." She grabbed a fistful of the girl's black wrapper and tugged her out into the hallway, then grasped her hand so she couldn't wriggle away as she pulled her along the hall. She knew that in her grief Safiya might not be so afraid of death, and she didn't intend to give her any opportunity for a meeting with the grim reaper under her roof.

When they reached the bottom of the stairs she saw little Snowflake the terrier standing there expectantly as if waiting for her. She snatched him up in her arms.

"The children are all in the herb garden, Mama." Her son Stephen came running back inside. "I'm off to check the hall."

"No, my love. Your bravery is a credit to you, but please tend your brothers and sisters instead. They can't stand to lose another great man in their lives. And I'm afraid the littlest ones might be fascinated by the flames and put themselves in danger."

Stephen looked ready to argue, then after a glance at her face, he nodded. They both turned and looked toward the fire. Flames and sparks leaped from the building that held the kitchens and the great hall. The servants had formed into a line, passing wooden buckets of water back and forth from the well to the blazing building. Ela moved toward them.

"The kitchen's all ablaze, my lady!" cried the cook, her face a mask of horror. "I don't know how it started. I left a small fire burning in the hearth to keep the stones warm for the morning's baking, but there wasn't enough wood on it to start a blaze."

Flames licked the kitchen's stone window frame. The window covering wasn't glass but waxed linen, already consumed by the flames except for a few tatters that tossed sparks to the breeze.

"Was anyone asleep within?"

"No, I don't like to leave anyone in my kitchen overnight making mischief with my ingredients."

"Did it spread to the great hall?" There was no way to see into the hall from here. It was down a corridor now filled with smoke. She'd have to run around the building and enter by the great arch to find out.

"I don't know, my lady."

Garrison soldiers rushed to and fro, picking up anything that could hold water and tossing it on the flames. One man batted at a patch of blazing thatch with a piece of old rush matting from a floor somewhere, and Ela watched in amazement as his odd weapon beat back the flames and doused the sparks rather than catching fire.

The battle waged on in the darkness, men and women with vessels of water—buckets and washbowls and milk jugs —fighting the flames and sparks, until the fire started to die back. Ela stood with her children gathered about her. Little Nicky had started to cry and was sucking his thumb for the first time in months. She didn't have the heart to scold him for it. "Is anyone dead, Mama?" asked Richard, in a tremulous voice. She could tell he was trying his best to be brave. He'd busied himself counting all the cats and dogs who'd mercifully escaped the smoke.

"I don't know, my love. We'll find that out when the smoke clears. She prayed that everyone escaped in time."

Gradually the flames dimmed and the sparks shimmered down onto the puddles of spilled water. Once the smoke thinned, people started to creep back into the building to see what remained after the blaze.

The first one out again was Cook, who let out a plaintive wail. "I fear everything in the kitchen has burned up and there's nothing left but the stone walls themselves."

"You may be right." Ela held sleepy Ellie pressed against her. "But at least the stone walls won't support a fire. The roof is stone, too, praise God." It had vaulted stone arches, possibly a design by a clever forbear of hers who knew that kitchens and fires went hand in hand.

But the great hall had a timber roof. A whole forest must have gone into building the high ceiling that seemed the very roof of the world when she was a child sitting on her father's lap and gazing up at it.

And the tapestries on the walls held so many memories. They'd belonged to her father, and his father, woven by some ancient ancestress.

Would they all be gone?

Smoke thickened the air even out here in the courtyard, making people cough and rub their eyes.

"The fire's defeated!" The first cry of victory caused an echo of joy to reverberate around the courtyard. Deschamps rushed up to Ela with the good news that the last embers were doused and the building saved.

"Where did the fire start?"

"In the kitchen, from the look of it. Most fires do. It spread toward the great hall and the armory, but there's no damage worse than smoke stains on the walls and ceiling in either room."

"Is anyone hurt? Smoke can fell a man as quick as flames."

"Albert the old porter has suffered the effects of smoke. He must have tried to raise the alarum but collapsed before he could."

"I must see to him at once. Where is he?"

Deschamps cleared his throat. "The mortuary, I'm afraid."

Oh, God. Ela crossed herself. "This is terrible news." Emotion welled in her chest. Albert had manned the great gateway for as long as she could remember and he was like a kindly old uncle to her, always quick to welcome her friends and make subtly rude excuses to her enemies. "May God rest his soul," she murmured, feeling tears prick her eyes. "Was anyone else hurt?"

"I don't think so, my lady. Can I help you to a seat?"

"I'm fine." She didn't want him to think her weak or overly emotional. "I must see the hall."

"You'd best wait until the smoke clears. No sense harming yourself when my men can air it out first."

Ela's nerves jangled. Did he simply want to protect her from smoke, or did he want to keep her from seeing something?

She nodded, as if she agreed, then walked away, going around behind the kitchens and up past the screens to enter the hall from another back entrance. The first light of day brightened the scene, illuminating all the smoke-stained faces around her.

Ela entered the hall to find it barely smoky at all. The fire must have been contained to the kitchens and the store rooms closest to it. Already soldiers lolled around in the great hall like it was an ordinary day, even as two maids flapped lengths of cloth to push the smoke out the open doorways.

Relieved to see the hall preserved, Ela headed to the kitchen to survey the damage. Immediately on entering she could see the walls blackened with smoke. The cook fussed and flapped about, already moving hot scorched items and exclaiming over lost ingredients and baskets. "If I was sleeping in here this would never have happened! I always used to say that a cook should sleep in her kitchen. I've grown soft in my old age and taken to my bed at nights, and I blame myself."

"Don't blame yourself. Thanks be to God you're not injured, which you certainly would be if you'd slept while the fire broke out," protested Ela. "As it is you're lucky the smoke didn't reach your chamber." The cook and her staff slept in a spacious room three doors down from the kitchen. Ela peered inside to find it undamaged and relatively smoke-free.

She walked through the adjacent rooms and along the corridors, waving the smoky air from her nose and relieved when she finally reached the relatively fresh air of the herb garden again.

One thing bothered her immensely. If the hall wasn't damaged—if nowhere had burned except the kitchen—why was Albert the porter injured?

And—yet more perplexing—why was dear Albert anywhere near the kitchens at all?

～

ELA MOVED next to the mortuary. On her way she passed Safiya, cloaked in black from head to toe, with even her eyes barely showing. She looked like a night creature startled from her burrow.

"Are you all right?" asked Ela.

"I feel scared."

"The fire's been put out. It seems that only one person was hurt."

"That is a blessing," said Safiya dully. She looked at a loose end, as people whirled around her, going about their business.

"Come with me." Ela beckoned Safiya. "I must pay my last respects to a man that's guarded our hall my whole life." She didn't want to leave Safiya standing there to be buffeted by people running to and fro.

Safiya mutely followed her, barely glancing at the chaos around them. She seemed to have sunk into herself in the days since her husband's death. Hardly surprising since her entire life revolved around him and she'd lived in a little cocoon, protected from other people until now.

Ela followed the cinder paths that led to the mortuary. She greeted the guard at the door, and he opened it for her. The dim, cool space didn't have the acrid smell of death that often greeted her there. Of course dear Albert had only been dead a short while. His body lay on the long table in the center of the room, already wrapped in a linen winding sheet.

Ela moved closer, closed her eyes, and started to pray, thanking the Lord for Albert's long life and thanking him for his faithful service. She was halfway through a Hail Mary when Safiya let out an ear-piercing scream.

CHAPTER 14

*E*la's prayer withered on her lips. "What ails you?" she looked at Safiya.

"He's risen from the dead." Safiya's words emerged from quivering lips.

Ela looked at the rumpled linen shroud wrapped around Albert's slight form. "Your senses deceive you."

"He moved, I swear it!" Safiya shrank toward the door.

"That's impossible. As impossible as a ghost being real."

"You believe in the Holy Spirit," said Safiya with a quavering voice. "Then why not an unholy spirit?" Her words shrank to a terrified whisper.

Ela frowned. She couldn't understand why Safiya was so spooked. The widow's eyes remained fixed on the corpse. Ela wondered if poor Safiya had suddenly lost her wits altogether, then she realized that—unless her eyes deceived her —Albert's chest rose and fell slightly.

Ela leaped forward and pulled at the winding sheet that covered his face. She pressed her ear to Albert's lips and immediately felt the warmth of his breath. "Dear God, he lives!" She tugged at the sheet, which someone had wrapped around him. Mercifully the linen had been thin enough for him to take breath through its weave. "Albert, it's Ela, can you hear me?"

A rattle sounded in his chest, then rose up to become a very weak cough. Emotion rushed through Ela. She chafed at his hand. More rattling in his chest preceded more coughing. Soon he was sitting up, spluttering, and taking deep lungfuls of air.

"Where am I?" He looked around, blinking. With only the scant dawn light coming through one tiny window, even Ela couldn't see much. No doubt that was why she hadn't noticed Albert was still breathing.

She hesitated. She didn't want to shock him, especially in this delicate state. But now he plucked at the linen winding sheet thrown hastily over him. He still wore his clothes because he hadn't been prepared for burial, just put in here amid the hubbub of the fire. "Is this the mortuary?" he asked at last.

"It is," admitted Ela. "There was a fire and you were found unconscious and thought to be dead."

Albert blinked. "A fire?" He looked confused. "I couldn't sleep because my aches were acting up, so I went outside for a look at the moon." His eyes narrowed as he reached for the memories. "And I saw a figure dressed in black sneaking into the kitchens."

Ela's breath quickened. "Could you tell who it was?"

"All dressed in black, he was, a black cloak." He glanced at Safiya. "Like hers."

Safiya clutched her black wrap around her. "It wasn't me."

"No, it wasn't her," agreed Albert. "It was someone tall and quite thin. Scuttling about as if he didn't want to be seen or heard."

"A man."

"I'd imagine so. I don't know of a woman that tall other

than Mistress Higpen, who moved to New Salisbury. Anyway, I followed him, because he had a look of someone up to no good."

"Why didn't you alert a guard?"

"Begging your pardon, my lady, but some of those ruffians aren't worth a mug of ale, especially at that time of night, when they've already had a mug or two."

Ela reflected that this dismal view of the garrison troops rather echoed her own. She'd have to have further stern words with Deschamps about changing their behavior to at the very least gain back the confidence of the castle staff.

"Did you see where he came from?"

"I thought he came from the hall, my lady, but I can't be sure. I was too far behind him. At first I hastened after him to ask him his business, but his furtive movements made me wary."

"He was sneaking about?"

"That's a good way of describing it."

"So you followed him to the kitchen. Did you go in?"

"He left the door open and I stood in the doorway, back in the shadows, where he couldn't see me." He raised a gnarled hand and rubbed at the back of his head. "The only light in the room was the glow of the kitchen fire. I saw him go over to the fire, still sneaking and looking around, and he took the tongs, ever so quiet, like, then scattered embers over the cook's baskets—"

He stopped. Ela waited.

"Then I don't know what happened next. But my head hurts. I think someone hit me over the head."

An icy chill descended over Ela, out of all proportion to the cool damp that hung in the air of the mortuary no matter how sunny the day outside. This fire was no accidental eruption, as Deschamps would have her believe. It appeared there were also two culprits.

"So the man starting the fire could not possibly have been the man who hit you?"

"Nay, because one was in front of me and one behind me."

Ela drew in a shaky breath. What could anyone hope to gain from starting a fire in the kitchen? It was a miracle that no one had been seriously hurt, especially those sleeping in the rooms nearby. And now two men were involved? Even if no one had died, she intended to treat this as seriously as a murder investigation.

"Praise be to God that the one who hit you merely took you for dead and didn't finish the job."

"I may be old, but I've got some fight left in me yet, my lady," he said with a grin. Albert still had a fine set of teeth and thick white hair and did indeed seem like one of those old men who might live to a biblical age.

"Thank Heaven for that, Albert, because I can't imagine Salisbury castle without you at its gates." She suddenly remembered Elsie's lost key. "Albert, Elsie says you found her key on its green ribbon. Where did you find it?"

"I didn't find it. Someone else did and they came and handed it to me, knowing that I'd know where it belonged."

"Who was that person?"

"That odd new fellow. The steward."

ELA ASKED Safiya to escort Albert back to his room, in case he was still unsteady on his feet. She also asked her to stay with him. Ela was worried that whoever had attacked him might return to finish the job. He protested up and down that he was right as rain but finally indulged her. Ela returned to the kitchen—the scene of the crime—to see if she could imagine why the strange man in black had started a fire.

The cook stood in the middle of the blackened mess, shouting orders and chivvying underlings as they scrubbed away the soot and ash. "All my baskets!" she exclaimed as Ela entered. "Every last one of them. And the fine herbs that your mother ordered from Provence!"

"We can buy more baskets and procure more herbs, Cook. I'm just grateful that no one was badly hurt." She didn't yet want to reveal that the fire was intentionally set. "Does anyone on your staff wear a black cloak?"

"I don't know, my lady," said the cook, fussing over a soot stain on the wall. "I can't say I look at their cloaks. I'm more concerned that their hands are clean and busy. Besides it's summer and too warm for cloaks, now, isn't it?"

True. A black cloak was hardly rare these days. But there was no good reason to wear a cloak on a relatively warm night. The wearer must have intended it to conceal his form and identity as he crept about the castle on his evil business.

"Some say I shouldn't leave hot embers unattended overnight," said Cook with a harried air. "But I'm always ever so careful to make sure that the fire is settled with no sparks flying or logs that might crumble and fall out on the hearth. Keeping the stones warm overnight makes such a difference when it comes to baking the morning pastries."

"I'm sure it does." Ela hesitated. Then decided it was time to call for a jury. "But don't trouble yourself because this fire did not start by accident."

Cook stared. "You think someone set it on purpose?"

"I know they did, because there was a witness."

WHILE THE JURY WAS SUMMONED, Ela repaired to her chamber to wash and dress. Elsie was surprisingly garrulous while she pinned Ela's barbette and fillet into place, then arranged the veil over them. "There's ever so many odd things happening lately, my lady. One after another!"

"Indeed there are."

"First a murder, then a scream in the night, then the chess set all out of sorts, with a pool of blood around the white queen and the white king gone missing and the knight cracked! And Bill Talbot's a knight, isn't he? And he almost got cracked when that stone fell on him from the arch. That arch must be a hundred years old and a stone never fell from it before. Someone's up to no good!"

Ela found herself holding her breath. The girl was just repeating the gossip she'd heard downstairs. It was hardly a surprise that everyone was muttering about the strange events of the past few days. Of course they were probably also complaining that the sheriff hadn't managed to catch the culprit.

"Elsie, have you noticed anyone downstairs that wears a black cloak?"

The girl paused and chewed her lip. "Well, I suppose quite a lot of them do, don't they? Your mama, for one."

A chuckle rose in Ela's chest at the idea of her absent mother being seen as a suspect.

Elsie continued. "But I suppose that the coroner wears one quite often. And that Deschamps man who commands the troops. And the steward seems to have a cloak in every color of the rainbow. I think he has a black one as well."

Ela pondered this information. She was fairly certain that Giles Haughton hadn't committed murder or arson or any of the other infractions, but Deschamps had been downright obstructive to her investigations thus far. His guards had apparently ignored a murder committed right on their watch. A gross dereliction of duty by their master as well as themselves, and one for which she could insist on punishment, should she choose.

She'd been careful not to aggravate Deschamps. He'd been garrison commander since her husband's time and was considered competent at his job. His role meant he had access to the king's justiciar and even the king himself. If anything, her position here was more precarious than his, despite her ancestral claim to the castle and the sheriffdom.

But was he taking advantage of his perceived security to permit or encourage crimes? And would he welcome the opportunity to present the castle as a chaotic environment in need of a strong hand to guide it? A strong male hand that might well try to wrest it from her own?

"Why are you staring so, my lady?" Elsie peered at her.

"Thinking." She certainly wasn't going to give her maid more to gossip about. "Do be sure to pay attention to any details that could help us solve these crimes." She took the girl's plump chin in her fingers. "But don't chatter about them with anyone."

"Of course not, my lady." Elsie's face heated. "I'd never gossip."

"I hesitate to tell you not to, as I'm so delighted by how much more talkative you've become." She stroked the girl's cheek with her thumb. "You're coming out of your shell."

"Thank you, my lady." Elsie looked embarrassed rather than pleased by this praise. "I hope I'm doing my job better as well. I'd never been a lady's maid before."

"I know. You were quite dropped into the role by your heels and you've picked it all up so well. I'm very pleased with you."

Now Elsie beamed.

Ela reflected that neither Elsie nor her flighty and spirited predecessor, Hilda, could hold a candle to her beloved Sibel. Sibel had never—in all her years of service—pricked Ela with the hairpins or accidentally slopped her washing water on the floor as she carried it in. Still, they tried the best they could.

"Oh, there is one other person who wears a black cloak. That widow, Safiya."

"Well, yes, a widow would wear a black cloak." Ela didn't need Elsie spreading rumors that Safiya had killed her own husband and started the fire. Given the local mistrust of foreigners it probably wouldn't take long for that to spread like a fire. "She helped Albert the porter back to his room. Please go check on him and see if he needs some breakfast brought."

"How will there be breakfast when the kitchen's in ruins?" Elsie stared at her, wide eyed.

"Don't you worry. Cook is very clever. If there's breakfast to be managed she'll find a way. And if not then we'll all be a little hungry."

~

DOWN IN THE hall Ela discovered that, as she'd expected, the cook had somehow managed to conjure a bubbling pot of oatmeal and plates of nuts and dried berries and even strips of cured bacon to eat with it. Her children were finishing their breakfast, and she told them to attend their tutors as usual and not be distracted by the events of the night.

Despite some minor smoke stains to the whitewashed walls of the hall, there was no real damage. Even the old tapestries seemed to take this new insult in stride, with their hunters and maidens and horses gazing down at her as always, a look of mild disappointment in their embroidered eyes.

Ela swallowed a quick breakfast as the jurors assembled. Once four of them had arrived she ascended her dais, sat in her chair, and summoned them.

"Fortunately no one is dead," she began. "But this fire is the latest in a chain of misdeeds and it's essential that we find and imprison the culprit immediately."

The jurors watched her mutely.

"The fire was deliberately set." Now they looked at one another. "And there is a witness to it. The arsonist was a tall person in a black cloak. Do any of you know who that might be?"

Thomas Price, the old thatcher, scratched his head. "Things haven't been quite right around here since that foreign merchant and his wife turned up."

Ela suppressed a sigh. "While that is indeed true, she is not a suspect. And naturally he isn't either on account of his being buried outside the walls."

"Why isn't she a suspect?" asked Will Dyer.

"For one thing she doesn't fit the description of the suspect."

"She wears a black cloak, I hear," argued Matthew Hart. A man of nearly four score years, he'd been on the jury as long as Ela could remember.

"But the witness described the person seen with the murder victim as a tall man. And there was a different witness to the act of arson that set the kitchen alight. The perpetrator was also described as a tall man in a black cloak. I'm sure you'll agree that Safiya, while by no means short, could not be mistaken for a tall man."

"Who was the witness?" asked Matthew Hart.

"Albert the porter. He saw the stranger skulking about and followed him, wanting to know his business. When the unknown person entered the kitchen, he kept quiet and watched him. He saw him pick up the fire tongs and scatter embers, and then someone knocked him over the head."

"Knocked old Albert over the head?" exclaimed Price.

Ela nodded. "He fell unconscious and was taken for dead."

"That means there are two miscreants?" asked Hal Price, the thatcher's son, who now did most of the thatching work in the town.

"It seems that way. Albert was left for dead and removed to the mortuary. Gerald Deschamps told me he'd been overcome by smoke. He lay wrapped in a winding sheet when Safiya and I attended him to pray over his body and she saw him breathing."

Will Dyer crossed himself.

"My lady." Noel Bazin crossed the room, dapper as always in a deep blue tunic edged in yellow. "Something odd has happened."

"I'm meeting with the jurors. Attend me later," she said in a scolding tone. She didn't want her steward—whose days were already numbered here in Salisbury—thinking he could interrupt her as she conducted business.

"It's a matter for the jury, my lady." The smug expression on his long beaky face further irritated her.

"Oh?" She peered down the length of her nose at him, wondering what could be so important as to merit this intrusion.

He whipped something out from behind his back. "This chess piece is scorched, my lady. As if it had been burned by fire." He held out the rook, shaped like the turret of a castle, which was indeed blackened by soot. "Which is odd since the chess set was safely secured in its box in the hall and not anywhere near the kitchen." He looked at her expectantly.

Noel Bazin is causing this mischief. The revelation dawned on her with thunderclap urgency. But why?

"Why do you feel the need to irk me with this nonsense when I'm conducting business?" she said tersely. "Practical jokes are not a matter for the sheriff to be concerned with."

"I—I thought you'd want to know." Her dismissive tone clearly surprised him.

"Do you own a black cloak, Master Bazin?"

"Uh—I—I suppose I do. My family are drapers from—"

"Your black cloak is the only one I'm interested in, Bazin."

"Yes, I have a black cloak, but I—"

"Guards! Arrest this man." Two soldiers stirred nearby and hurried over.

"But why? I was merely informing you of this damage that—"

"You are one of but a few people who have had access to my chess set the entire time and could use it to playact this foolishness. My mother informs me that you used to play practical jokes on her staff."

"I—I—"

"Be quiet. You shall have your day before the jury and for more than the destruction of my beautiful and expensive chess set. I now also suspect you of setting fire to my kitchen."

Bazin's mouth opened, but this time he didn't utter a protest. Instead, the blood drained from his face and he wobbled as if his knees might give way. Since a guard now held each of his arms, there was no danger of him slumping to the floor.

Ela looked around at the jurors. "Before he's taken to the dungeons, do any of you have questions for Master Bazin?"

The jurors look dumbstruck. "Is this the new steward, my lady?" asked Thomas Price.

"He was and came well recommended, too. Though my recent visit to my mother found her tempering her recommendation with advice that he harbors ambitions beyond his station."

Young Hal Price frowned at Bazin and walked toward him. "Would you care to tell us your motive?" he asked in a sneering tone.

"I did tamper with the chess set," he said hurriedly. "I admit that. I—I was told to do so."

"By whom?"

"I can't say."

"You'd better say unless you want to hang for him."

Bazin swallowed. "I don't know who it was."

Liar. "Did you start the fire?" Price stood as tall as Bazin and a good deal broader.

Bazin seemed to shrink before him. He hesitated, his cheeks hollow. "I did. I didn't mean to do more than cause a stir. No one was hurt, my lady." His voice was now a wheedling whine.

"Albert the porter, one of the oldest and most cherished members of my household, was brutally assaulted and rendered unconscious. It's only by the grace of God that he isn't dead," said Ela.

"I didn't mean for that to happen," he stammered.

"Who did?"

"I don't know." He blinked rapidly.

"If you happen to remember who murdered Ziyad and who knocked my porter over the head, then be sure to send me a missive. Until then you shall be locked in the dungeon."

She half expected him to fall to his knees, pleading for mercy. The dungeons were known to be cold and damp and the foul air down there could sicken a sturdier man than Noel Bazin. Then there were the rats and mice whose bites could fester.

"Why did you tamper with my chess set? You know its value."

"I didn't injure it, my lady. The soot will wash off."

"The knight piece is cracked."

"I had nothing to do with that."

"Why did you set the queen in a pool of blood?" She

didn't want to admit that she'd seen herself in the queen, with her husband gone and her knight wounded.

"Just some mischief, my lady. Something to amuse the youngsters." He attempted a terrible smile that made her stomach curdle.

"You're a liar." She looked right at him and took a deep breath before asking her question. With all these witnesses here, now was as good a time as any to extract a confession. "Did you kill Ziyad the merchant?"

CHAPTER 15

"*I*'m but a meek and mild steward. I could never kill a man." Bazin's protest quivered on his lips.

"You fit the description of the man in a black cloak seen accompanying Ziyad on his last journey up to the top of the wall. He was next seen lying strangled in the ditch below."

"Never, my lady. Never!" Bazin's voice trembled.

"You'd be surprised at how often murderers lie, Master Bazin," retorted Ela. "Almost always, in fact."

"But why would he kill the merchant?" asked hoary old Matthew Hart. "What is his motive?"

"Greed, perhaps? The merchant's cart contained many treasures and perhaps he met with him to bargain over one, only to kill him and take possession without paying. We must search his quarters."

A surge of energy thrust Ela from her seat and she took a step toward Bazin. Still on her dais, she looked down at him. "You must tell me who your master is."

"You, my lady." He attempted a bow, but the guards holding him stifled the movement.

"As of this morning you are no longer in my employ and

shall take no shelter in my mercy. Your co-conspirator stands accused of attempted murder. Albert saw you set the kitchen fire before someone knocked him on the head."

Bazin startled. "Albert is alive, I hear."

"No thanks to you. You didn't know he was watching you, did you?"

"No," he admitted with a gulp.

Ela didn't tell him that Albert had described only a tall man in a black cloak. He'd already confirmed that it was him by his lack of protest.

"Who was with you, that hit Albert over the head and left him for dead?"

Again, Bazin looked shocked, like he truly had no idea what she was talking about. "No one was with me. It was a silly act of mischief, that's all."

"Your words have almost sentenced you to a hanging for property destruction alone," she said in a voice so low it made her chest rumble. "You truly see setting fire to my kitchen and the cook's herbs and baskets as an act of mischief? You, who were charged with protecting and preserving the wealth of the household?"

Truly, it made no sense. This went far beyond mischief. "The fire could have spread and set the wooden roofs of the storerooms and sleeping chambers and even the great hall alight. You might have killed a hundred people with what you claim was an act of foolishness."

His head drooped slightly. "I see the error of my ways."

"Albert also said that you handed him Elsie's missing key. No doubt you used it to tamper with the seat of my garderobe. Did you hope for me to be killed, or just injured?"

His gaze rested on the floor.

"Who told you to do these things?"

"No one," he protested quickly. Too quickly. "I've always had a taste for jests. It's a weakness of character. I like to see how people will react, great people, when the carefully woven tapestry of their grand lives starts to fray. Your mother didn't mind my little practical jokes."

Ela blinked at him. Was it possible that such a man would risk his freedom and livelihood for such foolishness? He was like a gambler risking his own house on a wager. "My mother disliked your foolery and decided to rid herself of you. She admitted as much once I complained of you to her. I suppose I should have known better than to trust a steward who plays such a cunning game of chess." She looked at the guards. "Take him to the dungeons."

ELA BROUGHT the jurors with her to search Bazin's quarters. His large chamber lay in a different building than the one she shared with her children and their servants and guests. That structure housed the more senior male staff members, including Deschamps and other knights among the garrison and the castle staff.

Bill Talbot had lived here until her husband's death, when she'd asked him to move his residence to nearer her own rooms. That had caused some tongues to wag, but idle gossip didn't disturb her sleep.

She found Bazin's room locked so she sent a soldier to fetch a key. Normally she'd send for Albert, who kept a set of master keys, but he needed to rest and recover from his injuries.

When the soldier returned and unlocked the room, they found a painstakingly neat space. Instead of the treasure room she'd half imagined as they climbed the stairs, Ela found it spare as a monk's cell. A large dark oak chest with faded scrolling painted on it in gold was the only furniture beyond the basic bed and chair that furnished all the men's rooms.

"Open the chest," she commanded the guard.

"I don't think we have the key for it. It's not castle property but his personal possession."

"He must have the key on his person. Find him in the dungeon and secure it."

Once again, they waited. Bazin's bedcovers lay neatly folded back to air the mattress. Two spare pairs of leather boots sat in one corner, one black and one dark blue, clean and oiled. A plain brass cross hung by a ribbon from a single nail driven into the plastered wall above his bed. Nothing about his chamber spoke of avarice or cunning or a disturbance of the mind that would make a respected steward throw his life away for an amusement.

When the guard returned with Bazin's key, Ela watched with curiosity as he opened the trunk. As expected it contained his clothes, which she knew were varied and colorful. A red tunic, a blue one, hose in mustard yellow and green. He had a gray cloak and a blue cloak and tunics in almost every shade that cloth could be dyed. An astonishing array of garments befitting a noble of great status. It was hard to imagine he'd amassed such a fine wardrobe on a steward's wage, but if he came from a family of drapers that explained it. Will Dyer removed the items one by one, examined them, and placed them on the bed.

When he found the black cloak—not on top of the other clothes but tucked fairly deep in the folded pile, he shook it out. "This would be the black cloak seen by Albert the porter."

"It would indeed." Ela sniffed it and it did smell faintly of smoke. She hoped Albert would recognize the garment, so she sent the same guard to fetch him, giving instructions not to rush him and to bring Safiya as well if she still sat with him.

The trunk also contained two books—neither of them a prayer book. The first was a worn treatise on maintaining business accounts, written in Latin, possibly a copy of something penned back in Roman times. The name of its author sounded odd and unfamiliar to her. The other was a book of military strategy, this one decidedly less ancient and rather more well-thumbed than the first. Ela frowned as she glanced over the pages. "Why would a steward keep a book of military strategies?" The book contained drawings of how to arrange an army during a siege, with the soldiers and their war engines flanked around the castle walls like so many...*chess pieces.*

"Many a man dreams of fighting when he's sitting in the warmth of his own fire," said Matthew Hale. "Battle's more enjoyable when imagined than when experienced."

"Bazin is a master at the game of chess. I suspect he gleaned some of his cunning strategies from this book," said Ela. And what else did he gain from reading these plans for destruction and plunder?

She shuddered and closed the book. "I believe we've had a very dangerous man in our midst."

"If he killed the merchant, he'll hang for it," said Hal Price with an air of gloating. "And Salisbury will be well rid of his scheming."

"I daresay he could hang for setting fire to the castle," said Hale. "I've seen a man strung up for less."

"Indeed. His rash act could have taken many lives. I'm not in the least inclined to mercy," said Ela coolly. As sheriff she couldn't sentence a man to death, but she could recommend it to the traveling justice who came to Salisbury for the assizes.

She put the books down on the chair and reached deeper

into the trunk. Among Bazin's effects was a spool of sturdy thread. Ela studied the tightly wound cord, then held it out to Haughton. "Could this have been used to strangle Ziyad the merchant?"

Haughton took it and unspooled a length of it. "I suppose it could be. Though this cord isn't stretched, so it would likely be a similar piece and not this one."

They pulled the rest of Bazin's worldly goods from the trunk. She'd half expected to find a stash of jewels or other valuables that he'd bargained for with Ziyad, or even stolen from Safiya's caravan. But there was no sign of anything unexpected beyond his many garments.

Albert the porter arrived as Elsie was putting everything back in the trunk. Ela held up the cloak for him. "Is this the cloak the man you saw wore when he started the fire?"

"Aye, it is. I recognize the piping around the hood."

Ela glanced at the hood and saw dark wine-colored piping that she hadn't noticed before. "That confirms Bazin's guilt in setting the fire, though he didn't deny it when accused. But now we need to know if this cloak was also worn by the man who murdered Ziyad the merchant." Only one person saw the black-cloaked-stranger who walked on the wall with Ziyad—Rosie the prostitute.

Ela resolved to summon Rosie to the castle to discuss the matter with her and Giles Haughton.

THE NEXT MORNING, the hall thronged with people plying Ela with requests and pleas of various kinds. The loud banging of repairs from the kitchen rose over the hum of voices, and by Nones Ela's nerves were frayed.

She'd summoned jurors to attend her along with Rosie and Haughton, for she hoped to put to bed the matter of who had killed the merchant. If Rosie could confirm that she'd seen Bazin, Ela could press Bazin to find out why he'd killed Ziyad.

Bazin's black cloak sat folded in a basket near her, and Ela had Elsie shake it out as Haughton approached. "This cloak of Bazin's confirmed his identity as the one who set the fire. Albert knew it right away," said Ela. "Is Rosie the...the witness here yet?"

"I haven't seen her," replied Haughton. Ela glanced around the hall, looking for the woman's red dress and painted face. "Now that I think about it I haven't seen her in Salisbury lately."

"What?"

"She lives above the Bull and Bear. Or at least she did. As you know I eat my meals there when my wife is visiting her mother. She would often pass through the parlor of the inn on her way to and from her...business."

Ela was still shocked that a busy inn would allow such sinful traffic under its roof. Haughton seemed unbothered by it, though, so perhaps such women were common in such an environment. She'd spent as little time in inns as she could manage—only staying or eating in them while traveling—and she only frequented the most respectable and well-maintained establishments.

"When did you last see her? When you asked her about the night of the murder?"

"I never spoke to her about the murder," he said quietly. "I'd sent a message for her to come meet with me, promising payment for her time and information, but I never heard back. That was three or four days ago."

A nasty cool sensation trickled down Ela's spine. "She's the only one who saw the man who accompanied Ziyad up to the wall. She stood here in the hall and was publicly questioned. She didn't accuse anyone, though. She said she couldn't see the man's face because the hood of his cloak covered it."

"Still, perhaps the killer decided she was a liability." His voice sounded grim.

"You think she might be dead?"

"It's possible."

"We must raise the hue and cry."

"And then she'll be found sleeping in her bed with a headache. Perhaps we should make discreet inquiries, first."

"I suppose you're right, but I'm very uneasy about this. I'll send guards to the Bull and Bear to ask her whereabouts."

Haughton frowned. "That would send half the denizens there into hiding. I'll go there for a drink myself and make inquiries." Unsurprisingly, the two jurors volunteered to go with him, and the three men went off on their quest. Ela sat on her dais, surrounded by needy townspeople and the thumping and thudding of carpenters in the kitchen.

Was there truly another murder to investigate? And if so, could Noel Bazin have committed that one, too? When a man had killed once he was twice as likely to kill again. Already halfway along the road to hell, a murderer often thought little of taking another life to cover his tracks. She'd never have taken Bazin, odd though he was, as someone who would start a fire, so it wasn't impossible.

GILES HAUGHTON RETURNED to the hall in the late afternoon with the news that Rosie was indeed missing from the Bull and Bear. The innkeeper hadn't seen her in days and was already fussing about money she owed him.

"Did you ask to see her room?" asked Ela.

"I did and they took me up to it—a triangular-shaped

cubby right under the rafters. I expected to see her things there, just as she'd left them, but they were all gone."

"So she left of her own accord?"

"It seems that way. Or someone removed her belongings."

"I'd imagine that would be hard to do without attracting the attention of the innkeeper."

"Indeed."

Ela frowned. "Maybe her bills came due and that just happened to coincide with our need for her."

"And she may not have liked the scrutiny she came under at the castle. Notoriety is not an asset in her trade."

"We need her as a witness," said Ela. "Perhaps it's time to get John Dacus involved." An amiable man, Dacus was good at staying in the background and letting her command the role of sheriff, though they were supposed to be equals. She suspected he preferred fishing and hunting at his manor and was quite content to leave the hunt for justice to her. "I'll ask him to send men out to search for her."

Ela looked up to see her son Richard striding toward her, a purposeful look on his face and something concealed in his hands.

"What is it, my dear?" Ela didn't like to be interrupted when she was engaged in official business.

Richard moved closer and opened his hands to reveal one of the chess pieces—the rook—completely blackened with soot from the fire.

"Where did you find this?"

"It was in the box like this."

"I'm afraid it's no surprise to me since Bazin told me about it." Ela glanced at Haughton. "More nonsense with this chess set. I bought it from Ziyad the day he died, and since then mischief keeps befalling the pieces in a way that heralds the day's evil events. The knight piece was cracked the day before Bill was injured, and now this burned image of a castle was found after the kitchen is set on fire. Bazin has been playing games with me to amuse himself."

"He'll find hanging from a gibbet a very grim form of amusement. He must have scorched this one before he started the fire."

"I think I've had enough of this chess set," said Ela. The blackened rook left soot stains on her son's hands. She didn't even want to touch it.

"It's bad luck, isn't it?" asked Richard.

"Luck is superstition," said Ela firmly. "We're educated in the word of God and don't hold with fancies based on old fairy tales." She didn't want her children spreading foolish rumors throughout the castle. Though if she destroyed the chess set, was she actually playing into the idea that it was somehow cursed? "Noel Bazin is in our dungeon right now." She suspected he'd love for her to make a fuss about it the chess set being hexed and bringing bad luck on the castle. "So I doubt we'll have more trouble with it."

Though she'd certainly rather never see it again. Perhaps it could be repaired and regifted after Bazin's trial was over. If it was cursed—not that she believed in such things— perhaps she should give it to Hubert de Burgh?

"Go give it to Elsie to clean and then place it back with the rest of the pieces. They're to be kept safely put away, though with Bazin in charge of the set I'd left my geese with the wolf."

CHAPTER 16

*E*la summoned her co-sheriff, John Dacus, to the hall the following morning. When he arrived she took him into a private chamber and tried to summarize the odd chain of events that had put Bazin down in the dungeon and made Rosie vanish from Salisbury.

"What's this I hear about the chess set?" he asked.

Ela hadn't planned to mention such foolishness. The castle was already abuzz with rumors about curses and foreign witchcraft. "It seems that Bazin, who prided himself on his game of chess, thought to make sport of me by tinkering with the chess set entrusted to his care. Another reason for him to rot in the dungeon."

"Someone told me that the queen piece was found in a pool of blood," said Dacus. "Do you see that as a threat to your person?"

"I'm not the queen."

"You are the queen of Salisbury castle, my lady. And given that your knight has been injured and your castle burned, I suggest that you take care."

"Someone is deliberately trying to intimidate me, and I

refuse to let them succeed. Besides, an attempt to kill me in my private chamber was foiled by my maid Elsie."

She studied his face to see if he knew about the garderobe incident. She didn't relish going into descriptive detail. That rather seemed to play into the hands of the perpetrator who wished to humiliate her.

"I did hear about that. Praise be to God that no one was harmed."

"Indeed. And with Bazin now in custody I feel confident that such threats will cease."

Dacus looked doubtful. "Why would your steward want to injure you or Bill Talbot or Albert the porter? He can't have been acting alone."

"He wasn't." She'd almost forgotten the presence of a second man who'd clubbed Albert as he watched Bazin light the fire. "But he won't say who. We must extract the information about his co-conspirator from him."

"I hear the jailer is experienced at drawing the truth from men."

Ela shuddered slightly and hoped he didn't see it. "I don't believe in torture. It will fetch a lie as soon as the truth. I hope to tease the truth out of him before the jurors."

She'd lately discovered a minor talent for irritating men into revealing too much. There was something especially galling about being interrogated by a woman that made them lash out in anger and spill secrets they'd have done better to keep to themselves.

John Dacus regarded her with his steady open gaze. "Who in this castle would want to hurt you?"

Ela hesitated before admitting something that nagged at her conscience. "I suppose there might be men under my roof who resent my role as their leader. They'd prefer to see me replaced by a man and would be happy to see my authority undermined."

He didn't argue with her.

"Not you," said Ela quickly. "I'm grateful for your stalwart support and also that of Bill Talbot." She frowned. She could think of other men she trusted among the large castle staff, like Albert and a few faithful guards, but the army of soldiers that roamed about the castle and its village were mostly strangers to her. She'd already dealt with several failures of guards to adequately protect her and her household. It was too painful to state that aloud, however.

"What of Deschamps?" asked Dacus quietly.

"He's been garrison commander for a long time. He served my husband. If anything I'd say he handled the transition well, though he rankles when I try to limit the pleasures his men can enjoy in my castle." Much as she didn't like Deschamps enough to share intimacies over a cup of wine, she admired his abilities. "He has a difficult job, managing men from all walks of life hailing from all over the kingdom and beyond and keeping them in a state of readiness."

"Indeed," mused Dacus.

"Have you heard him say anything about me?" She hated to ask the question. She felt like a gossiping alewife.

"No, my lady." He hesitated. "But I observe that he's a man who enjoys power."

"I give him freedom to rule as he wishes in his own domain." She hated how defensive she sounded. "Though I suppose lately I have reprimanded him about the failure of his guards to prevent a murder on my castle walls."

Dacus didn't say anything.

Ela's mind grappled with the silence. "Are you suggesting that he told his guards to look aside?" She glanced at the door. There was a guard right outside—as always—and she hoped they'd been speaking quietly enough so he couldn't overhear. "Or that he was directly involved in the murder of Ziyad the merchant?"

Dacus's placid face barely moved. Just a slight twist of his mouth. "I hesitate to raise suspicion about a valued member of the castle staff, but I'd be remiss in my duty if I didn't speak my mind."

"I'm grateful for your candor, though I struggle to wrap my mind around the idea that my garrison commander should be under suspicion." She glanced at the door again. "Gerald Deschamps is almost as much a fixture of this castle as the tapestries in the hall and the halberds on the wall of the armory."

"Perhaps he has aspirations to be castellan?"

"Impossible. He's not a noble. If I were to die, my son William would inherit the title of Earl of Salisbury."

"An ambitious man might prefer a green youth in the role of castellan. Your son would lack experience and seek the opinion of a seasoned elder like Deschamps. Perhaps he might even be chosen as sheriff. He is a knight, even if not a noble."

"God willing, Bill Talbot would be here to guide young William in my absence. But my son is not yet ready to assume the role of Earl of Salisbury or castellan of this castle. If he were I would step aside and hand them to him. He has maturing to do and shall come into his inheritance when he's ripe for it."

Ela knew people talked about her depriving her son of his supposedly rightful position as heir to his namesake father. But too many people's lives and livelihoods were at stake for her to give command of Salisbury to a callow youth.

She glanced at the door again, wondering if the guard had his ear pressed to it. "Why would Deschamps want to kill Ziyad?"

"I can't imagine a reason why anyone would want to kill the merchant," said Dacus. "His wife has no idea who killed him?"

Ela shook her head. "She seems to know almost nothing of his affairs. He kept her tucked away in his wagon."

"Surely in such a position she would have heard his business."

"Not if he took his business up on the castle wall."

Dacus nodded. "It is strange that he accepted the invitation to walk up there. He must have trusted the person who took him."

"Perhaps he felt safe in the confines of the castle, which is under the protection of so many guards. How could he know they'd neglect their duty?" Ela pondered what they knew of the situation. "He was last seen with a man in a black cloak. Noel Bazin, the steward, was seen wearing a black cloak while he set the fire. There's an excellent chance that Noel Bazin is the man who accompanied him up on the wall and who killed him with a length of thread that was found in his possessions."

"Do you suspect Bazin of killing him to steal an object in his possession?"

"We didn't find anything suspicious when we searched his room. If he did steal an object, a valuable ruby, for example, it must be well hidden. We'll have to tease more information out of Bazin in front of the jury. He's a proud and arrogant man and may perhaps be pressed into boasting about his cunning."

She'd almost forgotten why she'd asked Dacus here. "I'd like you to find Rosie, the, er, woman who saw Ziyad walk into the tower that led up to the wall, and who was the only one to witness the black-cloaked stranger by his side. She's vanished from Salisbury and left nary a hairpin in her room above the Bull and Bear."

"That is odd. There aren't many places to ply her trade that boast such an ample supply of lonely men. Begging your pardon for my frankness, my lady."

"Don't ever apologize for speaking the truth. Rosie didn't say a word to anyone about leaving. She seemed excited that she was the only one who might hold the key to a murder and was seen running her mouth in the Bull and Bear and drinking cups of ale on the news before she disappeared."

"That is worrying," said Dacus. "I hope she isn't dead."

"You think she might have been killed by the murderer, who wished to rid himself of a potential witness? I also had that thought. But if she can be found, I wish you to find her forthwith. And if she can't be found I'd like to know what happened to her."

Now that Bazin couldn't inventory the goods in Safiya's wagon for resale, Ela reasoned that Safiya must do it herself. She visited the young woman in her bedchamber and was surprised when Safiya agreed. "I don't know the value of all the items," she admitted. "But I can read my husband's account books, which are written in Arabic, and come to some idea of them."

"Excellent," said Ela. "I don't trust anyone else to do it. Bill Talbot will stand watch as you make the inventory. He's the one person I'd trust with both my life and my purse. You should organize the items by type so we can look into how to resell them. I have contacts in London for the more valuable items. My former maid Sibel married a man who owns a shop that sells baskets and bottles. Perhaps he could help sell some of the cheaper items for a small share of the profits."

Safiya nodded.

"I'm glad to see you in better spirits today."

"Life goes on, even when we wish it didn't," said Safiya, rather flatly. "I don't want to be a burden to you any longer than I have to."

"You're not a burden," insisted Ela.

"The people here are all suspicious of me. They even say I killed my own husband. Why would they think that?"

"Some people are quick to be suspicious of a woman who gains her independence by a man's death. They may have muttered the same when my husband died."

"Was your husband murdered?"

Ela hesitated. "I believe so, but his killer was never prosecuted."

"Why?" Safiya looked perplexed.

"Some people are above the law." Ela could hardly believe she'd admitted this. Still, Safiya didn't know the key players and was unlikely to spread the gossip.

"Perhaps my husband's killer will escape punishment, too," said Safiya gravely.

"Noel Bazin is in the dungeon at this moment. He owns a black cloak and was seen wearing it while starting the fire in the kitchens. It seems likely that he's the man who was seen taking your husband up to the wall. We also found a long strip of twine in his trunk that could be used as a garotte."

"Will he be hanged?"

"If he's found guilty. Murderers are judged at the assizes, when the traveling justice comes to Salisbury. In the meantime the jurors and I will gather all the information we can to present to the justice when he arrives."

"I want to know why he would kill my husband." Safiya's smooth brow crumpled.

"I mean to question him and try to tease the truth out of him."

A sudden rap on the door made her jump and a man's voice called out, "My lady!"

Ela spun to face the door. She'd told the guards not to disturb her. "What is it?" She didn't want guards bursting into Safiya's room and frightening her.

"Noel Bazin is dead, my lady."

∿

ELA HURRIED down to the great hall. The hum of conversation stilled as she entered, and Ela felt heads turn to stare at her. As castellan and sheriff she was charged with keeping the peace in Salisbury and in her castle. Now it seemed that chaos reigned under her watch.

"Where is Deschamps?" She didn't hide her anger. She wanted to know how Bazin could have died in custody before they could properly interview him. As garrison commander Deschamps held responsibility for the management of the dungeons as well as the soldiers themselves and this death lay at his feet.

After some time, Deschamps strode into the hall with a grim expression on his face. "God has seen fit to take his servant Noel Bazin, my lady."

"How, exactly?" She didn't want him to blandish her with biblical allegories.

"Perhaps the cold and damp, my lady." He shrugged slightly. "It's not unusual for men to sicken to death down there."

"First of all, the weather is warm and dry. Second of all, Bazin is a young man of only thirty-five or so. He's been pampered by the rich and nourishing food of my household —and before that, my mother's household—and was in robust health. It's inconceivable that he could sicken and die overnight. I demand an autopsy and I've called for the coroner."

Deschamp's jaw stiffened. "I hardly think that will be necessary. The Lord has called him to pay for his crimes against—"

"The Lord has done nothing of the sort. Someone has

killed him, and I wish to know why." Deschamps shot to the top of her list of suspects. "And I blame you. I also blame you for the death of Ziyad the merchant up on the castle wall, which should have been under the watchful eyes of your guards. You are trusted with keeping this castle—the king's own garrison—safe, and you are failing at your duty."

Her voice rose during the last accusation, and she paused to watch its effect on him. "My lady, I am but a lowly commander and subject to the whims of those above me."

Now Deschamps was trying to blame her for this failure of leadership. She wished she could order him horsewhipped for his insolence. But such a fit of pique would draw unwelcome comparisons between her and her husband's ancestor Empress Matilda.

Still, she knew people would blame her for the deaths and disarray plaguing the castle of late.

Giles Haughton hurried in, hair disheveled as if he'd been riding hard. "Excuse the delay, my lady, I was in Amesbury on an errand for my wife. The messenger caught up with me, and I turned my horse and galloped the whole way back. He said it was an urgent matter but didn't say what the matter was."

Ela had given instructions for the messenger to be kept in the dark. She didn't need rumors of this new death leaking out of the castle and into the town until she understood it better.

"Noel Bazin has died down in the dungeon. I wish for you to examine him in close detail and determine the cause of death."

"He might have taken a chill—" began Deschamps, looking earnestly at Haughton.

"In one night? More likely he was murdered in cold blood," finished Ela. "And I wish to know how and by whom."

"I'll have his body brought to the mortuary," said Deschamps.

"No, leave him where he fell," replied Haughton. "I wish to see the circumstances of his death."

Ela studied Deschamps's face, but he kept his expression stony and neutral. "It's very dark down there."

"I'll bring a lantern."

~

ELA DECIDED to accompany Haughton down into the dungeon partly out of curiosity over the circumstances of Bazin's death and partly as a show of bravado. She didn't want Deschamps—or Haughton—to think that she shrank from visiting the fetid and clammy depths even when a dead body lay there.

She climbed gingerly down the ladder—which was rickety at best—holding her skirts so as not to trip on them. The musty odor of damp earth and bodily fluids assaulted her nostrils as she descended below ground level. Haughton had gone first and held up the lamp for her, so she could just make out the ground below as she stepped off the ladder. It felt unpleasantly mushy underfoot.

The menacing jailer who kept watch over the chained prisoners didn't hide his surprise at her arrival. Then he remembered himself and bowed his big, blocklike head.

He was a possible suspect. "Were you down here when Master Bazin died?" asked Ela.

"I don't rightly know when he died. He was alive when I gave him his slops last evening, and he was dead when I came around with the gruel this morning."

"Where is he?" ask Haughton. Ela could hear Deschamps begin his descent down the ladder behind them.

"Over here," said the gruff jailer, with a jerk of his head.

Haughton's lantern lit the way past two disconsolate prisoners, who didn't even lift their heads as she passed. She'd seen them up in the hall, before their confinement down here to wait for the assizes—a three-time poacher at risk of being hanged for his crimes and a farmer accused of punching his wife so hard that she died. As they approached the farthest corner, the pool of wavering yellow lantern light crept over the prostrate form of Noel Bazin.

He lay sprawled on the floor, his face completely hidden by his longish hair. His right ankle was still chained to the wall and his arms splayed out at his sides.

"Has he been moved since he was found?" asked Ela.

"We tried to wake him up," growled the jailer. "Shook him and all. Breath had left his body."

"Was he found in this position?" asked Haughton.

"More or less," said the jailer.

"It looks like he threw out his arms to catch himself as he fell. Almost as if he was pushed," said Ela slowly.

"Couldn't anyone have pushed him," said the jailer. "No one down here but me."

"You weren't relieved at night?" asked Ela.

"Nay. The night watchman fell sick, and I took his shift for an extra fivepence."

"Is that a common arrangement?" asked Ela.

"Aye. I don't mind working more time to earn a bit of extra coin."

Haughton knelt over the body and turned the head toward him. Bazin's dead eyes stared at them from his beaky face. Haughton peered into them, holding the lantern close, then he closed them with a sweep of his hand.

Ela crossed herself and muttered a quick prayer. For all his faults, Noel Bazin wasn't actually—yet—accused of murder and had not been sentenced to death so his end was untimely and ill-starred.

Haughton picked up each of the man's hands and peered at it. Ela wanted to ask questions, but there'd be time for that later. She could feel a sort of fuming energy rolling off Deschamps, as he stood there watching in silence.

Ela wanted to ask Deschamps if he'd visited the dungeon since last night, but since that would amount to an accusation of murder, she held her tongue. If she were to broadcast suspicions about the commander of the king's garrison she'd need a lot more to go on than idle conjecture by her fellow sheriff.

"There's bruising on his forehead," said Haughton at last. "It appears he fell and hit his head on the stone floor."

"Perhaps he tripped over the chain," said Deschamps. "New prisoners forget it's there."

Or perhaps he was shoved—hard—by the burly jailer who seems so keen to earn a few extra coins. Again, Ela kept her suspicions to herself. Even as sheriff, castellan, and Countess of Salisbury she knew her power had its limits.

"Did he eat his supper?" asked Ela. She was curious about the time of death.

"No, but I took the bowl away. Food left out attracts rats, and they can gnaw a prisoner's eyes out while they sleep." The jailer's eyes glittered as he replied to her.

"Was he prostrate on the floor at that time?"

"Nay. He were sitting all hunched up in the corner sobbing like a babby." His sneering voice mocked the dead man.

"Did he say anything?"

"Said there's been a mistake. That he's not supposed to be here. Kept saying it over and over." The jailer looked amused.

Ela felt Deschamps shift slightly at her side, and she turned to see him catch the jailer's eye. The jailer's smile vanished from his face.

"What kind of a mistake, I wonder?" asked Ela aloud,

mostly for Haughton's benefit. "Had he perhaps expected someone else to pay the punishment for his crimes?"

"I don't follow you, my lady," said Deschamps in an oily voice.

"Someone was seen with him when he set fire to the kitchens." This wasn't entirely true. It was truer that someone was felt—when they clubbed Albert over the head. She didn't want to mention this in case the information would put Albert in danger. She had a strong feeling that Bazin had been killed to protect his accomplice—or his master.

"Who would do such a terrible thing?" asked Deschamps.

"Who indeed?" asked Ela. "And why would Bazin, my gainfully employed and highly capable steward, risk his career and even his life over such a strange and incomprehensible crime?"

"The question boggles the mind, my lady." Deschamps looked coolly down at the prostrate body.

Haughton crouched over the corpse, examining the man's limbs and the area around him. The dungeon floor was damp earth, and Ela could almost swear that she could smell the rats who reportedly scurried across it at night. She itched to turn and run for the ladder but held herself steady.

Finally Haughton examined the iron cuff on Bazin's wrist that held him fast to the wall. "Bruising," he muttered. "Suggests force."

"As if his arm was wrenched hard?" asked Ela.

"Aye. Likely at the same time that he banged his head."

"When someone shoved him," suggested Ela.

"I daresay the same could happen if he slipped and fell," offered Deschamps.

Ela found Deschamps's repeated insistence on such an unlikely scenario downright suspicious.

"I've seen all I need to down here," said Haughton. "Have him brought up to the mortuary for further examination."

Relief flooded Ela's body. She couldn't wait to get out of this malodorous hellhole.

Deschamps gestured for her to lead the way and even held the rickety ladder for her as she climbed toward the light. Why did she feel like he'd love to knock it sideways and send her flying?

CHAPTER 17

*I*n the mortuary, Ela closed the door, shutting herself in with Haughton and leaving her guard outside. "Your thoughts?"

Haughton drew in a slow, deep breath, then let it out. "I agree with you that this man was likely murdered."

"And our list of suspects is very short."

"The guard claims there was no one down there but himself, thus stepping up toward the noose."

"Except that of course he insists it was just an accident. Is there any way to prove it wasn't?"

Haughton frowned. "Not with Deschamps defending him."

There was a long pause. Ela didn't know whether she could risk accusing Deschamps to Haughton. The two men had worked together a lot longer than she had worked with either of them.

Still…Haughton had opened the door with his comment. "You think Deschamps had reason to want Noel Bazin dead?"

"I certainly can't think of one." Haughton's inscrutable reply dampened her enthusiasm. Haughton looked at the body on the table, currently wound in a length of linen cloth. "Unless Deschamps told Bazin to start the fire."

He thought it was possible. "But why?" She hesitated again, not wanting to betray her fellow sheriff's confidence. Then she reminded herself that her utmost duty was to truth and justice. "John Dacus wonders if he resents having a female castellan installed over him."

She watched Haughton's chest rise as he took in another of his weighty breaths. "It's not impossible. Deschamps may even have cherished hopes of being sheriff and castellan himself. He's a knight and has served his king long and hard enough."

"But I hardly stole the role from him. I seized it back from the odious Simon de Hal. I never heard a word breathed about Deschamps becoming sheriff." Not that she would be included in such discussions. De Hal had been foisted on her by her powerful enemy, Hubert de Burgh.

A nasty sensation pricked her nerves. "I wonder if Deschamps's orders are coming from higher up the chain of command?"

Haughton frowned and peered at her. "De Burgh?" He spoke the words so softly she could barely hear them. Which was wise when her guard—a man under Deschamps's command—might have his ear pressed against the door.

She'd confided in Haughton about her suspicions that de Burgh had poisoned her husband. He'd even promised to slip the rumor into the air in the hope that the arrows of justice might somehow, eventually, find their target.

"I suppose de Burgh is furious that I thwarted his plans to install one of his cronies here in Salisbury. No doubt he hoped that installing de Hal as sheriff would banish me to a nunnery or to one of my distant manors. He apparently didn't reckon on my making a deal directly with the king."

"There aren't many who have both the clout and the

daring to do such a thing." Haughton's eyes shone. "If the man has any sense he should be afraid of you."

Ela wanted to laugh, but didn't. "If he's behind this murder inside my castle then he'd do well to be afraid of me."

"Unless we can't even prove that a murder was committed." Haughton leveled a steady gaze at her. "While Deschamps doesn't quite command the unassailable power of de Burgh, he's master of his own domain here."

"And if he's operating as de Burgh's functionary, then our quarrel is in fact with de Burgh himself." Ela's stomach tightened. How could a mortal man be so utterly above the law?

Haughton walked over to the body and carefully pulled back the sheet. Bazin, a thin and insubstantial man in life, looked positively skeletal under the stained remains of his fine clothes. His long beaky nose had turned a spectral blue, as had his lips.

"Has he been poisoned?" The color was unnerving.

"Nay. The blue color in his face indicates that he died face down. It's from the blood pooling there."

"How can we coax a confession from the jailer, if he is indeed the murderer? Is there anything to stop me from accusing him and chaining him to the walls of his own dungeon?"

Haughton blinked at her. "You could call him before a jury and question him on the matter. Though if I'm honest I'm not sure the jurors will be quick to see Bazin's death as murder. They may not care how Noel Bazin died now that he's known to have set fire to the castle and endangered lives in it."

"Except it suddenly seems that—chess master though he was—Bazin was merely a pawn in a larger game being played by someone else." Ela walked around the table, watching as Haughton started to remove Bazin's clothing. "And I'm starting to wonder if we are at checkmate if the conspirators can simply back up each other's lies."

Haughton cut through Bazin's tunic and peeled it back like he was paring an apple. "You must have a care for your own safety, my lady." Haughton's concern furrowed his brow.

"I wonder if making accusations would protect me from acts of ill intent, or make me more vulnerable?"

"Accusing Deschamps?"

"Yes." The prospect chilled her blood. Such an arrest would shake even the throne and possibly draw the ire of the young king and his closest confidant, de Burgh. "I would need definite proof that it was him."

Right now she had no proof at all. Just suspicion.

Haughton looked up from examining the corpse. "Why would either of these men want to set a fire in the castle kitchen?"

"If they were behind all the mischief with the chess set and my garderobe, I suspect that Deschamps ordered Bazin to foment trouble and get people whispering that I can't keep my castle under control." It pained her to say the words aloud, since they had a ring of truth to them. "I'd hoped that by arresting Bazin I had stopped the trouble."

"If Deschamps has lost his lackey he may struggle to continue his campaign against you."

"I can hardly live quietly with an enemy in my keep." The prospect of seeing Deschamps daily in her hall, issuing orders to him, hearing him call her "my lady"—while plotting her demise—made her stomach churn. "I need to arrest him."

"It won't hold without evidence."

"Even with my word?"

Haughton inhaled deeply. "I've been coroner for many years, and the jury at least must be convinced that a man is guilty. Deschamps is well-liked in Salisbury. He was close to your husband and is a favorite with the soldiers."

"Am I not well-liked?" She felt foolish asking the question, but suddenly she burned to know the answer.

Haughton lifted his hands from Bazin's body. "Of course you are well-liked, my lady."

"But?" She could hear it in his voice.

"As you said yourself, some men struggle with seeing a woman in a position of authority that they'd like to command themselves."

"Do you find it...difficult to work with a woman sheriff?"

"Not at all, my lady. I'm proud to work with you as coroner. You've a keener sense of justice and a sharper mind for the truth than most men I've worked with."

His words warmed her heart. "Thank you. I trust you to be honest with me, and I lean heavily on your experience and expertise."

"And I in turn appreciate that you value my knowledge. I can't say that's been my experience with every sheriff I've worked with."

Ela wondered how he felt about her husband in the role of sheriff. She decided not to ask. Her husband had many fine qualities, but he sometimes showed disinterest or even disdain for what he saw as minor local matters. He'd entrusted much of the work to subordinates. She suspected that everyone, including the king, expected her to leave most of the sheriff's duties up to John Dacus, but she felt keenly the responsibility to maintain peace and justice in Salisbury.

And now someone was trying to undermine everything she hoped to achieve.

Haughton examined Bazin's long, bony feet. His very dead nakedness made her shudder slightly. "What did Bazin hope to achieve from all this?"

Haughton looked up from Bazin's toes. "Money, power,

and sex are what motivate most men to commit crimes in my experience."

Ela blinked at his blunt response.

"That is, unless they're driven by genuine need. A desperate mother will do almost anything to feed her hungry child. But Bazin risked a comfortable existence for an elusive prize, and now he's paid the highest price."

"He seemed to have a taste for trouble. My mother mentioned that he played practical jokes on her staff. I suspect that his tendency toward mischief made him easy prey for someone who offered him a chance to make mischief for a reward."

"His master was someone he trusted," said Haughton gruffly. "Someone he thought would keep him out of the dungeon."

Like Deschamps.

Yet there was no evidence against Deschamps. He rested easy in bed knowing that she had no proof of his involvement, and now the man who'd done his dirty work could tell no tales to the jury.

"I'll have to arrest the jailer," she said after a long pause. Haughton peered at Bazin's fingernails, always spotless before his night in the dungeon but now rimmed with black. "I can't allow this scheme to unfold unimpeded. If the jailer won't confess, perhaps imprisoning him will force his master's hand."

"Perhaps he will confess."

She didn't hold out too much hope of that. "John Dacus is looking for Rosie the prostitute."

"You think she knows more than she said?"

"I think it's entirely possible that she's already been killed for what she knows," said Ela softly. "I pray that isn't the case, but if it is, then perhaps her death will lay a trail of footprints to her killer."

Done with his examination, Haughton pulled the winding sheet up over Bazin's head. "Have the jailer guarded by someone you trust. Or he may find himself going the route of Noel Bazin."

"Whoever is behind these deaths is callous enough to destroy all evidence, human or otherwise."

"And have a care for yourself, my lady."

"Indeed I shall."

~

"Arrest the jailer?" Deschamps's eyebrows shot up. "Whatever for?"

"Noel Bazin died on his watch. The coroner says his death was from injuries sustained in a violent fall. As you witnessed, the jailer insists that he was the only man present in the dungeon that night—aside from the other prisoners chained to the walls and out of reach of Bazin. Therefore the jailer must be the killer."

Deschamps attempted a grim smile. "Impossible, my lady. Wilf Baldric has been jailer here in Salisbury for nigh on fifteen years. I'd trust him with my own life."

"Arrest him." Would he continue to argue with her? As castellan of Salisbury and Sheriff of Wiltshire she was his superior and he had a duty to obey her.

"And put him where?" Deschamps continued to look incredulous and like he had no intention of following her orders.

"I've asked my co-sheriff to prepare a strong room for him. The location shall be kept secret for now."

"In the castle?" Deschamps's beady dark eyes unnerved her.

"Have him arrested immediately and brought to the hall. A jury has already been summoned to question him." She spoke slowly, her calm voice hiding the fire inside her. If he defied her again she'd have to pull rank. If he wanted a fight, she'd give it to him.

Perhaps he read danger in her gaze, because he mumbled, "As you wish, my lady," and walked away issuing orders.

That rattled him. Ela watched his back recede with some satisfaction. She planned to watch him like a hawk for any signs of weakness. Still, she didn't dare even hint to the jury that her main suspect in the killings was Deschamps. Such an accusation would be so explosive that it might destroy her if she didn't have irrefutable evidence of his guilt.

ELA SUMMONED Bill Talbot to her private writing room. "I have a task for you, if you're willing."

"If God is willing to give me the strength, I shall do any task you request of me."

"I've asked Deschamps to arrest the jailer who presided over Bazin's death. I believe this jailer struck the fatal blow. I also believe he did it in the employ of another, and I'm worried that his master may try to kill him as well."

"To destroy evidence of his crimes."

"Exactly. So rather than having him down in the dismal and inscrutable depths of the dungeon, where he might meet with an unfortunate end in the dark without anyone knowing what happened, I'd like him contained in the room at the top of the old tower."

"The one with no window?"

"Exactly. The floor and walls are stone more than six feet thick. He can't escape, and no one can get in. I'd like to ask you to guard him personally until we can assess his role in Bazin's death."

"I shall guard him with my life."

"And you should certainly take pains to protect your life. Be armed at all times." She leaned in close because there was no way to know if there was an ear pressed to the door. "It's possible that Deschamps is behind these killings. He controls the guards. Don't assume that they're on our side."

"Deschamps?" He blinked. "He's served here in Salisbury on and off almost as long as I have."

"Then perhaps he rankles in his inferior role after such long service."

Bill looked like she'd struck him over the head with a fire iron. "He's entrusted with the king's garrison."

"And Hubert de Burgh was entrusted with running the country during the king's minority." She didn't have to say aloud that de Burgh was a murderer. She'd shared her suspicions with Bill on the sworn promise that he'd never breathe a word of them to her children or anyone else.

Bill glanced at the door, ever conscious of the ears that might be listening. Ela knew she'd spoken low enough for privacy. Still, her accusations were every bit as dangerous to herself as to the men she accused.

"Why am I cursed to have the most powerful men in the land as my enemies?" she asked, half in jest.

"Why would Deschamps want to kill the merchant or Bazin?"

Ela rankled that Bill still found her accusation outrageous. "At risk of sounding conceited, I strongly suspect that his core motivation is in undermining my authority and removing me as sheriff."

Bill stared.

"Bazin set the fire and I suspect he tampered with the chess set. I don't know who chiseled the stone that fell on your head, but I assume it's part of the same set of calculated maneuvers designed to foment unease and distress among us. Since Bazin's sudden death and Deschamps's anxiety to declare it an accident, I now see Deschamps as the master-mind behind these events."

"You think Deschamps killed Bazin himself?"

"I suppose that is possible, but I think it more likely that he paid the jailer to do the deed for him. Hence my locking him up."

"With no proof?"

"What can I do? I can't ignore a murder that happens under my roof. The townspeople are already whispering about the man who was murdered on top of my castle wall. If I don't act swiftly and decisively they'll say I'm too soft because I'm a woman."

Ela hated to arrest anyone without solid proof, but in this case hesitancy could prove fatal. "If the jailer is arrested perhaps he'll talk."

"I doubt it. He's been here as long as Deschamps."

"But they're not equals. The jailer spends his days and nights in a dark, dripping cavern, while Deschamps sips wine with the gentry. There may be an element of resentment there that we can exploit."

Bill pondered this. "You want me to press him?"

"Start by observing him. See if you can get to know him and understand something about his motivations. All we need is a crack where the truth can shine through."

"We need proof."

"Or a reliable witness," said Ela.

"Or someone who'll betray the confidence of his master." Bill frowned. "I'd give my life before I betrayed you."

"I know that, but these men are greedy and driven by pride and a lust for power. Their base motivations make them vulnerable."

"Noel Bazin was clearly more vulnerable than he anticipated."

"And the jailer likewise. I don't want him to be found

mysteriously dead in the morning, which is why I want him under your watchful eyes and not those of the palace guards."

"Indeed. Those same guards watched over the wall while a murder was committed."

"They may even be witnesses or know more than they've admitted, but until the first wall is breached there's no way to get any of them to confess anything. They form a tight phalanx around their lord and defend him as he undermines my authority and plots my demise."

Much as she hated to utter the words aloud, she had to admit that this was the only set of motivations that made any real sense. "I suspect that the merchant had some valuable item that Deschamps wanted, possibly to help pave his path to power. Bishop Poore spoke of a precious ruby. If we can find the object in his possession that would provide evidence of his involvement in Ziyad al Wahid's murder."

"Can you order his rooms searched?" Talbot looked doubtful.

Ela shook her head. "Not without solid reason for suspicion. As you've said, he's too entrenched and entrusted. To root him out I'll have to extract a confession from the jailer or the guards, or find evidence of theft."

"At least there are several roads to the truth."

"Each one more winding than a Scottish mountain pass."

CHAPTER 18

*E*la slept fitfully that night, tossing and turning under her covers, the room unusually warm. The fire had left her uneasy. That someone she'd trusted—who'd come highly recommended—could have set fire to her castle and endangered lives was deeply unsettling.

And his master—his hands now red with blood—still walked free. What fresh havoc might be wrought tonight and discovered in the morning?

And she'd be blamed because as sheriff and castellan it was her job to maintain order at Salisbury castle and throughout all of Wiltshire. Even she agreed that failure to do so lay at her own feet.

After her morning rounds and a quick breakfast Ela resolved to press Safiya about any items valuable enough to have provoked her husband's murder. The girl had not come down to breakfast, so Ela walked up to her room and rapped on the door. "It's Ela. May I come in?"

"Yes."

Ela was disappointed to see Safiya tearful again. She'd hoped that she was coming to grips with her widowhood, but her red-rimmed eyes said otherwise. Ela put aside her headful of practical plans and laid a hand on Safiya's shoulder. "The nights are hard, I know."

"I heard his voice last night." Safiya's voice trembled.

"Your husband?" She knew it was impossible.

Safiya nodded, her eyes filled with tears. "I heard it as clear as your voice speaking to me."

"You must have been dreaming."

"I swear I was awake. I could hear him through the open window."

Ela frowned. "What did he say?"

"He said to find the precious jewel. The hidden jewel. I don't know what he was talking about. I've been through every drawer in the wagon, and there's nothing like that."

Ela walked over to the window. The leaded glass window pane was propped open and held in place by its iron latch. She opened it further and looked down toward the ground. They were on the second floor, above a passageway that led to the garden courtyard.

"Did you come to look out the window?"

Safiya shuddered involuntarily. "No! I'd be terrified to see his ghost."

Ela reflected that she wouldn't mind an encounter with the well-intentioned ghost of her own late husband. Not that she believed in such things.

"So you didn't look out the window?"

"I hid under the covers."

Ela peered down to the cobbles below. "I suspect someone climbed a ladder and spoke right under your window."

Safiya looked blank. "Why?"

"To put the idea in your head to look for a jewel. Perhaps it's someone who has reason to think there's great treasure among your husband's possessions that hasn't been found yet."

"Who would do such a thing?"

Ela hesitated. She didn't want to burden Safiya with her suspicions about a conspiracy involving Deschamps, Bazin, the jailer, the guards on the wall, and who knows how many other people. Such knowledge could endanger the girl's life. But still...

"It seems somewhat likely that your husband was killed over a precious item that a greedy man hoped to obtain without payment. Bishop Poore mentioned a magnificent ruby. Perhaps the murderer had killed Ziyad assuming it was on his person, then was disappointed to find that it wasn't."

"My husband never, ever carried valuables on him when he was away from our wagon."

"His killer may not have known that."

"But I went through all the contents with Sir William Talbot, and then again by myself. The gemstones are all smaller, strung beads and the like, nothing very valuable. They must have got the item, ruby or otherwise."

"If they had, they wouldn't be hanging on a ladder outside your window, attempting to imitate your husband's voice." The perpetrator must have showed a degree of cunning as, despite his good English, Ziyad still had a strong accent.

"It sounded just like him."

"The voice startled you from deep sleep. It's easy to be deceived in that state."

Who could have climbed the ladder? Might it be Deschamps himself?

"From now on, sleep with your window closed and latched despite the warm nights. And, while it may pain you,

I believe we must take your wagon apart, stick by stick, back to the bare axles."

"To look for hidden goods?"

"Exactly."

~

TRUSTED guards watched over the wagon under the faithful eyes of Albert the porter, so Ela was fairly certain no one had been able to ransack it where it stood in the courtyard between the great archway and the entrance to the hall. Still, she wanted it somewhere yet more private and guarded, away from the prying eyes of Deschamps—or whoever was behind all this—and his henchmen.

"Please have the donkey hitched to the cart and bring it around to the orchard yard." This walled garden lay along the inside of the castle's outer wall, its fruit trees protected from the stiff winds that raked the castle mound. It had doors at both ends, to protect the fruit from thieves, and would be easy to defend from unwanted eyes and light fingers.

Ela chose four guards who were not part of Deschamps's garrison but owed their allegiance entirely to Ela's family. She asked them to keep out any and all intruders, even the king himself if he asked, and to refuse entry to anyone at all unless they were in her company.

Then she employed her sons Richard and Stephen, with chisels and prybars and all the curiosity and energy of two bright young boys, to pick the wagon apart. They started by pulling back the canopy, which felt almost like peeling back a skin, exposing the highly decorated and formerly private interior to the harsh light of day.

Safiya—who Ela wanted to watch the entire proceedings closely—cringed as they pried the first set of drawers from the floor with a crowbar. The contents of the drawers had been safely removed and stored in Ela's strong room until such time as they could be sold to provide for Safiya's future.

The drawers stacked to one side, the boys went to work on the elaborate carved bed and a chest for storing clothes, all cleverly mortised to the existing structure.

"Take every single thing apart," said Ela. "If a piece of wood is as thick as a finger it could have a compartment in it that might hold a king's ransom in rubies."

They set to the built-in furniture with saws and chisels, and soon the entire wagon was reduced to a pile of sticks. Petronella came along to see why no one had come to Nones service and pointed out that the axles themselves were thick enough to contain goods.

Ela thought Safiya might collapse in a heap as Stephen sawed through the solid oak of the first axle, rendering the entire wagon beyond repair.

"It's hollow."

They all rushed over. "How could a hollow axle support all this weight?" asked Ela, before she could even see it.

"There's a narrow channel drilled through the middle," said Richard, peering at it. "Like the hole in the middle of a gemstone. And look, there's something in here."

Further excavations produced a treasure trove of small but valuable pearls and emeralds, both raw and polished, lined up in the hollow compartment in the middle of the axel. They must have been dropped in—one by one—from one end and then the whole sealed and fixed to the wheels. The second axle at first appeared to be solid, but minute examination revealed a portion had been chiseled away and then replaced with a massive polished ruby inside it.

Ela held the ruby, almost the size of a plum, in the palm of her hand. "I cannot begin to imagine how much this stone is worth. It's fit for a king."

"Safiya said that Ziyad was a favorite of the court," said Petronella.

This didn't surprise Ela. "I wonder who knew of this ruby, other than Bishop Poore, who was told of it but never saw it. I'd imagine Ziyad would keep such a precious prize very secret."

"He kept it a secret from me," admitted Safiya quietly. "And I don't blame him because I would have been afraid to sleep over such a prize."

"Your husband was a wealthy man," said Ela to Safiya. "Did he deal with bankers or own property?" It was hard to imagine the man who she'd previously seen as an itinerant peddler—albeit a successful one—in possession of such a fortune.

"No. He believed in reinvesting his profits into goods. I wore any unused coins under my gown, as you saw. He didn't trust anyone."

Ela wondered if Ziyad had planned to retire on the proceeds of this one voyage, which—if successful—would have left him with enough gold to build himself a retreat to rival the Moorish palace in Granada, where he could live with Safiya and sire a large brood.

"This stone, and the others, will secure your future should you live to be a hundred."

Safiya didn't look either pleased or relieved. "If my husband died because of these stones I want nothing to do with them."

Ela didn't argue with her but arranged for her sons and two of the guards to escort them to the strong room and secure them firmly.

Despite her efforts at secrecy, Ela suspected it wouldn't take long before word would spread around the castle that new treasure had been found.

∼

THEY SET the shredded remains of the wagon alight in the orchard yard. The smoke attracted conversation, and Ela hoped it would reach the nostrils of the men who hoped to profit from killing Ziyad.

She told all her allies to listen carefully for any talk about the gems, even curious gossip. And she encouraged them to make up tales about the jewels that would make men's eyes light up and draw any villains out into the light.

"Don't we have to place the jewels where someone can hope to snatch them?" Bill Talbot was taking a brief respite from his tiresome work of guarding the jailer, who'd remained almost completely mute and yielded no useful information.

"As a baited trap?" asked Ela. "It had better be a trap with a tight spring." She'd had the same thought but struggled to come up with a plan that didn't risk losing both the gems and the thief.

"I imagine that you need to get the gems valued," said Bill. "Why not call a jeweler to the palace to perform the task—in the great hall—then arrange a distraction that will give a thief the opportunity to steal it. He'll think he's unobserved, but at that moment myself or John Dacus will accuse him before all of Salisbury.

"Our would-be thief is a ruthless killer. This plot would put your lives in danger."

"Our lives are already in danger while this miscreant stalks the halls. I'd feel safer in hand-to-hand combat with the villain than I would waiting for him to jump out from behind a column."

"I suppose that having a plan gives us at least the chance at an upper hand. And the gems do need to be valued, though I'd prefer to do it in the safety of the strong room."

"That room is too small, and the hall too large and easy to escape. I think the armory would serve us best."

"All those weapons…is that really safe?"

"Sir John and I are knights of the realm. We are never safer than with sharp weapons at hand."

Ela inhaled sharply. She didn't want to insult Bill or hurt his feelings by pointing out that his reflexes might not be what they once were. "What if it isn't Deschamps? What if it's someone totally unexpected?"

"That would be a blessed relief. I don't relish the prospect of going to war with Deschamps, and I'm sure you don't either."

"I trust you to make arrangements with John Dacus that you'll keep each other safe and protect the gemstones."

"We won't let you down."

ELA'S NERVES jangled as they spread Safiya's future wealth out on the table in the armory a few days later. The man they'd hired for the valuation was Moses of Bracknell, a well-respected gem dealer who wouldn't risk his reputation on trying to cheat her.

Moses watched closely as they unwrapped the bundles and purses of the various gems and strings of beads. He used a piece of glass to peer more closely at the items and spoke the values—or at least that was what Ela suspected he was saying—in Hebrew to a boy who scratched them down on a piece of parchment.

"Is this your son?" asked Ela, watching the boy's keen attention and careful hand.

"Indeed it is, my lady. Abraham will one day take over my business so he must learn it from the bottom up."

"I completely agree," said Ela. "I try to involve my sons in all aspects of my affairs as well. Stephen and Richard helped to gather all these gems, some of which were very carefully concealed."

"They're a credit to you," said Moses. "This ruby in particular is worth a great deal." He picked up the stone that had enjoyed its own cart axle. Its deep color reminded her of new wine. "More than all the other goods put together." He spoke the value to the boy.

"How much?"

Moses regarded her for a moment as if he wasn't sure he should share such critical information.

"Safiya must know. She's the merchant's widow." Ela gestured to where Safiya stood mutely in the corner. "Her future depends on us getting a good price for these gems."

He glanced at Safiya, then back at Ela. "I'd value it at seven hundred pounds, if the right buyer can be found."

Ela's breath caught for a moment. "Is there a buyer other than the king who'd covet such a costly treasure?"

"Oh, yes." He looked amused. "Some London merchants are far richer than the king."

Ela blinked. She'd been surprised at the great wealth the modest Ziyad had carried with him. She'd always seen land as wealth, but perhaps movable goods allowed for a faster accumulation of profits. She'd have to ponder this as she planned her own affairs in the future.

The doors to the armory had been deliberately left open during the valuation. In addition to Bill and John Dacus, Ela's older sons both arrived, followed closely by Deschamps and several of his men, who took up positions near the table as if they were guarding the jewels.

Ela's heart beat faster, and she said a quick prayer that this gamble would pay off and not end in disaster.

When he'd valued all but a few less interesting trinkets, Ela decided it was time to make her planned move. She launched into a bout of feigned coughing that caused every head in the room to turn toward her.

"Oh dear, I'm taken ill." She swayed on her feet. They'd planned for Richard and Stephen to escort her to her room, causing enough of a commotion that the thief would make his move.

But instead Gerald Deschamps strode forward, swept Ela up in his arms, and barked for everyone to clear the way to the door.

CHAPTER 19

*D*eschamps's arms closed around Ela like the bands on a barrel, and she fought the urge to kick and scream. Once outside the armory, she summoned every bit of calm and composure she had in her, and said—as slowly as she could manage—"Put me down."

"I'm taking you to your solar, my lady." His strength surprised her. He carried her as if she were a newborn babe. "You shall rest in your bed, and your maid can bring smelling salts and revive you." His eyes glittered as they headed into the passageway that led to the stairs up to her solar.

Fear prickled over her. She didn't want to be alone in there with him.

"I can walk there myself, I'm quite recovered." Ela wasn't sure that he didn't have something up his sleeve, like tripping and falling hard on the stairs with her in his arms, or accidentally banging her head against a stone archway. "It was just a coughing fit." She pushed against his oak-hard chest. "I prefer to walk."

"Put my mother down right now," cried Richard. Ela turned her head and was relieved to see her two strong sons

225

close behind them. The willowy boys were almost a head shorter than Deschamps, but the fire in their eyes suggested they were ready to go after him like David after Goliath.

"Goodness, young man. Anyone would think I was trying to steal her away."

Deschamps eased Ela to her feet, which hit the stone flags gratefully.

"What put you in mind of stealing, Sir Gerald?" asked Ela coolly, as she struggled to regain her composure. She thought it an odd turn of phrase under the circumstances. No doubt he also had a plan to create a diversion so that one of his henchmen could grab a valuable item while he was away from all possibility of guilt and accusation.

Ela had learned that the dirtiest and darkest villains often hid behind others. They were also the hardest to accuse and convict, especially if they were quick to kill their own accomplices and witnesses.

Who had he used to commit the crime?

"I feel fully recovered. I shall return to the armory."

Deschamps protested forcefully, as she had expected. Still, without laying hands on her again, he couldn't prevent her.

Flanked by her indignant sons, Ela turned and marched back to the armory, where—not unexpectedly—chaos reigned.

One man lay prone on the floor just inside the door, with Bill Talbot's foot on his back. Ela couldn't see his face, but he wore the uniform of a garrison soldier.

"This man snatched the big ruby," growled Talbot. "Bold as brass." He tilted his head to the far corner of the room, where John Dacus stood over another man with his hands trussed behind his back. "And that one seized a fistful of the pearls."

Ela turned to see Deschamps's reaction, but he was nowhere to be seen. He must have slipped away, no doubt to distance himself from the scene of the crime. "Call a jury immediately," she cried. "And clap these men in irons so they can't escape."

～

SEVERAL JURORS ARRIVED SHORTLY after the hue and cry was raised. Servants arranged three long trestle tables into a U shape so they could all sit around the accused. The great hall hummed with excitement and outrage that such a daring robbery had been attempted under the nose of the castle guards—by the castle guards.

The jewel appraiser was forced to stay as a witness, as was Safiya. The jailer was brought down from his solitary confinement, partly just to make sure that nothing mysterious happened to him while Bill Talbot was busy elsewhere.

Once the thieves were secured in the hall, Talbot and Dacus oversaw the packing of the jewels and other valuables and made sure that all were accounted for and stored safely back in the strong room.

Ela summoned Safiya to sit in a chair at her right hand. John Dacus then sat at her left and Bill Talbot stood behind her. The general din grew so loud that Bill had to shout to shush the crowd into silence so Ela could start the proceedings.

"Who here was a witness to the theft of the ruby?" she asked.

"I saw this man take it," said Bill gruffly, gesturing at a burly man with light brown hair and squinty pale eyes. "I had my eyes on him already and saw his hand dart out. He had a special fold in his tunic prepared to hide the stone, and it disappeared so fast that if I hadn't been waiting for him to take it I'd never have seen it."

"What is your name?" Ela demanded of him.

"Thomas Belcher," he choked out. His teeth started to chatter.

"Why did you take it?" Ela peered at the man. She now recognized him as one of the guards who'd failed to prevent Ziyad's murder up on the wall.

"I wanted to sell it," said the man in a faint voice.

She didn't believe him. "Who did you plan to sell it to?"

The man blinked and his lips worked. "I don't know yet."

"You stole it for someone, didn't you?" Unable to sit still in her chair, Ela rose and walked around the tables, then approached him where he stood in the middle with his hands and legs chained together.

He swayed slightly as she approached. "He won't save you now," she said coldly. "Do you plan to hang for him?" She looked around, searching for Deschamps. "What does your master have to say about this? Where is Gerald Deschamps?" Her voice boomed out above the crowd.

Deschamps was nowhere to be seen. Ela sent trusted guards to find him and bring him to the hall, on the understanding that he was needed because two of his garrison soldiers were in trouble.

"What prize were you promised to commit this despicable act of theft? That ruby is worth more than you'll earn in your entire life. You'll almost certainly hang for the crime."

The man's knees buckled and a muscle worked in his jaw.

"But perhaps leniency can be arranged if you're honest enough to point your finger at the man you stole it for."

The man flinched, and Ela followed his gaze to see Deschamps striding into the hall through the main doors, face black as a thunderstorm.

Ela turned to face Deschamps. "Two of your men have been caught stealing valuables from the merchant's stores." She watched his face, which remained impassive, though his eyes shone with what might be fury. "What do you have to say about this?"

"They must be punished." He spoke flatly. "As their commander I will deal with them. Let them be brought to the dungeons at once."

Where you can kill them before they talk. "No, they shall reveal all in front of the assembled jurors," said Ela curtly. "They stole these gems on the instructions of someone else." She looked into his eyes. "And I intend to learn who that person is."

She watched as Deschamps shot a glance at each man. What had he promised them? Did he reassure them that he'd arrange their freedom if they got caught? That each would receive a payment which would allow him to retire in ease?

"It was him," said Belcher. He spoke so quietly that Ela asked him to repeat his words.

"It was who?"

"Him." The man jutted his stubbled chin at Deschamps. "Sir Gerald Deschamps. He made me do it, just as he made me turn my back when the merchant was up on the wall."

Ela inhaled a slow and steadying breath. This was going far too well. "Arrest Deschamps," she barked quickly.

No one moved. The guards couldn't conceive of arresting their powerful commander.

"This is nonsense," protested Deschamps. "This fool is trying to save his skin by blaming an innocent man. It's clear that he took it himself. I wasn't even in the room at the time."

"You were certainly keen to have me out of the room as well," said Ela. "Was your abduction of me planned simply to create a distraction or to remove me as a witness?" She looked around, glaring at the guards. "Arrest him!"

"I'll arrest him myself," said Bill. He walked up to Deschamps and locked his arms behind his back in a swift movement.

Ela wasn't sure if Deschamps, a younger and larger man, might fight back. Would the garrison soldiers side with him? Or would they obey their sheriff and countess and take him into custody?

"There's no need for this," Deschamps protested. She could see the roping muscles in his arms through his clothes, as if he itched to break free of Talbot's hold. "It's a misunderstanding. The men of the jury will see that."

The confidence in his voice gave Ela pause. Would they? A silver-tongued villain had talked his way out of a conviction more than once, she imagined. If Deschamps heard the accusations against him he had time to plan a rebuttal. He could also put on a further show of dismayed innocence that might sway the jurors.

She was tempted to put him down in the dungeon and deal with him later.

Still, if there was a moment to seize the truth by the throat, that moment was now.

Ela turned to the guard who said that Deschamps had asked him to turn his back on the wall. "Who killed Ziyad the merchant?"

Belcher snuck a glance at Deschamps, who looked back at him with a face like a stone statue. "I don't know."

"But Deschamps asked you to look away from whatever happened?"

"No. He told us to patrol the north end of the wall because there were reports of someone stealing sheep in the fields below it."

Ela peered at Deschamps. This suggested that the murder was planned. He'd chosen a location and made sure no one was watching. Did Deschamps kill Ziyad himself?

Ela did want him in irons. "Guards, Sir William Talbot should not be holding this prisoner in custody. Bring chains for him."

The guards shuffled their feet and looked at one another, and at Deschamps. Ela's gut churned. Their loyalties still lay with him. "Do it at once." She spoke to one guard in particular, an older man who'd been at the castle for years. The man turned and left the room.

She prayed he'd come back with chains and wasn't sure what she'd do if he didn't.

Then she turned to Deschamps, who now grimaced, likely because of the way Bill held him tight. "Why did you steal the jewels?"

"I didn't." His reply sounded calm and measured.

"You sent your minions to steal them. That is the same as stealing them yourself except that you also condemn another's soul to sin and damnation."

"I have no interest in the trinkets of Ziyad's wagon," said Deschamps.

"Speak only when you're spoken to," she retorted, though gritted teeth. She didn't intend to give him free rein to plead his case. "It's clear from this man's confession and accusation that you did. I suspect that you made an offer to Ziyad for the ruby, then met him up on the wall to seal the deal. There, you killed Ziyad to obtain the ruby without paying for it. When you found that he didn't have the stone on him, you attempted to find it but it was too well hidden."

She walked toward him. "I suspect it was you that climbed up to Safiya's window and pretended to be her husband, urging her to look for the hidden jewel."

A muscle twitched in his jaw.

"Members of the jury, do you see his reaction to this accusation?" She enjoyed a tiny flash of triumph. "I'd imagine that a man in your position has many expenses. You live surrounded by nobles with great fortunes, but you're forced to live off your wages, not the profits of an estate. These last few years of relative peace have perhaps deprived you of the ability to seize riches as spoils of war. Perhaps you found yourself in need of a way to feather your nest?"

Deschamps lips twitched. She could see that he wanted to respond but, having been commanded not to, he knew it would look ill if he did.

"I suspect that your ambitions outstripped your circumstances and you searched for a way to line your purse, even at the cost of your loyalty to the crown and of your immortal soul." She allowed her voice to boom out on the last words.

It occurred to her that he might want money to pay the king. A fine, such as she'd paid herself—might purchase him a better position, possibly as sheriff and castellan either here or somewhere else. Perhaps he even harbored ambitions to be Justiciar of Ireland or some such thing. Men of small means and grand ambition often cut their teeth in the wilds of Ireland, then returned to England in triumph. There were many routes to the top for a man of courage and determination. Hubert de Burgh, the king's justiciar, was an example of how the son of a lowly yeoman could rise to the highest office in the land.

"Men of the jury, please ask your questions of the guards first." She wanted to watch Deschamps stew in his own juices for a while before they questioned him.

Stephen Hale, the cordwainer, cleared his throat and looked at the two arrested guards. "What did Deschamps promise you if you stole the goods from the armory?"

Neither of them responded.

The guard Ela had dispatched returned with heavy, somewhat rusted irons. He placed the wrist cuffs carefully about Deschamps's wrists, looking sheepish as he did it, then secured the ankle cuffs to his feet.

Bill Talbot stepped back, clearly relieved to shed the duty of holding Deschamps in place. Now Talbot walked toward the guards. "You must answer the jurors."

"Money," said the smaller man, who hadn't spoken yet, in a very quiet voice. They'd established at some point that his name was Matthew Diggs. He was a ten-year veteran of the garrison with a flash of silver in his hair.

"Five pounds," said the other.

"That's a great sum," said Ela. "But a paltry fee if the act costs you your life."

The guards both glanced at Deschamps.

"Did you think your master so mighty that no one could touch him?" asked Ela. It wasn't hard to imagine Deschamps thinking that himself.

"He said he'd make sure we weren't arrested," said Belcher.

"He's clearly a liar, as well as a thief." Ela knew she was making bold statements about a man who'd not been either caught in the act or convicted by a jury. "And what of the jailer?" She looked at the heavyset man who'd been confined under lock and key for several days without any admission of guilt. "You can see your master won't be able to save you now. You'd better save yourself with an admission. Did you kill Noel Bazin, the steward, on his orders?"

The jailer's meaty face was unmoving as the standing stones in the old henge.

Loyalty? Or did he know he'd hang either way?

Or maybe he hoped that salvation might gallop in on a black charger...

"Are there others involved in this conspiracy?" Ela asked the guards. "How many of your fellow soldiers have been paid to look aside or to do your master's dirty work?"

Perhaps following the jailer's example, the guards just stared at her, tight-lipped.

Will Dyer, a barrelmaker with a head of shiny black hair, spoke up. "I can understand that a man might kill the merchant for a precious stone, but how does it connect to the steward's death?"

Ela was about to reply, but a glance from John Dacus told her that he wanted to respond. He stood up. "Noel Bazin was employed to sow the seeds of chaos and unrest in the castle. He was a man of mischievous tendencies, and Deschamps exploited that and encouraged him to tamper with the chess set and the garderobe and to start the fire so that he could undermine our sheriff's authority." He shot a stern look at Deschamps. "Perhaps with a view to claiming the role for himself."

"Never!" protested Deschamps, realizing that remaining silent at this point would be an admission of guilt. "My loyalties lie with the king and with his representatives in Wiltshire, our sheriffs."

"Your guards have accused you of planning a theft," said Ela. "Your loyalties have clearly strayed."

"The merchant was dead. Theft of his stone is not akin to murder."

"It is when the murder was planned to achieve it."

"Why would I kill him when I could simply have the stone stolen?"

"You couldn't. Ziyad was too clever for you. He traveled across Europe and beyond with a cart laden with treasure. He knew how to protect his goods so you couldn't take them while he was alive. And then once you killed him, you still couldn't find your prize."

"I didn't kill anyone," protested Deschamps. "No man can say I did."

"Then who killed Ziyad the merchant?" asked Ela.

"His wife, of course."

CHAPTER 20

Ela glanced at Safiya, who paled.

"Your accusation is baseless and offensive," Ela spat at Deschamps.

"Ask others in the castle and the village." Deschamps eyes had a sudden, unpleasant gleam to them. "You'll find they don't like her or trust her."

"They don't know her," retorted Ela. "They never even laid eyes on her until her husband went missing. He kept her hidden in his wagon. She's a victim, not a murderer."

"Or is she?" asked Deschamps, looking at the jurors. "Perhaps she rankled at her small and circumscribed existence and longed to take control of her own destiny."

Out of the corner of her eye, Ela saw Safiya start to tremble. She wished the girl would cry out, like Deschamps, and protest her innocence rather than looking like a cornered rat.

"What do you have to say for yourself, girl?" asked Hugh Clifford, the wine seller.

Safiya stared at him for a moment, then crumpled to the floor.

Safiya's fainting fit forced Ela to bring the session to a close. She could see that the line of inquiry had gone astray and once again, Safiya was being baited as quarry to deflect from the real villains.

With some trepidation, she ordered for all of them— Deschamps, the jailer, and the two thieves—to be put down in the dungeon and chained to the wall. Then she carefully chose two of her most faithful men to guard them all and not allow them to exchange as much as a single word on pain of being whipped bloody.

Alone with Bill Talbot in her solar, she paced the floor anxiously. "I must send word to the king at once that the commander of his garrison stands accused of theft and murder."

"I doubt he'll take it well," mused Bill. "Nor de Burgh, who was no doubt instrumental in placing him in the role."

"I know. But you and John Dacus witnessed the theft and the thieves accused him. The evidence against him is plain."

"Indeed it is," said Bill.

"But?"

Bill didn't respond, except with a ragged sigh.

Ela, assured that the king was at Windsor, sent her fastest messenger to inform him of events at the castle and to assure him that she had the matter well in hand. Deschamps would have to be tried by the traveling justice at the assizes since he stood accused of a capital crime.

In the meantime the garrison needed a new commander. Ela took the liberty of making three suggestions, all close allies and friends of her late husband. She prayed the new commander wouldn't prove to be a worse thorn in her side than Deschamps.

She waited somewhat anxiously for three days, hoping for a reply that would soothe. John Dacus stood in the role of Deschamps, but it was clearly an uncomfortable one for him. Though a knight, he didn't have the warlike disposition that impressed men at arms and Ela wasn't sure how well they'd respect his authority in a crisis.

Around midmorning on the third day, a guard on the hall spotted banners flying in the distance, amid a cloud of dust from thundering hooves. The castle stirred into action, and Ela herself climbed quickly to the top of the outer wall to get an early look at the man coming to command the troops in her castle.

The bright banners and shiny helmets glittered in the sunlight, and she couldn't make out the heraldic arms until they were almost at her gates.

"Oh, no." The words fled her mouth before she could stop them.

"Who is it?" Bill stood at her side. "My eyesight isn't what it used to be."

Ela's chest tightened, and she fought the urge to cry out with shock. "It's Hubert de Burgh."

BY THE TIME de Burgh and his entourage clattered into the courtyard, Ela had made her way back into the great hall. She took up her seat on her dais, ready to greet her enemy with all the composure she could summon.

Bill hovered nervously nearby and the servants rushed about, readying for the large company of guests about to arrive.

Ela regretted her gentle upbringing and her sex at this

moment. How she'd love to challenge de Burgh to a fight to the death, right here and now in the hall.

But he was the king's closest advisor and likely here on the king's business, so such aggression—even if it were feasible—would seal death warrants for her and likely all of her children.

Discretion is the better part of valor.

She'd heard as much muttered under the breath of her father, her mother, and even her husband, who never shrank from a battle he could win.

She debated whether to rise as Albert announced her foe and ushered him into the hall. No. She remained seated and waited for him to approach, glad of her decision as he wound his way slowly across the hall greeting others before her as if she were just another occupant of the king's garrison.

"Ah, my lady Ela," he said at last, as if surprised to see her here, in her own hall. He approached, bowed low, and took her hand.

Ela fought the urge to snatch it back or slap his bony cheek with it. She tried to force a pleasant—or at least neutral—expression to her face.

"Good afternoon, my lord de Burgh. What brings you to Salisbury?"

He looked at her as if to say, *I think we both know the answer to that question.* "Why, the urgent matter of managing the king's garrison, of course. It appears that Salisbury is in disarray, and I'm here to restore order. Won't you sit down?"

Ela seethed but did retake her seat. "You'll find that order has been restored by the arrest of the garrison commander, who had embarked on a rampage of murder and thievery, employing the men under his command to commit his foul deeds."

De Burgh studied her for a moment, then one side of his

mouth lifted slightly. "Come now, my lady. Gerald Deschamps has served king and country with honor and valor all his life. There is a misunderstanding and I shall get to the bottom of it."

"There is no misunderstanding," hissed Ela. "Sir William Talbot and my co-sheriff John Dacus were witnesses to the theft he attempted against a guest of my household."

"A theft committed by two common soldiers. Simple men apt to be swayed by the sight of a glittering object."

"These simple men admitted, in front of a jury, that Deschamps had paid them to take the jewels."

"Of course they did." He pinned her with his beady gaze. "They wished to shuck the noose from around their necks and place it around a more powerful one. I daresay many men would do the same in their place."

"Since you seem to know some details of the case, I'm sure you're aware that the merchant who owned the gems was murdered in cold blood on the wall of my castle, while Deschamps's men were ordered to keep watch over an empty field on the other side of the castle."

"You accuse Deschamps of murdering him?"

"A witness saw a man in a black cloak accompany the victim up to the wall."

De Burgh lifted a brow. "Half the men in England own a black cloak. And where is this witness?"

Ela drew in a steadying breath. Despite John Dacus hunting high and low, Rosie had disappeared and no one had seen hide nor hair of her. "The witness, a popular resident of this town"—this was not a lie—"has disappeared without warning and vanished so completely that I begin to suspect she has also been murdered."

"A prostitute." He spat the word as if it tasted foul in his mouth. "You can hardly believe the word of a woman who lives by sin."

"She had no reason to lie." Ela wondered who had filled de Burgh in on all these details of the case.

"But she didn't identify Deschamps as the killer, did she?"

"No, that is true, but it's likely that he used a proxy to commit the crime in order to keep his hands clean. He did as much when he killed my steward, whom he'd employed to create acts of mischief, including setting fire to my kitchens."

De Burgh had the temerity to look amused. "Why would your steward set fire to the kitchens? Such a thing makes no sense."

To create chaos and undermine my authority. She wasn't going to give him that on a platter. "I daresay Deschamps paid him to do so for his own reasons."

"I wish to speak to Deschamps." He spoke calmly as if he'd asked for a cup of wine.

"You may speak with him in my hall if there is a jury present." Ela didn't intend to give him an opportunity to make a secret deal with her captive. "We can summon one for tomorrow morning."

"I can't wait that long. The matter is urgent. I must restore the leadership of the king's garrison."

Ela couldn't believe this. "Do my ears deceive me, or did you just state an intent to set my prisoner free?"

"You have no evidence of his guilt, and he's needed to manage the king's men." De Burgh removed his gloves as if getting ready to relax and settle in.

Ela stood, towering over him on her dais. "By my authority as High Sheriff of Wiltshire I insist that the prisoner remain in the dungeon until he can be tried at the assizes. Any communication between him and yourself must happen here in my hall under the watchful eyes of a jury or not at all."

Ela saw a vein rise in de Burgh's forehead. "You are only sheriff and castellan for one year."

Ela swallowed. This was true. She'd paid the hefty fine of five hundred pounds for that one precious year in the hope that once she could get her foot back in the castle door and take up the reins as sheriff she could prove to the king that she was the right person for the job.

De Burgh peered up at her. "It's clear that your castle is in disarray, with two unsolved murders, an arson fire, stones tumbling from your archway, and a girl falling down the garderobe—not to mention an infidel living under your roof. Perhaps the merchant's mysterious and taciturn wife is the true source of all these woes? Regardless, this castle is being mismanaged and should soon be back in capable hands."

His insults stung. *Who is your source?* How did de Burgh know this much? Had Deschamps filled him in on all the troubles in the castle?

"This unrest has been deliberately sowed."

"Surely that in itself is a problem. If you were in charge of your castle and respected by its denizens, such a thing would be impossible."

"I am in charge of my castle, and I have solved the murders. They were commanded by Deschamps, who no doubt masterminded the other mischief that's plagued us."

De Burgh lifted his chin and fixed her with a withering glare. "You are wrong."

Am I? His confidence forced her to consider the possibility. "Then who, pray tell, is behind all this?"

It's you.

The realization struck her with thunderbolt force. Deschamps had boldly bribed the guards and flouted the rules, even burning her castle, because he trusted in the protection of a powerful master.

More powerful even than the sheriff.

De Burgh had put him up to this.

He wants revenge.

241

It wasn't enough that de Burgh had murdered her husband, he still rankled at her refusal to bend to his will and marry his feckless nephew, and now he planned to destroy her—one way or another.

"I must ask you to leave my castle." The words chilled her as they left her lips. She knew their import. They were a declaration of war.

"This castle is the king's garrison. As the king's justiciar I have a commanding role here, especially since the garrison commander is wrongfully imprisoned in your dungeon."

He refused to leave. Could she force him to? Or would she be the one taken from here in chains?

This is a very dangerous game.

She held her ground. "I shall order my guards to remove you."

His mouth twitched. "Your guards are members of the king's garrison and are thus under my command."

"They are under my command as castellan." She turned to the nearest guards, who all listened with rapt attention. The entire hall had fallen so quiet you could have heard a fart. Ela knew that all eyes were on her and that what happened next would determine whether she managed to keep her authority and her role as sheriff. "Guards, please escort the king's justiciar to the gates and help him find his way back to the London road. Ensure that he does *not* see the prisoners or have any contact with them by letter or otherwise."

The guards stepped forward. She sensed their hesitation —would they have to seize the kings' justiciar and forcibly remove him from the palace? They might wonder if that could open them up to a charge of treason. It was a true test of their loyalty.

But they passed it.

As the guards drew closer, de Burgh turned back toward the main door into the hall. He walked a few steps—rather slowly—then turned. "You error in judgment will cost you dearly, my lady."

"It is no error, and the justice at the assizes shall determine guilt or innocence according to the laws of the land." *Which you are quick to bend to your own ends.*

This would cost her, though. One way or another. There was no doubt of that.

CHAPTER 21

*N*o sooner had de Burgh and his henchmen ridden off, Ela asked John Dacus to urgently determine the whereabouts of the king. Since de Burgh was his closest advisor and traveled with him, he might well be close by. She must visit him immediately, preferably before de Burgh had time to plead his case.

Henry spent much time in Westminster, but Ela knew he'd lately been expanding and embellishing his palace at Clarendon, less than three miles east of Salisbury. If he was there, she could seek an audience with him at once.

Dacus rushed back with the news that the king was indeed at Clarendon.

God is with me, thought Ela, who'd already dressed in finery and prepared herself for an audience with the king on the off chance that he might be nearby. *God knows I seek only to do his work in Salisbury.*

She left John Dacus to keep watch over the castle, the prisoners, and the guards—who might have allies of Deschamps or de Burgh in their ranks, and mounted Freya. Bill Talbot rode at her side, along with eight faithful guards.

Ela's knees trembled slightly as she alighted from Freya in the courtyard at Clarendon. The palace bustled with activity, and servants hefted two fat sides of ham from a cart as she stood waiting to enter.

The tall, studded oak doors opened, and she and her entourage passed into a great hall, smaller than her own but with the walls plastered smooth and painted in bright colors.

"Ela, Countess of Salisbury," boomed the porter's voice.

"I wish to speak with the king in private," said Ela with all the calm and authority she could muster. "About a very urgent matter relating to his garrison troops."

Men hurried back and forth, speaking in low tones, and a page ushered her forward, with Bill following close behind her. They passed through the hall and out into a bright courtyard ringed by fruit trees in stone planters, then into another airy room with colorful patterns painted on the walls and ceiling.

Ela found herself glancing nervously around, looking for de Burgh. Had he rushed here before her to plead for Deschamps's freedom? She didn't see him anywhere. She saw the young king across the room, wiping his hands on a fresh linen cloth proffered by an attendant. He handed the cloth back and turned to her with a smile.

"Dear Ela, so good to see you."

Ela reflected that if he was so delighted by her company he might have sent word that he was coming to Clarendon and invited her to call on him. But perhaps it was awkward for a man—especially a young, unmarried one—to send for a widowed woman with no husband or father to escort her.

She muttered the usual greetings, then took a deep breath. "I'm here about Gerald Deschamps."

"Oh?" He gestured for her to walk toward a seating area near the fireplace. There was no fire due to the warmth of the season. "Let us sit."

"I'd prefer to discuss the matter in private if possible." The hall held at least two dozen people and, with the fashions of the day tending toward plainness, it could be hard to tell a noble from a well-turned-out servant. For all she knew the people around them could be spies of de Burgh.

Henry frowned, then sighed. Then, to Ela's relief, he led her through an arched doorway into a small, surprisingly cold chamber just off the great hall. "An unpleasant closet of a room, I'm afraid, but it does offer protection from prying ears." Bill Talbot followed them in and then closed the door.

"You speak of the garrison commander?" The king gestured for her to sit.

She would have rather stood, since nervous energy clawed at her, but the young king might be too polite to sit until she did so she lowered herself onto an intricately carved wooden chair. "Yes. You received my missive about his arrest, I presume."

"His arrest?" Henry's eyes widened.

"You didn't get my letter? I sent it some days ago." She was sure the arrival of her letter had—unfortunately—summoned de Burgh to her hall.

"I've had no letter from you. What do you mean, his arrest?"

Ela inhaled a long, slow breath. The king's closest companion and most trusted advisor had kept him in the dark. She must be careful not to tread on the king's pride as she revealed this. "Deschamps was discovered to be behind the theft of a most precious jewel and is also suspected of murdering the merchant who owned it and then ordering the killing of my steward."

Henry stared at her like she'd grown another eye. "Gerald Deschamps? Who's commanded the garrison for years?"

"It's come as a terrible surprise to us at the castle. But Sir

William Talbot and my co-sheriff, John Dacus, are both witnesses to the plot that unfurled under my roof. I had no choice but to confine Deschamps to the dungeon along with two guards and a jailer whom he hired to do his foul deeds for him."

King Henry glanced at Bill Talbot, then back to Ela. "I must speak to de Burgh about this. He left here to return to Westminster this morning."

Ela's gut clenched. "Hubert de Burgh visited me at my castle this morning. If you were not in receipt of my letter, which I sent to Westminster on the understanding that you were there, it's likely because he intercepted it and decided to handle the matter himself." She watched his reaction carefully.

"De Burgh is charged with handling affairs that I need not trouble myself with—" Henry frowned. "But I'm surprised he wouldn't mention something so serious as a charge against the garrison commander."

"De Burgh wouldn't even hear the evidence against Deschamps. As you can imagine, all proceedings involving so important a member of our community and our nation were handled in the presence of a jury. Two guards confessed, in front of the jury, that Deschamps hired them to steal gemstones."

She waited a moment for that to sink in. Then she continued. "De Burgh refused to even countenance the charges. He insisted that Deschamps could not possibly be guilty of the crimes and must be freed from the dungeon at once so he could resume his duties as commander of your troops."

Henry's young face took on an odd, taut quality. "This is a very serious charge."

"Indeed it is. And I find I have a murderous villain in

charge of the armed men within my walls, which is an alarming state of affairs. I'm sure you understand that I could not release Deschamps from the dungeon."

"Indeed. He must be tried at the assizes and the justice's decisions shall be final." The king spoke with calm conviction that relieved Ela. "But in the meantime there must be a new garrison commander."

"I propose that Sir William Talbot serve as commander, at least until a suitable candidate can be found." Ela had not discussed this with Bill and she avoided turning to see his reaction. She wasn't sure he'd be too thrilled about this new role, but she dreaded the arrival of some odious new individual who might have his own reasons for freeing Deschamps before his trial.

Henry looked at Bill and nodded, a serious expression on his thin face. "Since he's already installed at the castle and has distinguished himself in battle, I agree. At least until a more permanent decision can be made."

"And—since de Burgh raised the matter—I wish to discuss my continuing in the roles of sheriff and castellan after my first year-long term ends."

"The fine you paid did cover only one year of service as sheriff and castellan." The way he said this suggested that he and de Burgh had recently discussed the possibility of demanding another fine. No doubt de Burgh looked forward to the opportunity to throw her out of her ancestral castle again. Henry probably just wanted more cash to wage campaigns to regain the lands his father had lost in France. "Perhaps we can come to some further arrangement."

Ela did not beat around the bush. "To my initial fine of five hundred pounds I propose adding a further two hundred pounds." She paused to watch his reaction to this sum. His eyes widened slightly. "On the understanding and written agreement that this second fine will secure me the role of castellan in perpetuity, and that I will have the right to assume to role of sheriff as I see fit. I've executed the role with justice and fairness and I am confident that no honest man in Salisbury would argue that point."

She hoped he wouldn't ask these honest men since it was entirely possible that several of them resented the mere existence of a woman managing her own life and fortune, free from the rule of a man. No doubt some of them cursed into their ale that their sheriff was a woman, for no more reason than jealousy and pique.

"I have indeed heard good reports of your work in the role." *Not from de Burgh, I'd wager.* "And on the rare occasions when I've heard whispers of complaint, I've had reason to doubt their legitimacy."

"Complaint?" Ela burned to know who her other enemies might be.

"You rattled the nerves of some members of the clergy with your investigation into the missing children who were found in the care of an abbot."

Ah, Bishop Poore's nose might have been bent out of shape. Especially since he himself was closely associated with the care and grooming of children in the school he'd founded.

"But I commend your bravery in rooting out corruption where it grows like a weed in the garden of our holy church."

"I seek to do God's work here on earth," she replied.

Two hundred pounds was a great deal of money. Her finances were still pinched and strained by the effort of raising five hundred pounds only a few months earlier. She wasn't entirely sure how she'd raise two hundred more in a hurry. While she'd inherited and skillfully maintained a great fortune from her father, her wealth was tied up in land and not readily available to pour into leather bags or pile in wooden chests. What would she do if he asked for more?

"You do God's work ably, and I accept your offer." He smiled. "And I commend you for making it, cousin."

Ela wanted to clutch the boy to her chest and weep with gratitude. His familial greeting warmed her heart. "You shall not have cause to regret your decision."

But what of de Burgh? The man was a thorn in her side. She'd love to pluck it out once and for all. "And will you forbid your justiciar from overriding the careful progress of the turning wheels of justice? I fear that he'll try to subvert the process again."

"He came to your castle today?" Henry still didn't seem to believe her.

"Yes." Now the king knew that de Burgh was keeping his own correspondence—from his cousin by marriage—from him, and sneaking around behind his back.

"I shall have words with him. If Deschamps stands accused of murder, he shall remain in your jail until he is tried at the assizes."

Ela maintained her serious expression, but a tiny bud of hope unfurled in her heart. De Burgh's arrogance might yet cause him to dig his own grave. She could already imagine him striding back and forth in Henry's chamber, berating her and extolling the virtues of Deschamps, while pointing out that the dead merchant was a mere foreigner and not worth wasting their time on.

"The murder victim was Ziyad al Wahid, a trusted businessman from whom I've bought a number of valuable items over the years. I suspect you know him yourself."

"Indeed I do." Henry looked rather shocked. "I expected him to attend me here. I'd asked him to bring me some unique gems to decorate the scabbard of a ceremonial sword. I wondered why he never arrived."

"He was garroted on the top of my castle wall and thrown into the moat. It seems that Deschamps coveted a rare ruby that Ziyad possessed but wasn't willing or able to pay for it. He—or someone he hired—killed the merchant, hoping to take possession of it. Since the gem wasn't on Ziyad's person, I suspect he and his henchmen then tried to find them in his cart, which was under guard in my courtyard. They didn't manage, because Ziyad's rarest valuables were cleverly secreted inside the cart axles. Once the jewels were discovered, Deschamps paid two guards to steal them while they were being valued. With the guards' confessions I think there's a good chance he'll be convicted."

Henry looked thoughtful. "I wonder why such a loyal, long-term servant of the crown, well paid in his position, would risk everything for avarice?"

Because de Burgh promised him status and power if he could pay for it? Perhaps he saw himself as sheriff in my place? It was only a suspicion, and she had no way to prove it.

"I hope he can be compelled to confess if there is sufficient incentive."

"If a man is likely to hang, there's a sure inducement that would loosen his tongue," said the king.

"The prospect of saving his life," agreed Ela. If Deschamps would confess that de Burgh promised him an inducement to murder, she could shoot a fatal—or at least terminal—arrow into her enemy's side.

"But to what end? Why save a man who deserves to hang?" The king inhaled. "And perhaps the story is more complex than it appears and he's innocent of the murder."

"He seems to have seduced my steward into his employ, then had him killed—to silence him—as he sat in my dungeon awaiting trial."

"You have proof of this?"

Ela's heart sank slightly. "Not yet. The jailer was the only

251

man present who could have taken my steward's life, but he's maintained his silence."

The justice at the assizes would likely be the only man who could offer a murderer his life in exchange for a confession. Though no doubt a letter from the king would provide sufficient encouragement.

"Again, I hardly see the point of giving them a way out. Let them all twist in the wind, if they're guilty."

Ela didn't reply. There was at least a possibility that none of them would twist in the wind. Murder was a capital offense and there was no solid evidence to convict either Deschamps or the jailer of the actual killings. For now, her main priority was keeping them imprisoned until justice could be sought. "Indeed, your grace. I shall leave justice in the capable hands of the traveling justice. My main concern is that my prisoners shall not be freed before justice has run its course."

"Rest assured, my lady, I shall personally ensure that they aren't."

"I'm so grateful for your support in this matter." Ela wished she could heave a sigh of relief at this pronouncement. But for all his bold statements, Henry relied on others to execute his wishes. If they were to betray him, he had little recourse other than to accuse them of treason and throw them in his own dungeon, and then where did that leave him? The prospect of another barons' revolt was a specter that must always hover at the edges of the king's imagination.

"I wonder," she continued. "Do you know who the traveling justice on this circuit is to be?"

Henry frowned. "I'm afraid I don't. I'm sure de Burgh would know, though. He sometimes selects them himself."

Ela's heart sank right through the bottom of her polished

leather boots and into the intricately tiled mosaic floor. *Of course he does.* There went any prospect of finding justice in the murder of Ziyad al Wahid or Noel Bazin and all of her hopes that de Burgh might finally meet his comeuppance.

Unless she could come up with a cunning plan....

CHAPTER 22

Salisbury, July 1227
The assizes were announced sooner than expected. No doubt de Burgh had arranged this in the hope of subverting justice and releasing Deschamps from jail forthwith.

In a way it was good. The prisoners had to be watched all day and all night to make sure they couldn't communicate, since they were already co-conspirators. Every day or two, Ela had one of them summoned to the hall for inquisition by a jury, in the hope that she could glean more details of their plot.

However, now that they were all locked up together, the two guards who'd been somewhat forthcoming had clamped their lips shut. Perhaps they hoped that with their master— the powerful keeper of the king's garrison—among them, they'd all be released if they played their parts.

"We must find Rosie. Dead or alive." Ela had sent her men out to hunt for the fallen woman, but they found no trace of her. Which, on reflection, wasn't surprising. A woman who lived below the law would hardly reveal herself to intrusive horsemen. After two weeks of failure to uncover any clues to her whereabouts—or any evidence of her murder—Ela turned to female accomplices.

Within three days, there was news. The alewife, Una Thornhill, who Ela now plied with orders for fresh ale for the castle, revealed that she'd spoken to a girl who knew Rosie. Ela stood in her shop and politely refused a cup of the bitter ale. "What is her name and where can I find her?"

"They call her Matilda, but I don't think that's her real name," said Mistress Thornhill. Her chapped hands rested below her ample bosom. "She's a close friend to Rosie and says they spoke of the night of the murder."

Ela's skin prickled. "I must meet with her."

The alewife's mouth pursed slightly. "She's afraid to meet with the sheriff." There was a hint of scolding in her voice. "She thinks nothing good can come of the news she bears."

Ela frowned. "How so?"

"It points the finger of accusation at a powerful man and such a thing bodes ill for a poor girl, especially one who breaks the law and God's Commandments to earn her bread. If she's a friend of Rosie's she's likely a woman of…ill repute."

"I shall swear to protect her. If I can use her information without bringing her before the jury, I shall do so. I simply seek to gather information. Does she know if Rosie is alive or dead?"

"She doesn't know for sure, but she thinks she's dead. And she fears the same fate for herself."

"She confessed this to you?"

"Yes, when she came to my shop looking for news of her missing friend."

Ela breathed out slowly. "I shall go to her in private. Where might I find her?"

Mistress Thornhill laughed. "In private? With a phalanx

of guards trailing behind you and everyone in the village whispering? She won't want to meet you in the town."

Ela glanced back at the door to the alehouse. Two guards stood outside the door, waiting for her. "Unfortunately I find a bodyguard necessary for my safety."

The alewife's ruddy face softened. "I heard there was an attempt on your life last year. I don't envy you the job of locking up all the ne'er-do-wells of the county. I know of a place where you can meet her without being observed. If you'll tell me the time in advance, I can relay it to her."

Ela's chest swelled with gratitude. "I appreciate your contribution to the cause of justice."

"I like good to triumph over evil as well as any man, but as a woman I'll never be called to serve on a jury." Una Thornhill's chin tilted up a little.

Ela nodded. She'd like to sympathize further, but it wouldn't be appropriate to her station. "I can meet her after the bells for Nones tomorrow. Where shall I find her?"

"Do you know Cripple's Well?"

"The tumbledown cottage outside Fuggleston?"

"That's the one. She'll meet you there in the hope that no one else will know about it."

"Reassure her that I shall keep our meeting entirely private."

THE NEXT MORNING, Ela asked Bill Talbot to accompany her, so she could leave the guards behind. She'd vowed to protect this girl from prying eyes and wagging tongues, and she intended to keep her promise.

The bells for Nones rang as they set out on the road, Ela riding Freya and Bill on a bay palfrey. Once they left the castle gate she noticed Bill scanning the landscape around them. "Do you expect brigands to jump from the bushes?"

"I'm not sure what to expect with Deschamps in the jail. His presence there itches like a festering boil."

"One reason why I didn't bring the guards. I don't know who to trust these days."

The bright blue sky of the summer day should have cheered her heart, but instead the sun was a little too bright, the ground too hard. Ela found herself glancing suspiciously around. She was glad when the short ride brought them to a knot of woods where the remains of a small cottage were crumbling back into the earth.

She still remembered the old woman who used to live here, though the name Cripple's Well probably predated her by some generations. The former resident was sound in body, if not in mind, at the end. The roof had fallen in some five years ago and the wattle-and-daub walls had crumbled almost back to the ground. The round stone well stood firm even in its state of overgrown neglect.

"What an odd spot." Bill glanced around, still on edge.

"No one comes here," said Ela. "So we won't be seen." She looked around. Was the mysterious Matilda here? She didn't see anyone. But the sight of a countess and her knight riding up might intimidate anyone. "Let's dismount and put our horses in the shade."

They left the horses standing under a spreading oak tree and walked toward the ruin of the house. A figure appeared from the woods. Ela jumped in spite of herself. The new arrival was a young girl, white as a ghost, her hair wrapped in a white kerchief. She wore a faded blue gown with no ornamentation and not a speck of paint on her face. "Are you Matilda?"

"My name is Mary, my lady. We've met before."

Ela frowned, trying to place her. This woman wasn't at all what she'd expected. "Where?"

"I used to work at Nance's dairy." She pulled back her kerchief, revealing curly red-gold hair. Ela remembered talking to her and another dairymaid while trying to find a murderer the year before.

"I do remember you now. You're a dairymaid."

The girl looked down. "I was. Not anymore. I got pregnant, and Nance threw me out."

Ela's mind whirled. She had a bad feeling about Nance, but the girls had made a point of stating that he didn't interfere with them. "Who is the father of your babe?"

"Myles Lassiter."

Ela knew the name. He was one of the castle guards now accused of being part of Deschamps plot because he'd been up on the wall the night of the murder. "He's in my jail."

"I know. He said he was going to marry me…" Her face reddened and she broke off. Ela noticed that she was at least six months pregnant. Her loose gown had concealed it at first.

If Lassiter was convicted he'd likely hang. "Why didn't he marry you before now?"

"I don't know, my lady." The girl's mortification was evident in every word. "I don't suppose he ever was going to. And after I lost my place at the dairy I had nowhere to go and Rosie found me crying in the streets and took me under her wing."

Ela cringed inwardly. "She taught you her…trade?"

"No!" The girl looked appalled. "She let me sleep in her room with her. She never brought men back there. The landlord of the Bull and Bear wouldn't have it."

"Were you there with her by the wall the night of the murder?"

"No, but she told me about it when she got back. She was

tipsy so I'm not even sure she knew what she was saying. She said she went there looking for Myles to give him a piece of her mind, but he wasn't at his post. She saw two men there, one foreign and one very high and mighty who spat at her as she passed."

Was it Deschamps? "Did she recognize the second man?"

"She didn't know his name, but she said he was the one who bossed all the soldiers about."

It was. Ela needed this girl as a witness. "Why didn't she tell me this the next day?"

"She may not have remembered it. When she drinks too much she sometimes doesn't remember a whole day."

"Do you know where Rosie is now?"

Mary shook her head.

"Did she tell you where she was going?"

"She didn't. She went out to look for customers one night and never came back. The next day two soldiers came and took all her things away. I was in the room, and they told me to get lost."

Ela's gut seized. Had Deschamps sent two of his lackeys to do his dirty work? "Do you know who they were?"

Mary shook her head again. Ela remembered the former dairymaid as shy and taciturn and had a feeling she was about to run dry of words altogether.

"Where are you living now?"

"The mistress of the Bull and Bear is letting me work in the kitchens and sleep on the floor there. As long as I stay out of sight of the customers I can scrub the cups and clean the floors for my bread."

Ela's heart went out to the girl. She didn't know the innkeeper's wife well enough to know if her act was inspired by Christian charity or if she intended to steal the girl's baby away from her once it was born. She'd heard of women giving a home to a desperate pregnant girl, then once the child was born they'd sell it to a childless couple and the mother would never see it again.

"Did anyone see you come here?"

"No. At least I don't think so."

"You're in danger." Ela inhaled sharply. "I'm fairly sure that Rosie was murdered to prevent her from telling what she saw. If anyone finds out that you know what she witnessed, they might come after you. Will you return with me to stay at the castle?"

The girl blinked in confusion. "But I can't afford to lose my place at the Bull and Bear. Where will I go?"

"I can find you a place in my household. My girls are always leaving to get married." Perhaps she could even find the girl a husband. But she was certainly willing to take on a new member of her household if it meant a chance of seeing the charges stick to Deschamps.

CHAPTER 23

People crowded into the great hall on the first day of the assizes. The traveling justice had brought an entourage, and curtained partitions were set up at one end of the hall to give the justice private chambers surrounded by his men.

Much to Ela's dismay, the justice arrived with Hubert de Burgh.

"Ela!" De Burgh insulted her with the informal use of her first name in front of a stranger. Still, she didn't want to prejudice the justice against her before the trials even started, so she forced a smile to her face.

"My Lord de Burgh. Welcome to Salisbury." She hoped her words didn't sound as insincere as they felt.

"This is Sir Robert de Lisle. The traveling justice on this circuit has taken ill, and Sir Robert has kindly agreed to stand in for us."

Ela fought the urge to frown. Where had they dug up this man? The trial of Deschamps was arguably the most important in the land, and de Burgh had somehow managed to remove the experienced and able justice she'd expected?

Of course he had.

"A great pleasure to meet you, my lady." De Lisle spoke slowly, and with a slight tremor to his voice. The justice was a tall man, with wispy blondish hair, watery pale eyes and a head like a big loaf of bread. He bowed low to Ela. "It was my great honor to know your late husband, one of the finest men in England."

"May God be with you, Sir Robert. Your words warm my heart. How did you know my husband?" She didn't remember meeting this man before. With his rather extraordinary looks, she surely would have.

"We fought in Wales against Llywelyn with King John."

"Ah yes." An awkward time, with Llywelyn's wife, Joan, being a half-sister to both King John and her husband. That lady had in fact brokered the delicate peace that had held ever since. "Would that he were here to welcome you to Salisbury."

"Sir Robert harbors ambitions to become Justiciar of Galloway," said de Burgh.

What an odd thing to say, thought Ela.

"My family estates are in those parts and I feel a strong affinity for the region," said de Lisle.

A remote and desolate part of the world, thought Ela. Then she realized why de Burgh had mentioned his goals. *De Lisle is here to deliver what de Burgh desires, so that he can gain what he desires.*

The implied arrangement made her heart sink. It suggested that the results of the trial were a foregone conclusion, with de Burgh telling his puppet what to think and how to rule.

Still, the justice would be obliged to sit through the trial and if the facts were presented in a convincing manner by the jury and herself, then he could hardly dismiss them without a thought, could he?

~

Servants arranged the tables in a U shape, this time rather larger than usual, with room to accommodate a full twelve jurors and space in the middle for the bevy of defendants still locked up down in the dungeon.

Everyone dined, and Ela did her best to entertain the justice and his acolytes. De Lisle's stories of his Welsh adventures with her husband were rather sparse, so she suspected he'd seen him mostly from afar. The justice had a lugubrious air that probably wouldn't have endeared him to William. In fact, she could readily imagine her husband making fun of him. Still, she smiled and feigned interest, all the while praying there was a heart beating under his well-cut gray tunic.

Flanked by guards, the prisoners entered, scrubbed and shaved for the occasion. None of them seemed that much the worse for their weeks of confinement, but Ela could feel enmity rising from them like a foul smell. Especially from Deschamps. His gaze had the bite of a steel blade when it met hers, and almost made her catch her breath.

She watched him glance at de Burgh, and she turned to catch de Burgh's reaction—a look of stony disinterest. Artful, perhaps, unless he planned to let the garrison commander hang for his own reasons.

Bill Talbot silenced the assembled men, and Ela, seated next to her co-sheriff, cleared her throat. "The first trial of the day concerns the death of a traveling merchant, Ziyad al Wahid, who was strangled atop the outer wall of this castle and thrown into the ditch below. The last person to see the merchant alive saw him ascend to the wall with a tall man in a black cloak, who I now believe to be Gerald Deschamps, the garrison's commander."

De Lisle didn't seem at all surprised by this announcement, suggesting that de Burgh had already bent his ear with his version of the facts of the case. He asked the jurors about the various findings—the merchant's origins, his familiarity to the castle residents, whether he'd been pushed or thrown from the wall. Then he turned to Ela. "What makes you think that the tall man in a black cloak was Gerald Deschamps, when it could have been another man fitting that description?" He looked at de Burgh.

Who positively glowed. "Indeed. Does not your steward, Noel Bazin, fit the bill? I hear he had debts that might have pressed him to an act of desperation."

Ela had heard nothing of Bazin's debts. Though debts would explain how easily Deschamps bought his participation, they were irrelevant and she refused to let this news distract the justice. "My late steward was a tall man, but a new witness is able to point the finger of blame squarely at Deschamps."

"A new witness?" asked de Burgh.

"Indeed," said Ela. "Which is fortunate since our previous witness cannot be here."

"Can you produce the witness?" asked de Lisle, in his bumbling way.

"Indeed I can." Ela gestured to Mary, who—dressed in plain gray clothing not unlike a nun's habit and with a wide white veil covering most of her face—sat quietly in a corner of the hall. The girl came forward, and Ela could see her trembling from the movement at the edge of her veil. "Please tell us what you saw and heard."

Mary repeated Rosie's story that she'd told of seeing two men, one foreign and one very high and mighty.

De Burgh snorted. "To a low woman like that, Noel Bazin the steward seems high and mighty."

"Except that there's another detail," said Ela. She looked at the girl, praying she'd say the right words.

Mary's veil shook again. "Rosie said that the man she saw was the one who bossed all the soldiers about."

"My steward certainly didn't do that," said Ela.

"Even if the merchant was seen with Deschamps, that's hardly proof that he killed him," said de Burgh.

"Did Deschamps hire you as a lawyer to represent him?" asked Ela, looking pointedly at de Burgh.

His dry laugh hurt her ears. "I'm merely trying to bring some common sense to these proceedings. Perhaps we should hear what the accused has to say for himself?"

Deschamps was brought forward. A tall, broad-shouldered man with thick, dark hair barely touched with silver, he had the distinguished air of a man in command. His weeks in the jail had barely dimmed it.

Before he could speak, Ela cleared her throat. "Gerald Deschamps commanded the troops that patrol the castle's outer walls. On the night of the murder, the three guards charged with that duty were ordered to the far end of the wall."

"Is this true?" asked de Lisle.

Deschamps stony features barely moved. "It is. There were reports of cattle theft in a field that could be viewed from that location."

"So you left a large portion of the wall unguarded?" De Lisle watched him with his big, watery eyes.

"We're not at war. No enemies were expected at the gate. I saw no reason to anticipate trouble," Deschamps protested.

Ela continued. "The merchant, who would soon be found dead, was seen ascending the wall with the tall man in a black cloak. The eyewitness was a prostitute, known to the men, who frequented this spot. I spoke with her myself."

"She stated that she saw Deschamps?"

"She didn't identify him by name. She only made that statement to her friend, directly after the event. It's possible that she was afraid of repercussions if she accused the garrison commander. She made her living coaxing change from Deschamps's men and would soon find herself penniless, or worse, if she was banished from the castle."

"Why is this prostitute not hear to testify for the court?"

"She's vanished, my lord," said Ela. "She'd lived at the Bull and Bear, a tavern in town, for some months, and was well-known in Salisbury. After she witnessed this crime and testified about it here in this hall, she disappeared. She'd given Mary here shelter in her room, and the girl witnessed garrison soldiers removing her effects. We didn't learn this until just recently."

De Lisle frowned at Deschamps. "Did you instruct your soldiers to remove her effects?"

"Why would I do such a thing? I care nothing for a common prostitute."

"No one has seen her since," said Ela. "We suspect that she's been killed, to silence her."

The justice inhaled slowly, peering at Deschamps down the length of his long nose. Deschamps shifted slightly, as if his knees gave out a little.

"The suspect is thus accused of killing the merchant, then arranging for the deaths of my steward and of the prostitute. He also ordered the theft of the jewels."

De Lisle had a piece of parchment at his elbow, and Ela watched him scratch some words on it. "Let's jump ahead to the theft." He shot a piercing pale gaze at Deschamps. "The countess informed me that your men accused you of instructing them to steal these jewels. What was your reason?"

Again, Deschamps faltered. He glanced at de Burgh, then dragged his eyes back to de Lisle. "I needed to raise money." He spoke softly, and the noise in the hall, which was barely a whisper when he started, hushed to a dead silence.

He's confessed! Ela's heart started to race, and she schooled herself to remain calm. Did he fear that his staunch defender had abandoned him? Or did guilt at betraying his men's trust finally overtake him?

"I needed to raise money to pay to the king to secure for myself the post of Sheriff of Nottingham." Now he looked at de Burgh, a question in his eyes.

De Burgh barely blinked, but Ela could tell the statement took him by surprise. It took de Lisle by surprise as well, and he looked from one man to the other. "The king had promised you the post of Sheriff of Nottingham if you raised a particular sum of money?"

"The king's justiciar had promised me the post. One hundred pounds was the sum proposed."

One hundred pounds? When she'd paid five hundred pounds to secure the castle and position that should be her birthright. Ela struggled to keep herself calm. Was this her chance to tie de Burgh into a plot against her? She drew in a breath and turned to her enemy. "My Lord de Burgh, is this true?"

"I find your pique rather surprising, my lady, given that you paid for the privilege of occupying this very castle and assuming your position as sheriff."

Ela bristled. "My castle and position have been in my family since the time of William the Conqueror. Any fines I paid to the king were a courtesy, not a bribe." Still, de Burgh had deftly and effectively cut off this line of enquiry. She'd better get the focus back on Deschamps's crimes to be sure he didn't wriggle free of the hook as well. She turned to Deschamps. "So, to give the king his due, you decided to steal a gemstone belonging to another man?"

"No, of course not," blustered Deschamps.

Ela wondered how he'd walk back his confession.

"I intended to buy it from him and have it made into a

valuable item that I would resell to secure the desired profit. I promised him an excellent offer if he'd meet me that night and sell me the stone."

Unlikely story. How would he raise the funds to buy such a stone? "You must have offered a great deal of money to draw him away from his wife's side in the night," said Ela.

Deschamps eyes narrowed. "I promised him every penny the stone was worth, but then he tried to cheat me."

Ela looked at De Lisle. He was the justice, and she didn't want to be seen taking the proceedings out of his hands and subverting the process.

"The merchant tried to cheat you?" De Lisle lifted his chin.

"Yes. He doubled the promised price. He said he had interest from another party."

Probably Bishop Poore, thought Ela.

"So you grew angry and killed him," said de Lisle flatly. "Which would be quite understandable under the circumstances. After all, he'd promised you a price and now he reneged on the deal—and from what I hear he was a foreigner and an infidel."

Ela's heart sank again. The knights of the round table always circled and propped up their power and wealth for good or ill.

Deschamps brightened. "I didn't intend to kill him. We argued, and then he fell from the ramparts during the discussion."

Giles Haughton rose to his feet and cleared his throat loudly. "We've just heard a confession from Gerald Deschamps. Under the circumstances it amounts to a confession of murder because the merchant's neck bore a ligature mark. He was strangled before being thrown from the wall."

Deschamps sagged slightly. "He was indeed a foreigner and an—"

"Silence!" barked de Lisle, louder than Ela would have imagined he could speak. "You are the prisoner and will speak only when you are spoken to. The Lord your God commands you to welcome the foreigner as one of your own and to treat him as an equal. You've revealed that instead you killed him with the intent to steal from him, and then were disappointed in your efforts." He looked at the jury. "Does this contradict any of the evidence you've heard since the murder was committed?"

They all shook their heads, cowed into silence by de Lisle's new, commanding manner. Ela realized he'd deliberately set a trap for Deschamps by appearing to sympathize with him. Her chest swelled with hope.

The justice rose to his feet. "Given this damning evidence that fell from Gerald Deschamps's own lips, I now pronounce him guilty of murder. Since he is a knight of the realm and a valued servant of our king, I shall temper my sentence with mercy."

Ela's heart sank. Would he let Deschamps walk free? She'd seen it happen before. She could feel de Burgh willing it from where he sat just down the table from her.

"Instead of hanging he shall be beheaded." De Lisle's quiet words hung in the air.

Ela sagged with relief. Beheading would dispatch him to meet his maker faster than hanging. Although Deschamps deserved to suffer for what he'd done to Ziyad, as well as Noel Bazin and—most likely—Rosie, she didn't relish torture, even of a man doomed to die for his crimes.

"I'm most satisfied with this sentence," said Ela quietly. She glanced at de Burgh, expecting him to launch a protest of some kind.

"As am I," he said gruffly. "I'm appalled that he hoped to steal the wealth to buy himself a position as one of the king's sheriffs." Clearly he did not want to hitch his wagon to a dead horse. He avoided Ela's gaze.

She glowed with a clear feeling of triumph.

Deschamps, to his credit, did not cry out in protest or fall to the floor in a faint. He took it as he might have taken a fatal blow in battle, and his stern face held a look of resignation.

Ela looked at the jailer. His champion as good as dead, would he now give up his protests of innocence? His beady dark eyes gleamed in his massive head.

She turned to de Lisle. "This large man here was the jailer who guarded Noel Bazin down in the dungeon on the night he died. Unless Deschamps killed my steward himself, this man must be guilty of dispatching him to meet his maker. He even took money to replace the man who should have been on that shift."

De Lisle watched the jailer with his big, liquid eyes. "What is your name?"

"Burt Wallis, sir," said the man gruffly, as if his voice was rusty from disuse.

"Has the jury asked him about his guilt?" asked de Lisle. "Let me hear from them."

One by one the jurors described how they'd visited the jailer in the dungeon, and he'd maintained his innocence and insisted that Bazin had tripped over his chain and banged his head on the floor. De Lisle finally lifted his chin and looked at Deschamps. "You're already sentenced to die. The Lord shall judge your sins here on earth. If you do not wish to compound them you must tell the absolute truth. Did you order the jailer to kill Noel Bazin?"

"No." Deschamps spoke with quick conviction. "I killed him myself."

A whisper rushed around the room.

Ela frowned. She didn't believe him. No doubt he felt that claiming guilt for himself was an honorable act.

De Lisle made Deschamps describe the manner of death, and—since he knew all the details of the case and had seen the body slumped where it fell—he was able to present a convincing argument that he'd done the deed himself.

Ela watched the jurors, who looked surprised but not unhappy with this new development. "May I ask a question, my lord?" she asked of de Lisle.

He nodded.

She turned to the jailer. "Did you see Gerald Deschamps in the dungeon that night?" If he was there—as had been clearly established—he must have witnessed the murder.

Wallis looked nervously at Deschamps. "Yes?" The question in his voice belied his answer.

Deschamps held his jaw locked and he avoided looking at any of them, but stared off toward the great main door as if he might spirit himself out of it.

"You didn't mention that when I questioned you over the body, in the presence of Giles Haughton, the coroner, and Deschamps himself," said Ela.

The jailer looked confused, especially when he looked at Deschamps again and found him still staring off into the distance. "He told me not to tell."

"So you were a conspirator in his plot," said de Lisle. It wasn't a question.

The jailer blinked, and his fat chin quivered.

Ela expected him to continue questioning Wallis, but instead he turned to the two guards who'd stolen the jewels. "And you, also, were conspirators in this deadly scheme."

"I never killed anyone!" protested Thomas Belcher.

"You were on the wall, guarding the wrong side of it, when Ziyad the merchant was strangled and thrown from the ramparts," said de Lisle. "So you were also a conspirator in this murderous conspiracy."

"I didn't know anyone would be killed," he whined. "And Lassiter and Wilks were there, too. He told us all to watch the fields below. We didn't find out about the murder until the next morning when we saw the body down in the moat."

De Lisle turned to Deschamps. "Did they know you planned to kill the merchant?"

"I didn't plan to kill the merchant," said Deschamps. "I planned to buy his ruby, as I discussed earlier." His calm demeanor impressed Ela. She was sure he was lying about his intentions to scavenge what remained of his honor, but otherwise he seemed to have accepted his fate.

"Did they know about the ruby?" asked de Lisle.

"Not until I asked them to steal it for me," said Deschamps, coolly.

"Why would they agree to do such a thing?" pressed the justice.

Deschamps hesitated. His eyes didn't stray from the judge's face. "Loyalty. They're good men who obeyed their commander."

The soldiers he'd dragged into his scheme displayed no emotion. Perhaps they still clung to shreds of loyalty for this man who'd risked their lives for his greed. The garrison commander had betrayed their trust, her trust, and, ultimately, the king's trust.

Ela glanced at de Burgh. His usually impassive face had turned dark with fury. Perhaps he'd hoped Deschamps would put up a more valiant defense of his own honor.

"It appears that Gerald Deschamps hatched this plot by himself and executed the worst of it without help," said de Lisle. He looked at Deschamps. "Did you kill the missing prostitute as well?"

Now Deschamps hesitated. "I don't know anything about her."

"Your men were sent to remove her belongings from her room at the Bull and Bear," said Ela.

"You're already sentenced to die," said de Lisle. "Do you wish for another man to hang for your crimes?"

Deschamps paused, and his stony expression melted slightly. Clearly ideas of chivalry and loyalty still played across his mind. "I killed her. I strangled her with a shoelace and buried her in a copse not far from the castle walls."

Ela crossed herself. "May God rest her soul."

De Burgh let out an audible sigh.

"As you can see, your defense of our garrison commander was grievously misplaced," said Ela to de Burgh, unable to resist the opportunity to thrust even this small dagger into his ribs.

"Indeed it was," he said slowly. Still, Ela had a strong feeling that de Lisle would never be Justiciar of Galloway now.

CHAPTER 24

*E*xecution day

Most of the denizens of the castle and at least half the residents of new Salisbury clustered in the market square around a newly built scaffold and a thick block of wood with a neck-shaped groove in it. A sunny summer day. Children played, dogs barked and people munched roasted nuts from a nearby market stall.

Deschamps was one of three men to die after the assizes. A villager who'd beaten his wife to death in front of their children was hanged, with de Lisle ordering the executioner to make sure that his scaffold was low and the drop short, in order to prolong his death. Ela had been surprised by such bloodthirstiness from the bookish, pale-eyed man.

While the wife killer still kicked and twisted in agony, Deschamps knelt before the execution block. The executioner pointed for him to place his head on the scarred surface. The man had a big broadaxe at his side, dull from many years of use except for the freshly honed edge that gleamed in the sunlight as he picked up the wooden handle and raised it over his head.

Ela's stomach churned and she closed her eyes and dove into prayer, beseeching the Blessed Mother to pray for us sinners now and at the hour of our death. She heard the swish of the axe, then the crunch of bone and the thunk of Deschamps's head as it hit the ground. She opened her eyes in time to see the head roll a short distance before coming to rest against the leg of a small, shaggy terrier, who sniffed at it with curiosity.

∼

LONDON, *August 1227*

"It's hard to believe that one small stone could cause so much trouble." Ela watched as the gem dealer counted out gold coins to pay for the ruby. "I hope it finds a home where it can bring glory to God." The gem dealer simply nodded and kept counting.

Ela departed with the money secured in a discreet box and headed straight for her banker, whose chambers lay a short distance away. The streets of London teemed with people, horses, and dogs and the smell of the city in the summer heat grew oppressive as they walked.

"I'd like a house with a garden," said Safiya.

"Prices in London are high. You could afford a much larger house in some quiet part of the country," said Ela. She disliked the oppressive atmosphere and almost constant noise of the city, and the incessant hovering smoke from a thousand cooking fires.

"I like it here," said Safiya with a small smile. She still swathed herself in black, but her face had regained its youthful glow and she showed at least a little enthusiasm for her future. "There are people from every country living in this city, and men and women plying all trades you can imagine. I feel I could live here without being harassed to remarry or tormented for being a foreigner."

"I understand completely." They'd decided—in consultation with Mary—that Mary should accompany her to London and live with her as her maid. Safiya's excitement over the impending arrival of Mary's baby had finally brought her out of her fog of grief.

Mary was grateful for the opportunity to keep a roof over her head and raise her baby without censure, and the two women had become fast friends. The prospect that they could comfort and support each other cheered Ela as much as it heartened each of them.

They deposited the chest of coins from the sale of the ruby with Ela's banker, who gave Safiya an accounting of her wealth. All the goods from the wagon had been sold and—as if her husband had planned it—she had enough to support herself in comfort for the rest of her life.

"I may start a small business making beadwork decorations," said Safiya, as they emerged back into the busy street. "I used to do that when I was a girl. It gives me pleasure to create pretty patterns."

"I think that's a wonderful idea," said Ela. "I'm sure I'd enjoy buying some myself on my visits to London. I do hope you'll be willing to entertain me at your house."

"It would be my very great pleasure," said Safiya, with a broad smile. "After the long time you've entertained me at yours."

"Sometimes I felt I had you imprisoned there."

"I used to wish I had never laid eyes on Salisbury," said Safiya, with a sigh, "but you've shown me that there's life after my husband's death. I also appreciate the risk you took in pursuing the conviction of a powerful man."

"That powerful man intended to discredit me and undermine my authority. I fully believe he intended to demonstrate my unworthiness, then buy the position of sheriff from the king and banish me from the castle again—this time for good. While your husband's death was a horrible tragedy, it revealed the cancer of greed and corruption that threatened to unseat me. I owe him a debt of gratitude for that."

All the soldiers involved in Deschamps's plot had been sent far from Salisbury, and those involved in crimes had been punished—though not with the loss of their lives. Mary didn't shed a single tear when she learned that her former lover had been sent to a remote outpost in Ireland.

The jailer never admitted to the murder of Bazin, but it was demonstrated that—at the very least—he'd allowed Deschamps to kill Bazin on his watch, so he was hanged on the same day Deschamps was put to death. Thus Ela felt that her steward had received a measure of justice. Some would argue that Noel Bazin didn't deserve justice since he'd signed his own death warrant by agreeing to be a puppet of Deschamps.

"I'm still learning how to make my way in the world as a widow," said Ela. "I'm not sure I'll ever adjust to it entirely, but life is full of great and small pleasures."

"I know one thing for sure," said Safiya. "I shall never play chess. That game is a source of so much worry and confusion. I once saw a fight break out between two soldiers who had a disagreement about the rules."

"Men will always find something to fight over. At least no one will fight over that bone chess set under my roof again. I had it repaired and gave it to Hubert de Burgh as a gift."

Since the thing seemed cursed, she could think of no better recipient. As a good Christian, she didn't really believe in curses, but just in case...

THE END

AUTHOR'S NOTE

This story was partly inspired by the cover image of a merchant with his wares—and his sweet donkey—from the Codex Manesse, an illustrated book of songs now in the Heidelberg University Library. The images in this manuscript portray the clothing style of Ela's time, and the belts for sale look much like those we'd buy today. While Bill Talbot, John Dacus, Bishop Poore, Hubert de Burgh and Ela's children are all historical figures, some of the key players in this story including Gerald Deschamps, Noel Bazin, Ziyad al Wahid and his wife, Safiya, are products of my invention.

The villain's motivation in this tale was inspired by a cataclysmic series of events that befell a later descendant of Ela's. Mervyn Tuchet, the second Earl of Castlehaven, was hanged for rape and sodomy in 1631. I won't go into the wild details of the story behind these accusations—for those you can read *A House in Gross Disorder: Sex, Law, and the Second Earl of Castlehaven* by Cynthia B. Herrup—but to a great extent he was executed for allowing chaos to reign in his household. A noble household was a microcosm of the entire monarchic society, with its delicate balance of fealty and respect. For an earl to lose the respect of his wife, servants, and son was a failure of his authority and ability to maintain his noble status—and condemned him to death on charges that he denied to the end.

As High Sheriff of Wiltshire, Ela was entrusted with maintaining order not only in her own household but in all of Wiltshire. It's easy to imagine how jealous men could have hoped that she'd fail and even actively worked toward that end. The king, likely on Hubert de Burgh's advice, had already once ousted Ela from her castle and installed the aggressive and corrupt Simon de Hal in her place. The "fines" that Ela paid, an initial five hundred pounds to regain shrievalty over her castle and the sheriffdom, followed by two hundred pounds to keep them in perpetuity, are recorded in the Fine Rolls of Henry III, and demonstrate that money could quite literally buy power. Ela inherited great wealth and used it—along with what must have been incredible strength of will—to consolidate and hold the authority enjoyed by her male ancestors.

Surely her enemies rankled after she managed to wrest her castle and position back and hold them with force. It's a testament to Ela's commitment to self-determination that she remained Countess of Salisbury until her death, never relinquishing the earldom even to her oldest son, William, whom she outlived. William tried to become earl, and even wrote a begging letter to Pope Innocent IV complaining that the king wouldn't grant him his estates. King Henry III—whose long reign continued until 1272—never went back on his deal with Ela, refusing to grant William the earldom while Ela still claimed it.

If you have questions or comments, please get in touch at jglewis@stoneheartpress.com.

ABOUT THE AUTHOR

J. G. Lewis grew up in London, England. She came to the U.S. for college and a career as a museum curator.

Her mysteries evolved from the idea of bringing almost-forgotten but fascinating historical figures to life by creating stories for them. The Ela of Salisbury series features the formidable Ela Longespée, wife of King Henry II's illegitimate son William. The widowed mother of eight children, Ela served as High Sheriff of Wiltshire and castellan of Salisbury and ultimately founder and abbess of Lacock Abbey.

Cover image includes: detail from Codex Manesse, ca. 1300, Heidelberg University Library; decorative detail from Beatus of Liébana, Fecundus Codex of 1047, Biblioteca Nacional de España; detail with Longespée coat of arms from Matthew Parris, *Historia Anglorum,* ca. 1250, British Museum.